W9-ACM-890

WITHDRAWN

ESCAPE TO FORT ABERCROMBIE

ESCAPE TO
FORT ABERCROMBIE

CANDACE SIMAR

FIVE STAR
A part of Gale, a Cengage Company

Farmington Hills, Mich • San Francisco • New York • Waterville, Maine
Meriden, Conn • Mason, Ohio • Chicago

LIBRARY OF CONGRESS CATALOGING-IN-PUBLICATION DATA

Names: Simar, Candace, author.
Title: Escape to Fort Abercrombie / Candace Simar.
Description: First edition. | Waterville, Maine : Five Star Publishing, [2018]
Identifiers: LCCN 2017039678 | ISBN 9781432838188 (hardcover) | ISBN 1432838180 (hardcover) | ISBN 9781432838065 (Ebook) | ISBN 1432838067 (Ebook) | ISBN 9781432838058 (Ebook) | ISBN 1432838059 (Ebook)
Subjects: | BISAC: FICTION / Historical. | FICTION / Westerns. | GSAFD: Western stories.
Classification: LCC PS3619.I5565 E75 2018 | DDC 813/.6—dc23
LC record available at https://lccn.loc.gov/2017039678

First Edition. First Printing: February 2018
Find us on Facebook–https://www.facebook.com/FiveStarCengage
Visit our website–http://www.gale.cengage.com/fivestar/
Contact Five Star™ Publishing at FiveStar@cengage.com

Printed in the United States of America
1 2 3 4 5 6 7 22 21 20 19 18

Escape to Fort Abercrombie

CHAPTER 1

Ryker Landstad leaned on the rake handle and swatted a horsefly feasting on the back of his neck. If only the rake were a rifle, and he were old enough to run away and join his brother in the Union army.

The moaning wind and scraping rakes created a strange melody. Whoosh, moan, whoosh. Ryker raked long strokes in rhythm with the song under the merciless sun. He mentally composed a poem about the smell of newly cut hay, and how a wooden handle rubbed blisters into calluses.

"Look," his nine-year-old brother, Sven, said while pointing to a fat cloud in the pale sky. "An angel!"

Sven's words jolted the poem out of Ryker's mind. He shrugged an irritated gesture and bent into his work, trying to remember the beautiful phrase now slipped away. "Don't be silly." His brother's constant chatter made him crazy. "Angels are pretend."

"See its wings?" Sven's thin face wore a rapturous expression. "A real angel, right in front of us." A shaft of sunlight reflected off his blond head and surrounded him like a halo. He reminded Ryker of a picture in their teacher's book about martyrs. "Look." Sven pointed again.

Ryker squinted into the bright sky, anything to keep his pesky brother quiet. A cloud puffed like a giant kernel of popcorn, but Ryker saw nothing else. He was fourteen, after all, almost a grown man, and too old for superstition.

"Mama says angels squeeze through the gates of heaven and slide down to us on sunbeams," Sven said. He shaded his eyes and pointed again. "Says they protect us wherever we go."

"You're crazy," Ryker said and raked another swath of grass into a neat pile to dry.

Meadowlarks warbled, and a brisk breeze ruffled his hair. The prairie grass grew taller than Papa and enclosed them like a green fortress, stretching in every direction around their homestead on the western rim of Minnesota. No wonder Mama told them to look skyward. It was their only freedom.

Fort Abercrombie needed beef to feed Union soldiers and hay to fatten the beef. Papa wouldn't rest until every stem of prairie grass was piled into haystacks. Papa declared hay an easy cash crop. He said the blackbirds left it alone, it grew without planting or cultivating, and it required no expensive equipment.

It didn't feel easy. Ryker's skinny arms bulged muscles like walnuts from long days working under the merciless sun. Calluses turned his bare feet into leather. Last winter the flour ran out before Christmas. Thank God for springtime suckers in Whiskey Creek. They froze their hands spearing the ugly fish, but Mama salted a whole barrel. It proved enough to keep them going. The family remained desperate for food, clothing, shoes, and everything. Grass was their only abundance.

"Think Martin saw the elephant?" Sven said.

"Probably," Ryker said with a shrug. "His last letter said they were gearing for battle."

Martin was the lucky one, off fighting Rebs while Ryker was stuck working. He hoped the war would last a long time, at least until he was old enough to pass for a man. Anything to get away from the farm and its never ending chores.

Sven's face was as sharp as a butcher's cleaver, with his narrow chin and protruding teeth. Ryker watched as his brother lifted the wooden rake and aimed the handle toward their brown and black dog, Beller, sniffing behind him. Beller looked filthy, bedraggled, mangy, and half-starved. With times so hard, he survived on whatever he could catch: gophers, rabbits, or naked hatchlings hidden in the grass.

"Bang, bang," Sven said. "You're dead."

A blue-coated soldier stepped out of the tall grass onto the hayfield. One minute they were alone, and the next a young soldier stood beside them. At first Ryker thought it might be Martin returning home. But it wasn't his brother. The soldier looked not much older than Martin, proved by his lack of whiskers and pimply cheeks. His eyes puffed swollen. Surely not from crying. Soldiers didn't cry.

"You scared me," Sven said. He spoke in Norwegian until he remembered his manners. He continued in English. "I was play-ing soldier, not expecting to see one." Sven stepped toward the young man and fingered the buttons on his blue jacket.

"You like it?" the young soldier said. He had a wheezy voice, as if he had climbed a mountain. He looked toward the soddy where Mama looked their way, shielding her eyes with the back of her hand. "I'll trade my jacket for one of your Pa's old shirts."

No soldier would trade his uniform jacket.

"I'm leaving and don't want to travel in this heavy garb."

"Going to see the elephant?" Sven said. "You'll need your uniform."

"Not going to fight." The soldier looked away, and Ryker noticed a flush rising on his neck. "Enlistment is up," the boy said, and his Adam's apple bobbed hard in his throat. "My pa needs help with the harvest."

"Where's home?" Sven said.

"Hush," Ryker said. "Don't bother the poor man to death." It was a charitable thing to call the young soldier a man. He was surely a runaway. With the War of Rebellion, no one was discharged from the army.

The young man slapped a fly off his hair and shifted his weight from one foot to the other. He turned toward the tall grass when he saw their mama coming their way. Klara followed with Elsa on her hip. Papa called commands to the ox team in the farthest field.

"Wait," Ryker said. "My mother won't tell."

The soldier looked at Ryker in alarm, his face turning as red as the pimples on his cheeks. He stepped backwards but tripped over Beller, who had sneaked up behind him, falling to the ground in a blue tangle of arms and legs.

Beller barked and then promptly licked the young man's face, straddling the soldier so he couldn't get up again.

"Get off me!" the soldier said. "Stinky mutt."

Beller growled a low warning. He held the soldier down until Mama got there.

"Beller!" she said.

Beller leapt at the sound of his name, always hopeful Mama might have a scrap of food.

"Shame," Mama said in Norwegian. "That's no way to treat company."

She wore a faded dress and a ragged apron. Mama's eyes glittered blue as the ocean. Her smile showed a gap with a missing bottom tooth. She smiled a gentle smile at the young man, and Ryker explained that his mother didn't speak English.

The soldier stood to his feet and brushed off his backside, rubbing his right elbow with a grimace.

Mama asked his name, and Ryker interpreted.

"Hannibal Mumford," the soldier said. "From Pig's Eye."

"Hannibal," Mama said with a nod. She smiled and introduced herself and her children. "You must be hungry. Come to the house for something to eat."

The soldier grinned when Ryker translated and followed Mama back to the soddy.

"He wants to trade his jacket for an old shirt," Ryker said in whispered Norwegian as Mama poured buttermilk into a tin cup. "I think he's a runaway."

Mama nodded quietly. She handed the young man the cup as if she were thinking what to say. "Tell him we are poor immigrants without clothing to spare." She sat on the bench next to the wooden table and motioned Hannibal to sit beside her. "And that my son also serves with the Union, fighting in the South."

Mama gave Hannibal a raw turnip and a small dish of leftover porridge from breakfast. She shooed the younger children outside but motioned for Ryker to remain and translate.

Mama looked to make sure the children were out of hearing and then pressed her lips together—a sure sign she would speak her mind. Once Mama decided to speak, there was no telling what she would say.

"Tell him that it is not so bad to serve at Fort Abercrombie, away from the fighting," Mama said. "Tell him that we wish our son were there."

Ryker translated while Hannibal twirled his empty cup on the table, making a scraping sound on the rough-hewn logs. "It's just that I've never been away from home before," Hannibal said. His lips quivered, and he pushed the empty dish away. He looked down at the dirt floor.

"Ya, ya," Mama said with a click of her tongue. "Homesickness is a terrible thing." She went on to tell him about the mountains of Norway, and the trouble learning English words. She laughed her tinkling laugh, as Ryker hurried to translate. "But no one dies from it."

She reached over and took the young man's hand. "I'm living proof."

Hannibal did not reply.

"They will look for you at your family home," she said. "If

you leave, you must travel far away to stay out of jail." She took a deep breath. "Shame will follow you all your days." She reached for the buttermilk jug and filled his cup again. "You would be homesick in Canada, too, or wherever you might hide."

Ryker translated the words. They hung in the dim room like circling birds.

"If you go back, you'll be released with honor at the end of the war, making your mama and papa proud to have such a fine son," Mama said. Her face crumpled, and Ryker knew she thought of Martin as she spoke. "Make them proud, Hannibal Mumford."

The soldier sat quietly for a long moment and then stood to his feet. He made a slight bow to Mama. "Thank you, Mrs. Landstad," he said. "I'll return to my duties, miserable as they are."

When Ryker translated, Mama reached over and kissed him on his cheek. "I will pray," she said. "Angels will watch over you."

No one knew what to say. The soldier straightened his shoulders and walked out of the dark soddy, squinting at the bright sunlight. Clouds drifted in a clear sky. Mama and Ryker walked with Hannibal to the edge of the hayfield. The children and Beller chased gophers and butterflies.

"Will you be in trouble?" Ryker said. Soldiers were shot for desertion during war time.

"I don't think so," Hannibal said with a shake of the head. "Not much anyway. Not if I go back of my own free will."

"Maybe we'll see you again sometime," Mama said.

Hannibal hesitated, muttered his thanks, and faded into the tall grass, heading northwest toward Fort Abercrombie.

"I wanted his jacket," Sven said. "How come you didn't trade?"

"Hush now," Mama said. "He's a good boy."

Over supper, Mama told Papa about their young visitor. Ryker noticed she spared important details.

"What was he doing so far from the fort?" Papa said, pushing porridge into his mouth. "Odd to be alone and afoot."

"Must have had business for the commander," Mama said. "He hurried back to his duties."

"He wanted to trade—" Sven started to say, but Ryker jabbed him under the table with his knee and sent a warning glance.

"Maybe there will be a letter from Martin," Mama said. "Mr. Schmitz is going to the fort and said he would check for mail."

CHAPTER 2

The next morning, Ryker dragged reluctant feet to the hayfield where Papa had left at least an acre of freshly cut grass. The fragrance of drying hay and the chorus of meadowlarks did nothing to lift Ryker's spirits. The sun crept higher in the east, and it seemed he and his little brother could never rake fast enough to appease their papa's bad mood.

"Supper!" Sven held a decapitated prairie hen with a bloody neck. Sven held the bird away from his overalls and bent a sun-bleached head toward the bird with a loud sniff. "Papa must have nicked it while cutting hay this morning."

Papa always scythed in the early morning when the dew softened the tough prairie grass. He started before daylight with his sickle honed sharp as a razor. No doubt he hadn't noticed the hen.

Ryker shrugged. Meat was meat, and they were always hungry. "Take it to Mama but come right back." He raked sun-dried windrows into haycocks, turning the hay to make sure it dried completely. The small piles dotted the prairie like cowlicks.

Papa had no one to help with the cutting since Martin joined the Union. Ryker could do it, but Papa believed a scythe man needed to be sixteen years old before being entrusted with the dangerous blade, and tall enough to see over the grass.

"Not yet," Papa had said. "You'll learn to get your head out of your hinder before I trust you with the scythe."

Ryker stood on tiptoe but could not see over the grass. He'd

14

have to rake all his life at this rate. The family spent the summer cutting, raking windrows, then haycocks, and lastly gathering the haycocks into large stacks. Six tons carried their oxen and milk cow through the cold winter. Remaining hay meant hard cash. The grass grew unbothered by the flocks of marauding blackbirds that robbed most of their corn and grain.

"You boys finish up before noon, and no foolery," Papa had said before he left to plow fire breaks. Papa spoke Norwegian at home, though he knew enough English to get by.

Last year, a prairie fire had burned half a haystack promised to Fort Abercrombie. All their work gone in a flash of flame. Papa vowed it wouldn't happen again. The army waited until freezing weather to move the hay on huge sledges. It was up to the family to keep it safe from hungry animals, wild fire, and prairie winds.

"Mama saw it plain as the nose on your face," Sven said as he returned from the soddy. He marched between the windrows, pretending to be a soldier, his boy-sized hoe propped over his thin shoulder. "She says angels fly on prairie winds as messengers of God."

"You heard what Papa said."

Sven aimed the rake handle at the dog and pretended to shoot. "Bang, you're dead, you dirty Reb." Beller crouched on filthy haunches and turned a quizzical, friendly look toward Sven.

Sven aimed the hoe handle again in another volley of pretend shooting.

Reluctantly, Sven turned back to his windrow. Ryker neared the end of his row, but Sven had barely started. "I wonder what Martin is doing," Sven said.

Their father stepped out of the tall grass onto the hayfield. Ryker raked as fast as he could.

"Sven!" Papa said in a tone that meant he would tolerate no

foolishness. His heavy eyebrows knit together above his long nose and dark eyes. His beard showed white shadows among the red. Papa wore his oldest trousers and hobnail boots. His chambray shirt showed huge sweat stains under both arms and down the center of his chest. "Quit your horseplay, and finish your work." Beller ran into the tall grass at the sound of the angry voice. "Ryker, your mother needs you at the house. No dallying."

Ryker propped the rake over his shoulder and trotted toward the sod house, delighted for any excuse to leave the field. The grass grew a little shorter over the slough and, of course, around the yard, where it was trampled by the constant movements of family and animals.

Marigold, the red cow with a blinded eye, would freshen any day. Papa kept her close lest a coyote snatch the new calf. Poor Marigold turned her head from side to side as often as she swished her tail, on constant watch for danger.

Marigold chomped weeds next to the chicken coop and swished her tail at swarms of flies around her. A rooster crowed. Hens scratched in the weeds beside the sod barn, and swallows swooped around the eaves, feeding worms to their naked babies in mud nests. Patsy, the broody black hen, skirted the manure pile. Mama suspected Patsy had a hidden nest. *Katt* crouched nearby, waiting to pounce on a fledgling unlucky enough to fall from the nest into his hungry mouth.

"I thought you'd never come," Mama said. "I need your muscles." She perched on a chunk of firewood in front of the door while harvesting feathers from an uncooperative gander clamped head down between her knees. Mama's skirts secured its head, but even so, the large male goose hissed, honked, and flapped strong wings in her face, leaving a mark as red as a slap on Mama's pretty cheek.

Ryker pulled Mama's apron tighter over the goose's flapping

wings and held it tight. The giant bird nipped his leg right through the cloth and flailed for release. Ryker stretched his body across the struggling bird.

It took all Ryker's strength to hold it down, as Mama plucked handfuls of downy feathers from the gander's fuzzy backside. She pulled only the smaller, downy feathers, avoiding those with sharp spines. She dropped feathers into an empty sack until the goose's bumpy skin lay exposed and naked. The gander hissed and struggled, nipping Ryker's hand.

"Now, now, *gasse*," Mama crooned in the same voice she used with sick children. Ryker repositioned his hold, as Mama plucked along its neck and reached under its wings. "Only a few feathers we take. They'll grow back. No need to fuss." The breeze swirled an August snowstorm of pin feathers around them. *Katt* abandoned her quest for barn swallows and batted a stray feather with nimble paws.

Mama nodded. Ryker released the half-naked bird in a flurry of wings and angry honking. It was as if the majestic bird felt ashamed. It flapped and sulked behind the outhouse.

Ryker reached up and jerked a single hair out of his head, wondering if pulling feathers hurt the goose.

"There now, the gander finished. Fetch me the *gas*." Mama pushed blond tendrils beneath her blue kerchief. The embroidered scarf matched the color of her eyes. Before moving to the prairie, Mama wore the kerchief only on special occasions. But when Mama first stepped inside the drab soddy with its dirt walls and floors, she pulled the kerchief from the trunk and announced she would wear it every day. She said they needed a bit of color to cheer them on the prairie.

"Back home the goats pasture around our mountain cottage," Mama said with a far-away look in her eyes. "*Bestemor*, Grandmother, fills the *stabbuhr* with *gjetost* brown cheese."

Ryker chased and cornered the female goose against the side

of the outhouse and brought it to his mother's waiting hands.

"Dark winter days, back in Norway," she said with a sigh. "At least we have sunshine every day on the prairie."

Mama never seemed to hurry, but her hands always busied. She spent her days cooking, sewing, washing, cleaning, and making a home in the wilderness. She spent the dark evenings knitting or spinning. How often Ryker had fallen asleep to the music of her clicking needles.

"Mama," Ryker said, "someday I will tell stories about the Old Country to my children." He took a firmer hold on the flailing goose.

Mama laughed a tinkling laugh, but Ryker noticed the sadness in her eyes. She grabbed the flapping bird and forced its long neck between her knees. Ryker wrapped Mama's apron around its wings and head in defense of the nipping beak. She grimaced, clutching her side.

"Are you all right?" Ryker said. Lately Mama complained of feeling poorly.

"I'm fine." She waved a feathered hand. "*Bestemor* made many a down comforter. Nothing warmer for cold nights." She took a deep breath and began plucking more feathers. "Of course, we had a huge flock of geese. Enough to sell barrels of feathers to the village store."

Mama told stories about their Norwegian homeland as they plucked feathers. Once she paused to wipe a tear from her cheek.

"Are you sick?" Ryker said as the near-naked goose ran behind the barn.

"Homesick," Mama said with a laugh. "Nothing serious."

Papa strode up to the yard wearing a worried expression. His face was smudged black, and his old straw hat carried a hole from a rat bite.

"Something troubles Brimstone," he said, wiping sweat off his forehead with the back of his shirtsleeve. It left a black streak across the faded linen cloth. Fire and Brimstone were their oxen team. Papa had worked an entire winter at a Wisconsin logging camp to pay for them before they moved to western Minnesota. Losing an ox would be far worse than losing a haystack.

"He's choking," Papa said. "Ryker, come."

Ryker dared not refuse his father's command but looked toward his mother with a helpless gesture. Her face was lined with fatigue, and the slouch of her shoulders showed exhaustion. Papa must have noticed, too, for he leaned over and kissed Mama on the top of her head.

"What's wrong?" Papa said.

"Go along," Mama said. She clutched her side again. "I'll manage."

"Maybe Klara could help," Ryker said, though Klara, Sven's nine-year-old twin, was terrified of hissing geese and not strong enough to do much good.

"She took Elsa to the garden," Mama said. "Don't worry. I'll be all right."

Ryker ran to catch up with Papa on the other side of the barn.

Brimstone shook his massive head from side to side, and drool dripped from the sides of his mouth. From time to time he made a choking sound and the muscles of his throat rippled beneath his black and white spotted hide. "Hold him while I take a look."

Ryker stood to the side, careful lest the ox trample his bare feet, and grabbed hold of the curved horns, as his father poked a stick between its back teeth and pried open the ox's mouth. The beast lowed and bellowed, as Papa stuck his fingers between its teeth and felt the back of its throat. "I feel something stuck but can't see it."

Ryker used all his weight to pull back the restless beast's

head as Papa peered into his mouth. "I hope it's not a piece of wire," Papa said. "My God, it couldn't happen at a worse time." He shoved his fingers deeper into the ox's throat. It gagged a horrible wheezing sound.

"A turnip?" Papa grasped a green leaf. "A whole damn turnip stuck in his throat." He jerked a green stem, and it broke off in his hand. "Damnation! Hold him tighter."

Ryker used all his weight to steady the ox's head, but he was no match for its massive strength.

"Hold him, I said." Papa reached deeper into the ox's throat. "I almost got it." He jammed his entire hand down the ox's throat. It gagged, flailing to get away. Then the huge beast swallowed the turnip in a single, strangled gulp.

"Good God, no," Papa said. He loosed a string of words that would make a preacher blush. "He'll founder, for sure."

Brimstone pulled away and stood trembling with his head down. Fire, the other ox, nuzzled Brimstone's side as if in sympathy, then lifted his tail, and did his business with a splat. Ryker stepped out of the way, wrinkling his nose at the smell.

"Are you sure it was a turnip?" Ryker said. He examined the bit of slimy green stem thrown to the ground. It could have been any plant.

His father gave him a look of disdain. "What kind of farmer will you make if you don't know your elbow from a turnip green?"

Papa swore until he ran out of bad words and then shook his fist toward heaven. "Do you see me, Old Woman? You wanted me to have land, and, by God, I have it now. What good is it? I should have starved in Norway for all the luck I've had in this damned country."

Bestemor had urged Papa and Mama to come to America. Papa always blamed his mother when things went wrong, even though she now slept in the Norwegian churchyard. Ryker remembered her soft lap and tight knot of hair at the back of her neck. The old woman had smelled of cheese and sour milk. It made no sense for Papa to blame his dead mother for a choking ox.

Ryker knew better than speak when Papa was mad. Instead, he planned his future. Ryker would be a professor, a scholar, or even a poet. He couldn't wait to leave the farm. Of course, he would miss Mama, but he wouldn't miss Papa at all.

His father returned to the ox, jerked back its head, and looked down its throat again.

"If I know my business, he'll bloat." Papa screwed up his mouth in concentration. "How did he get into the turnips?" He looked at Ryker with a piercing glance.

"Don't look at me," Ryker said. It was always Papa's way to find and fix blame.

At that time, Baby Elsa toddled by. Klara, Sven's twin sister, followed, holding several turnips in her hand.

"Did you give turnips to the oxen?" Papa thundered.

Klara cringed before his angry words. She first shook her head. Then she slowly nodded, as the tears dripped down her thin face. She was taller than Sven but had the same white hair and blue eyes. Her faded dress hung above her knees, she had grown so tall.

"He was hungry," she blubbered.

"Good God, girl," Papa said. "Are you trying to ruin me?" He unbuckled his belt. "You know better than to go near the team." The look of terror in Klara's eyes made Ryker's insides shiver.

Ryker should do something. Martin would have gone toe to toe with Papa and gotten away with it. He'd done it before, that time Klara spilled the night pot, and when she let the baby get too near the fire. But Ryker just stood there and watched the strap blaze a red mark across his sister's skinny legs as she yelped in pain. Baby Elsa screamed and ran into the weeds by the coop.

"Enough, Johann," Mama said, coming toward the pen. She always showed up when Papa lost his temper. "It was an accident." She scooped up the baby from the weeds and smoothed Elsa's wispy hair. "Come to the house, Klara. We must find Patsy's nest."

Klara fled sobbing after her mother. Ryker felt a surge of hatred toward his father and his cruel ways. Papa had laughed at Martin's escapades. And it seemed Papa was less stringent with Sven. Ryker and Klara took the brunt of his father's bad moods. Mama said it was just Papa's way and did not mean he loved them less.

Their family used to be happy. Ryker carried a wonderful memory of riding on Papa's shoulders to the fish market in Norway. Papa danced a jig and sang songs about bears and trolls, then pretended to be a bear and chased Sissel and Bertina into the house. Papa quit laughing after smallpox took both girls. And then the difficult move to America, their time grubbing stumps in Dodge County, their first hungry winter on the prairie, and Martin running away to join the Union. Maybe they would find happiness again when the war ended and Martin returned home.

Papa cinched his belt and returned to the ox. The storm ended. Ryker watched while Papa felt under the ox's belly and around the sides of its chest. Funny that Papa wasn't as tender with his children as with the animals. "We should have stayed in Norway." Papa shook his head. "We're ruined."

Overhead the clouds drifted into ribbons and wispy tails.

"I'll leave Brimstone to you," Papa said. Sweat dripped muddy rivulets down his dirty face and off the edge of his beard. "God knows how we'd replace him."

"What can I do?" Ryker's voice quivered. Papa said things

only once. Maybe Papa had already told him, and Ryker hadn't paid attention. Ryker braced himself, but Papa seemed pleased with Ryker's question. He pulled a folding knife from the front pocket of his overalls and handed it to Ryker with a stern warning not to lose it.

"Watch him like a mother over a sick child." Papa motioned Ryker closer. He pointed to a white spot on Brimstone's side. "Stick him when he bloats." Papa shouldered his scythe. "He'll die if you don't."

Ryker stood silently, holding the knife in his hand. The Schmitz heifer had once foundered in their cornfield. Johnny bragged how his father allowed him to push a blade into the heifer's flank. That heifer survived, and everyone knew Johnny was as clumsy as a bear.

Ryker imagined jabbing the knife into poor Brimstone's side. Would it draw blood? Would it hurt the poor animal? What if he stabbed too deep, or too shallow? Ryker faced consequences if he did something wrong, missed obeying his father to the letter, daydreamed and forgot to concentrate. "What if I poke the wrong place?" Ryker asked as his father tied a lead rope on Fire to return to his field work. Poor Fire must do the work of both oxen.

"You won't." Papa stepped closer and patted Brimstone's flank. "Aim for this white patch. You can do it."

Ryker wasn't sure that he could.

Papa with Fire in tow was twenty rods away when he turned and called back to Ryker. "And for God's sake, watch the little ones before they do something else to ruin us."

The task felt like a thundercloud hanging over his head.

CHAPTER 3

Papa was right. Brimstone bloated within the hour. Ryker took the knife from his pocket, relieved that he had not lost it, gritted his teeth, and jabbed the ox in the center of the white patch on his lower side.

Brimstone bellowed and kicked. Ryker had not expected the stinky cloud of gas that hissed into his face from the puncture. Ryker turned and retched, as Brimstone went running into the tall grass. It hadn't hurt the poor animal. Though he felt sick to his stomach, Ryker felt proud. He had done it. He would save the ox if it were the last thing he did.

The prairie rolled around him like a green carpet, but this time of the year, Ryker could not see over the grass to enjoy the view. He sometimes climbed to the top of the willow tree next to their house for a better look. The prairie reminded him of the rolling ocean waves. Ryker had been five years old during their ocean voyage to America, but the image imprinted on his mind as clearly as a painting hanging on a wall.

The prairie moved like that ocean, wave after wave of dipping and blowing grass. The ocean waves rolled blue, gray, and green. The prairie showed green, yellow, or blue, with pink splashes of wild roses. It turned gold in the dry season and after the first frost. Like the ocean, the prairie was never still, always tickled and pushed by the winds that swept in from the west.

The image brought words for another story into his mind.

He pushed through the tall grass, like a jungle, following the path left by the ox. He pretended to be a safari hunter in Africa. He followed the sound of the ox charging through the thick grass, pretending he followed an elephant. Meadowlarks sang, and the sounds of spring peepers grew louder as he followed the ox to the far edge of the slough, a marshy spot hidden from their farmstead by cattails.

Brimstone wallowed in muddy water up to his knees, chewing on water lilies. A dab of dried blood showed in the middle of the white spot like a bull's-eye. Brimstone dipped his nose into the green scum floating on the water. Then the ox turned reproachful eyes toward Ryker.

"I'm saving your life," Ryker said. "You don't have to be mad."

Ryker waded into the cool mud of the slough, stretching his toes and swatting mosquitoes. How good it felt to be away from his pesky brother and demanding father. Ryker remembered living in a real house with windows and white walls, clean floors, and real beds. Life in the soddy crammed all of them together without a moment's privacy. Today brought the unexpected gift of being alone.

The grasses dipped like peasants before a king. The thought pleased him, though Ryker knew better than to share this image. His father would tell him to get his head out of his hinder and concentrate on his work. Ryker might share a poem with Teacher, but Papa wouldn't let them attend school until after harvest. Mrs. Tingvold always had a three-week summer session in August. Mama said going to school was the only way for the children to succeed in America. Sometimes she got her way.

The only English word he knew that rhymed with peasants was pheasants. It seemed impossible to add a bird to his poem. Mrs. Tingvold once shared a newspaper article about pheasants. She sketched its graceful tail, explaining how the exotic birds were found in city zoos and in the yards of rich people.

Someday Ryker would be rich and have pheasants, even peacocks, strutting around his yard. He would have enough hens to cook eggs for breakfast every day of the year. He would have two cows, to ensure a steady milk supply, enough to drink without watering it down. And butter to spare. And flour, bread, and cake every day.

Overhead a mountain of white cloud billowed against a clear, blue sky. A bittern harrumphed at the far edge of the slough, and Ryker strained to get a look at the large bird blending into the cattails. He spied it standing still as a stone with its beak held straight up among the reeds, singing its deep, gulping melody.

He and Martin had often played in the slough, having mud fights and trying to swim in the shallow water. Afterwards they picked bloodsuckers from their legs and feet, plastering mud on their many mosquito bites. Lately, Ryker tried not to think about his older brother.

Martin and Frank Schmitz ran away to join the army last summer, though they were only sixteen and lied about their ages. Papa stormed over to the fort and demanded Martin's release. Many boys lied about their ages, and the Union needed every one. At least that's what Captain Vander Horck told Papa at Fort Abercrombie. The enlistment was only for three months, he had said. Martin would be home before winter.

Winter came and went, and Martin was still gone. Mama blamed Papa that Martin ran away in the first place. Sometimes, when they were supposed to be asleep, Ryker heard them argue. Mama said that Papa should have been firm with Captain Vander Horck and demanded Martin's return. Papa argued that nothing would keep a sixteen-year-old boy home if he didn't want to stay.

The heavy weight of Martin's chores fell on Ryker and Sven. Of course, Klara took care of their baby sister. She also kept the manure pail filled with dried cow pies for fuel and watched over Marigold.

Elsa toddled away if left alone for even a second. She always had the croup or earache, fussing and crying from morning until night. And Marigold's escape into the Schmitz's barley field had earned poor Klara a good switching. Every day Klara chased after the cow and baby until she wore down to a frazzle.

Ryker sighed and wished for a book to read. His stomach growled. He reached over to the edge of the swamp and plucked pink rose petals. They tasted tart like sweet lemons, or maybe oranges. Once, in Norway, they had each received a whole orange for Christmas. Ryker couldn't exactly remember how oranges tasted, but he remembered the feeling of sticky juice dripping down his chin.

No doubt, Sven's prairie chicken stewed over the cooking fire just outside the soddy. Mama let the stove go cold during the summer to keep the house cooler. They lived cooped like moles all winter, Mama said, and she determined to be outside as much as possible the rest of the year.

"Have you noticed how dark and dreary man's world is?" Mama said. "God's world overflows with blooming flowers, sun on water, green grass, and blue sky." She did all her summer cooking and laundry outdoors on an old grate set over a fire pit.

His stomach growled again. No bread, of course, until after the harvest, but turnips added a good taste to the stew. Just thinking of turnips reminded him of his task. He waded toward Brimstone and patted his belly. It swelled hard and tight as a watermelon. This time Ryker knew to look away and hold his breath when he made the jab. The knife pierced the thick hide. Brimstone lunged, and Ryker stepped back to avoid a kicking hoof, tripping on a hummock and landing on his backside in the mucky slough with a splash. The water stank, and Ryker wrinkled his nose.

Someone giggled. Ryker expected to see Klara but was surprised to see an Indian family watching from the edge of the grass. A woman holding a cradle board stood smiling beside a man mounted on a spotted pony. The man looked down at Ryker with dark eyes. The woman wore a leather dress and moccasins. Two naked boys, about the age of the twins, laughed and pointed. One had missing front teeth. They said something in their language, as Ryker struggled to his feet.

Indians sometimes visited their farm. This same woman sometimes came to the homestead, asking for food. When Papa complained, Mama said the late treaty payments to the Sioux were a crying shame, and it was her Christian duty to do something about it. She gave the woman a few eggs, even though the hens were in a molt and laying poorly. Mama said they were good people just trying to feed their families. Ryker had noticed that Mama was always more generous to the Indians when Papa wasn't around. Once she gave them the last loaf of baking. The Indians had patted Elsa's yellow curls with approving clucks.

If Mama had been afraid, she hadn't acted like it. "The Bible says to be kind to the poor," she said. "Perhaps angels at our door."

Papa had cast a disapproving look but wouldn't contradict her in front of the children. Besides, it was hard to go against the Bible, whether or not it was their last loaf of bread. Sometimes the Indians brought small game or berries to trade. Once they left a haunch of buffalo on their doorstep. Mama said a kindness always returned in the end.

Ryker wiped the mud off the back of his pants and dried his hands on his shirt.

Johnny Schmitz warned that savages scalped people caught napping. When Sven had repeated this over supper, Papa shrugged his shoulders and said the Indians seemed friendly enough.

The watching Indian family made no move to scalp Ryker.

Scalped, with a knife. Panic made him forget the Indians. Where was his father's knife? Ryker reached into empty pockets. He must have dropped it when he fell into the mud. Papa would kill him if he lost such a precious possession. Ryker knelt in the mud and felt the murky bottom with both hands. He had to find it.

The woman spoke in her language. It seemed she was asking what he was looking for. Ryker made cutting motions as if he held a knife, then splashing noises to show it had fallen into the water. The woman nodded and placed the cradle board in the grass. She and the boys waded into the muck and looked intently around their feet. The man walked his pony into the slough and said something to his wife. She followed his pointed finger and reached down. She held up the knife with a grin.

"Mange takk," Ryker said, taking the knife from her hand. "Many thanks." She had saved his bacon. He gripped the knife in his muddy hand and wiped it on the seat of his trousers before closing the knife. Then he put it into his deepest pocket, checking that no hole would lose it again. "Thank you," he said again, embarrassed to feel a tear of relief leak out of his eye.

The man nodded. Without warning, Beller charged out of the tall grass, barking and growling as the pony snorted and pranced. The woman called her boys, snatched the cradle board out of the grass, and handed it to the man.

"Hush," Ryker said. "Here, boy." He grabbed the dog by the scruff of the neck and held him back from the Indians. "They're friends," he said. "Nothing to be upset about."

After a long moment, the dog quieted, and Ryker released him. He wagged his tail and played with the children, who chased after water bugs. Elsa toddled toward the slough with Klara close on her heels. The man on the horse pointed toward Brimstone, who wallowed in the center of the slough. He made a questioning gesture and then a stabbing motion in Brimstone's direction, then another questioning gesture.

They must think he had lost his mind. Of course it looked foolish. Ryker grinned. He waded out toward Brimstone, who shied away, but in the end allowed Ryker to come near. The Indian pony stood nearby as Ryker examined the ox's belly, patting the bulging side. Ryker wondered how long it would take for the turnip to digest. He took a deep breath, removed the knife from his pocket, and unfolded the blade.

"Ah," said the man beside him. Then Ryker held his nose to show that it was going to stink and pushed the blade into the bull's-eye on Brimstone's side. A terrible smell erupted, along with a long, groaning noise. Brimstone bellowed but did not run away. Ryker patted his now deflated side.

"Ah," the man said as he held his nose. He handed the cradle board back to the woman and called the boys. Beller snatched a frog from the water and swallowed it in a single gulp. The man turned his horse out of the swamp. His family followed. They disappeared into the wall of grass.

Ryker might write a story about this Indian family. He would call the man, Finds the Knife, with his wife, Good Person. He would name the older boy Laughing Boy, and the younger, Little Dog. Through the rest of the long afternoon while he watched over Brimstone, Ryker imagined the story of the Sioux family, who would have died except for the generous gifts of a pioneer woman from Norway. The Norwegian woman wore a blue kerchief. One day when her baby was sick and near starving, she found a buffalo haunch lying on the doorstep. In his story, the white family saved the Indians, who in turn saved them during a terrible blizzard. It would have been an ideal afternoon if only Ryker had paper and pencil to write it all down.

Ryker determined to tell Mama the story and the new names

he had given to the Indian family. He wouldn't mention it to Papa.

Ryker stayed by Brimstone's side for two days. He slept with him in the sod barn. The ox groaned whenever his stomach distended, waking Ryker from his fitful sleep.

By late the second day, Brimstone returned to health.

"You did it," Papa said. He clapped Ryker on the shoulder with a grin that showed all of his teeth. "You might make a farmer yet."

Ryker knew the truth. He would never be a farmer.

CHAPTER 4

"I'm thinking what Martin said about Mama's letter," Sven said the next day as they raked hay together. Sven had not been able to keep up alone, and fallen grass stretched around them in every direction.

One of his letters told how Martin stayed awake during guard duty by memorizing one of Mama's letters. In the letter, Mama told him to think twice before shooting anyone, because "that rebel boy has a mother, too." Just then a Confederate soldier, a boy about Martin's age, stumbled out of the trees.

Martin said they stood looking at each other. Martin saw fear in the boy's face and admitted to feeling more than a little afraid himself. After a long moment, the Reb asked why Martin didn't shoot. Martin told him about his mama's letter. They agreed to each go his way without killing the other and exchanged names to reconnect after the war.

"I think we'll be friends," Martin had written. "If we live."

"Mr. Schmitz!" Sven pointed toward the path where their neighbor rode horseback toward their farmstead. "I knew there would be another letter today!"

The Schmitz family lived closest to them on the prairie. Even if they were German, they were friendly. At least the parents were friendly. Johnny was a bully. The way he tormented the twins was a shame. Frank had convinced Martin to run away with him. Martin would not have done it alone. Sometimes Ryker hated Frank Schmitz.

Mr. Schmitz climbed off his horse and removed his hat. He held the reins as he greeted their parents. Ryker heard their voices, but the prairie wind carried away the words. Gray clouds gathered in the western sky like gray hens perching on their roost. Rain would ruin the downed hay.

"Let's go see," Sven said.

"No," Ryker said. He knew better than disobey his father. They could go after the windrows were raked into haycocks, and not before. Even so, Ryker raked with his eyes fixed on the grown-ups by the soddy.

Mr. Schmitz handed Papa a piece of paper. It fluttered in the breeze. Papa could read a letter from Martin without problem, as Martin would write home in Norwegian. Ryker was the only one in the family who could read a letter written in English. Ryker raked as fast as he could with one eye kept on the adults in case Papa called him to translate. Though Ryker strained to hear, he could not make out a single word.

Mama screamed. The unexpected sound cut through the stillness louder than the honking gander, like a rebel yell or an Indian war whoop. Beller disappeared into the grass. Marigold lifted her head from grazing. Mama collapsed to her knees, her blue kerchief reflecting the color of the sky.

"No," Sven said. His face blanched, and his voice turned to a strangled whisper. "Not Martin."

For the first time Ryker realized his childish foolishness in longing for the excitement of war. Soldiers died. Maybe the war had taken his older brother.

Ryker threw the rake to the ground. Whipping or not, he had to know what was happening. Ryker ran toward Mama with Sven at his heels. It seemed he ran forever without getting anywhere, like in a dream. Mama rocked back and forth on her knees, her apron thrown over her head, praying and wailing like a crazy person.

"Dear Jesus," she prayed again and again. "Not my baby."

Mr. Schmitz stood holding his hat, looking apologetic and uncomfortable. A toothpick stuck out of one side of his mouth. He wore work-worn overalls and hobnail boots but rode the best horse in the community. "Frank wouldn't an untruth tell," he said in his heavy German accent, and in the peculiar sentence structure of their people. "What he knows, he speaks."

"*Mange takk* for bringing word," Papa said, his voice hollowed and strained. The letter trembled in his hands like a brown-eyed Susan in the prairie wind. "It was good of you to take time from your work." Papa's voice failed, and he swallowed hard enough that his Adam's apple bobbed. He didn't seem to notice the boys had left the field.

"The letter you may keep," Mr. Schmitz said. He turned to climb on his horse. The saddle squeaked as he settled his weight, and he flicked the reins. "I'll tell you when more I hear."

Mr. Schmitz disappeared behind the tall grass. Papa knelt beside Mama and patted her back. "It's not certain," he said. "Martin will return, you wait and see."

She threw her arms around Papa's neck and wailed into his chest. "I told you not to let him go." Her kerchief fell into the grass, a blue teardrop against the green grass still scattered with gray goose down.

"Hush now," Papa said. "Martin will be all right."

"You could have stopped him," she said. Her embrace turned into flailing fists on Papa's chest. "It's your fault." Elsa wailed, and the twins stared with open mouths. Ryker had seen his mother cry when his sisters died of smallpox back in Norway, but he had rarely seen Mama disagree with Papa, let alone strike him. "I'll never forgive you if something happened to him."

It was a foolish statement. She must know it wasn't Papa's fault that Martin had run off. She should blame Martin for being led astray by that mouthy Frank Schmitz. Mama, so kind and gentle, seemed incapable of holding a grudge against anyone, especially Papa. She prayed the Lord's Prayer every day, "Forgive us our trespasses as we forgive those who trespass against us."

"Ryker." Papa handed the letter to him. "Read it again."

Ryker carefully unfolded the single sheet of paper. Frank's handwriting climbed up and down across the page like dipping waves. Frank had never been a good student, always causing trouble instead of working his sums. It showed in his clumsy childish script with ink blots, and a drip of what looked like mustard on the corner. It was mostly written in English, and Ryker must translate to Norwegian as he read. Somehow his brain refused to think straight. He scrambled to find the part about Martin.

"Mostly in German," Ryker said.

"Then the English part!" Papa said. His voice quivered with impatience. "Just read the goddamn letter."

Ryker struggled to catch his breath. It was harder with Papa waiting. He read slowly and haltingly, translating as he went, changing the American words into Norwegian ones.

"I am unharmed, but bring bad news of Martin Landstad. We fought at the battle of Pittsburgh Landing in a place called the Hornet's Nest. I was sent with a message for the general. I got back just as the enemy surrounded the battery. I hid in a thicket and watched their surrender, barely escaping being captured myself. I could see clearly that Martin wasn't among those captured. I searched a nearby field hospital, but Martin was not among the wounded. I found Clyde Jensen from Breckinridge. He lost a leg. Please tell his family of his wounds, and that he has survived. Martin was not among the dead, though there were many, and some could not be identified. The dead and wounded number in the tens of thousands. The Reb general

was killed. We will not face him again in battle.

We had hoped to be home by harvest time but are no closer to an end than when we started this mess. We march for Corinth soon, in pursuit of Beauregard's army."

Ryker looked up from the page. "He ends with a paragraph written in German and his signature."

"Nothing more?" Papa said. "Did you miss anything?"

"No," Ryker said, looking over the paper to make sure. It was always that way with Papa.

"Don't cry, Mama," Sven said and retrieved his mother's kerchief. She wiped her eyes with it before sticking it in her apron pocket. "Missing isn't dead. Is it Papa?"

Klara carried the squirming Elsa in her arms. Klara set her down, and Elsa toddled across the yard chasing after a brown hen. The hen squawked, and Elsa chuckled a deep, throaty laugh. The midday sun shone white off her baby curls.

"Mind your sister," Papa said to Klara with a sharp voice. "Snakes hide in the grass."

"Yes, Papa," Klara said. She chased the little girl toddling toward the slough.

The cattails bowed in the prairie wind, and frogs croaked from the slough. The bittern harrumphed, and Ryker looked for it among the reeds. Clouds drifted overhead, hiding the sun.

"We'll eat," Mama said as she got to her feet. Her voice sounded small and breathy. She tied the kerchief back over her hair, and small yellow curls escaped on the sides of her face. Her puffy eyes leaked tears. She wiped them with the back of her chapped hand.

Frank and Johnny Schmitz had been cruel about their mother's kerchief. They said Yankees wore sunbonnets. They said their mother must return to the Old Country if she dressed like a Norwegian square-head and refused to talk American.

It seemed impossible that anyone would despise their mother

because of her pretty blue kerchief. Ryker had stood with gaping mouth, unsure what to do about the insult. Martin didn't hesitate but went nose to nose with Frank with fists curled, even though Frank was built like an ox and outweighed Martin by a stone.

"You pig-dogs know nothing. Our mother is a saint." Martin held his fist under Frank's nose. "Take it back or I'll give you a *chiliwink* you'll never forget." Martin knew how to handle situations.

Papa's voice intruded. "Get back to work."

Mama interrupted, something she rarely did. "*Nei*, not today. I need my children beside me this day." She pulled Ryker close enough that he could smell the lye soap on her skin. Then she squared her shoulders and gave Papa a stern look. "They'll not go back to the fields until after the noon meal."

Papa shrugged. He looked up at the cloudy sky. Without a word, he plodded out to the hay field with stooped shoulders and heavy footsteps. A strange burden settled on Ryker's chest.

Although Ryker didn't understand the German paragraph in Frank's letter, he recognized two words used by boys at school. *Todt* meant dead. It was next to Martin's name. Then *hoffnungslos*, the German word for hopeless, like the Norwegian word *vonlaus*. Ryker wouldn't tell his parents that Frank believed Martin to be dead. Surely the army would contact them soon enough with the facts, whether good or bad.

Hoffnungslos. Hopeless. Martin felt most *vonlaus* about Martin's return.

CHAPTER 5

"Klara!" Ryker called to his sister as he finished the next morning's milking. Klara came out of the outhouse just in time to stop Elsa from following Patsy into the tall grass next to the barn.

"Watch the baby!" Ryker said, as he gave Marigold's udders a final squeeze. "We'd never find her on the prairie."

Marigold had freshened the same day they learned of Martin going missing, giving birth to a beautiful little heifer that would grow up to build their dairy herd. Mama named the little calf Rosebud.

"I can't even go to the outhouse in peace," Klara said with a pout. "How am I supposed to pick berries, find Patsy's nest, herd Marigold, and mind the baby all at once?"

"Come," Ryker said, and motioned for her to dip a cupful of warm milk from the bucket, a rare and welcome treat. "You'll feel better after a drink."

Elsa howled in protest and struggled to escape. Klara drank a long swallow, then held the cup for Elsa to drink. "Try it," Klara said. "You're big enough. You can drink from a cup. Mmm . . . milk."

Elsa batted the cup, and Klara pulled it back. "Say it. Milk."

Elsa screeched, and Mama stuck her head out the door. "Try again. I'm too busy to nurse her right now."

Klara held the cup, but Elsa slapped it away, spilling milk over Klara's apron. Elsa threw herself down on the ground in a tantrum. Mama called for Klara to bring the baby to nurse.

"All right," Klara said. She picked up the screaming baby and whispered loudly into her ear. "Spoiled brat."

Ryker was glad he didn't have Klara's job. He headed toward the soddy with the full bucket, almost tripping over Sven, who wrestled with Beller by the door.

"Papa said to weed the cucumbers and melons before he gets home from the fort," Ryker said. Sven was always trying to wiggle out of chores.

"First we work, and then we work some more," Sven said. "Johnny gets to play. Not slave like us." He motioned for Klara. "Let's go to the hideout until Papa gets back."

Sven and Klara sometimes played in the empty root cellar beneath the branches of the willow tree. This time of year it stood empty of potatoes and, though dark and musty, felt cool and welcoming. Best of all, it was out of sight from adults who always found more chores for them to do, hidden by the drooping branches that obscured the wooden trapdoor.

"*Nei*," Ryker said. He corrected himself and spoke in English. "You will do your chores, or I'll tell Papa."

"Tattletale," Sven said. "Martin would never snitch."

The Landstad family had barely survived the last three years on the prairie. Their first five years in America were spent working for Papa's cousin in Dodge County. Mostly Papa and the boys grubbed stumps, mucked stalls, and did the chores no one else wanted to do. Backbreaking work, and little to show for it, except room and board for the family. Papa spent winters working at a Wisconsin logging camp. There he earned real money. He came back from the pinery that spring of 1859 with a bounce in his step and a burst of confidence.

"We're going to the prairie, Marie," Papa said. "Pack the trunk. We've a place of our own."

"The prairie," Mama said. It seemed she turned pale at the

mention of such a place. "A land without trees?"

"The best part," Papa had said with a laugh. "I've grubbed my last stump. Wide open plains with plenty of room for growing things. Hardly a stone."

"But, Johann," Mama had pleaded, "are you sure?"

"It's done," Papa said with a laugh and picked her up and twirled her around until her skirts fluttered like butterfly wings. Then he kissed her on the mouth right in broad daylight. "We're landowners, just like we've dreamed."

"But Indians," she stammered. "And schools . . ."

"Don't worry," Papa said. "Fort Abercrombie takes care of the Indians." He smiled at Martin and Ryker. "Farmers don't need schooling," he said. "These boys can figure sums and read enough to manage. They'll teach the younger ones."

Ryker's heart sank. His teacher in Dodge County had taught him both to speak and read English. Every Friday they memorized beautiful poems, and the best student received a stick of horehound candy. Ryker had earned three pieces of candy that year, but even sweeter on his tongue were the English words, so lovely and deep.

In the end, Mama agreed in spite of her anxiety. Papa was the man of the house, she had said to the children as they packed their meager possessions to leave for the unknown. "We trust God," she had said with a shaky smile.

Mama followed Papa to America, and Ryker figured she would follow him to the moon had he asked.

Ryker remembered all these things as he brought the milk bucket into the soddy, where his mother nursed the baby.

"This baby needs to learn to drink from a cup," Mama said with a sigh. "I don't have time to nurse with all the work there is to do."

She told Ryker to strain the milk against flies. He poured the rich milk into a porcelain pan and measured rennet, made from a dried calf stomach, being diligent to follow his mother's directions. He stirred it carefully and covered it with a towel. By morning, Mama would heat the junket, pour the mixture into an empty salt sack, drain off the whey, and press it with a prairie stone. The whey would have been saved for pancakes if they had flour but would instead be given to the chickens. Eventually it would become *gjetost*.

Ryker brushed a green weed growing down from the dirt ceiling away from his face. Mama allowed the weeds to grow unhindered, saying that she enjoyed a splash of color against the dark walls. The one-room dugout had a table built into one wall, and a bed built into the opposite wall. The children slept on pallets spread on the dirt floor. A small stove and stovepipe stood in the far corner, with the stovepipe stretching up through the thatched roof. A shelf built into the wall held a scattering of crockery and cooking utensils. A copper boiler sat on top of the stove. Above the door were pegs holding Papa's long rifle. Snakes or gophers sometimes burrowed into the warm room, and Mama's screams of discovery often woke the children in early morning.

His mother ordered him to rinse the milk bucket and place it in the sun to dry. "Cover it with a rag against the flies," she said, her face lined with fatigue.

Little Jimmy Henderson's mother died of fever last year, and his father talked of sending the two-year-old to an orphanage in St. Cloud. Ryker could think of nothing worse than being an orphan.

Ryker impulsively kissed his mother's cheek. "I love you, Mama."

She turned in surprise. "You're growing up," she said, and placed her warm hand on his arm. Her blue eyes swam with tears. "Almost a man." She looked at him with tenderness. "Trust God to help you through the hard times." She choked back a sob. "He will never leave you, if you put your trust in Him." Her words like a caress.

It was an awkward moment, open affection rarely shown in their family. Papa's voice bellowed from the barnyard, calling him to the cucumber patch.

"Your father is a good man," she said as if reading Ryker's mind. "He's hard on you, but that's the way he was raised. He worries you know . . . it almost killed him to lose your sisters . . ." She bit her lip. "And now this business with your brother . . ." She turned to hide her tears.

Ryker obeyed his father, of course. What choice did he have? A fierce anger boiled toward Martin who had so selfishly broken their mother's heart. Then it spilled toward his father, who acted like God Almighty. Ryker vowed to be different than they. He would never make his wife live in a dirt shack, dark and impossible to clean. He would treat his children with respect. He would not browbeat them or make them drudge in the fields like slaves. He would be different.

He daydreamed as he hacked weeds among the cucumber vines. The twins crawled around the plants, gathering cucumbers for their mother's pickle crock. Elsa toddled between the rows, getting in the way. She howled from a bee sting, and Ryker stopped hoeing long enough to jiggle her on his hip to stop her crying.

Someday he would be rich and live in a town big enough to have a library. One thing was certain: he would not be a farmer. When he grew up, he would never, ever, pick up a hoe or a rake again.

CHAPTER 6

Mr. Tingvold stopped by the field in late August when it seemed they would never finish making hay. The summer session of school had started without them.

Papa walked over to Mr. Tingvold but nodded toward the boys to keep working. *"God dag!"* he said in the traditional Norwegian greeting. "Good day."

"Playing hooky, I see," Mr. Tingvold said with a jolly laugh. His wife was the teacher of their little school, but sometimes Ryker wished Mr. Tingvold were instead. Mrs. Tingvold seemed a cheerless, harsh person; Mr. Tingvold, always jolly in contrast.

"Work to do," Papa said with a frown. "No time for school."

They were gathering haycocks into huge stacks. At first it had felt like a game to jump on the growing stack to compact the hay as tightly as possible. But hot weather and monotony soon turned it into plain, hard work. By the end of a day of trampling haystacks, their legs ached and it seemed they felt the tiredness in every muscle of their bodies. They trampled it as tight as possible to prevent the wind from carrying it away. Then Papa fashioned the top layer of the stack to shed water or snow.

Damp hay molded and ruined the value of the fodder. Fort Abercrombie wanted only sweet hay, sun dried and healthy. Ryker had calculated the amount of hay the fort needed to feed its large herds of horses and cattle. At least two tons for every animal. Papa acted like they would supply every ton.

Two haystacks stood finished already, and Papa hoped to do

another before snow. Another stack would carry them through the winter, even if their barley crop failed. It was their insurance against hunger. Ryker prayed a desperate prayer that they would never again suffer hunger and cold as they had that first winter on the prairie.

Mr. Tingvold shared local gossip while Ryker pitched haycocks on top of the growing stack. Sven jumped to compact the hay into the stack. Ryker kept his ear cocked toward the men's conversation and caught most of what was said. He heard the word *Sioux* several times and also the word *war.*

"Just come from Slabtown," Mr. Tingvold said.

Slabtown stood on the eastern edge of Fort Abercrombie, just across the Red River. Logging companies in the Big Woods floated giant logs down the Otter Tail River to where it connected with the Bois de Sioux River that became the Red River of the North. A large blade turned the logs into boards freighted away on riverboats. Papa said Minnesota logs were building cities across America. Huge piles of slabs and chopped stacks of cordwood supplied the boats with fuel. Immigrants lived there, enjoying the work and close proximity of the fort. Johnny said saloons and gambling houses outnumbered private homes. He whispered about upstairs women willing to sell their bodies, even to boys their age if they had the money.

"Payments to the Sioux are late," Mr. Tingvold said. He and Papa always spoke to each other in Norwegian. "Seems Honest Abe needs the money for the war."

Murmuring voices kept low.

"What are they saying?" Sven said and slid down the side of the stack, mopping sweat from his red face with his shirttail. He picked up a rake and gathered the scattered bits of hay lying around the base of the stack.

"Don't know," Ryker said. "Hush, so we can hear."

"Me, neither," Papa said clearly. "With the fort so close, I can't imagine there would be a problem out here." Papa looked their way and lowered his voice. Obviously, he did not want the boys to hear.

"Maybe they're talking about Martin," Sven said with a determined set of his jaw. "I'm going to sneak closer."

"You'll get in trouble," Ryker said. "Papa said to finish this stack before another rainstorm heads this way." Each stack took almost a month of work. If they pulled together, they might even finish another before frost ended the haying season.

Sven propped his rake over his shoulder and hurried toward the men.

"Where are you going, young man?" Papa said with a growl.

"The outhouse," Sven said while pointing with his jaw toward the home place, rubbing his tummy and making a sour face. "Don't feel so good."

Papa scowled but assented. "Make haste. Work to do."

Ryker pitched another haycock but kept an eye on his brother. Sven ran toward the out-house but ducked into the tall grass beyond the men. The turkey-foot grasses wiggled, showing Sven's movement to circle back closer to where they stood. Then only the wind rippled across the green prairie.

The sun beat mercilessly down. Just another row and Ryker would be finished. Maybe then Papa would allow him to go to school. He tried to remember the words for a poem he had learned last year. Something about a village blacksmith.

Mr. Tingvold turned to leave, and Sven sneaked back toward the path. He stood and headed back toward the haystack.

"Feeling better?" Mr. Tingvold called out to Sven. "Got the Tennessee Trots." He laughed at his own joke. He cautioned about the dangers of bad food and water. The conversation drifted to a close.

Mr. Tingvold hitched up his suspenders. "Boys, the missus says come back to school, or there'll be hell to pay."

Papa walked with Mr. Tingvold for a short distance down the path.

"What did he say?" Ryker said.

"Trouble with the Sioux," Sven said. "Papa says we're close enough to the fort, so we don't have to worry."

Something wasn't right. They were ten miles from Fort Abercrombie, too far away for the soldiers to be much help. He remembered Finds the Knife with his steely glance, sharp arrows, and hunting knife.

Sven whispered that Clyde Jensen had died from his wounds at Shiloh. His missus got the news that week. War news was all bad, and Mr. Tingvold said Lincoln was botching the war and needed to be voted out before it was too late.

That night, Ryker had just fallen asleep when his parents' whispering woke him.

"What's wrong, Johann?" Mama said. "Don't cry so."

Ryker listened. Muffled sobs came from their parents' bed. "It's my fault," Papa said. "We never should have come to this God-forsaken place."

"Hush now," Mama soothed. "Martin will come home; surely the angels care for him."

"And this whole business with schooling." Papa sniffed, and Ryker heard the edge of anger creep back into his father's voice. "Of course they should be in school, but what's a man to do?" Papa said. A creaking and rustling of corn shucks. "I can't keep up without Martin's help. Selling hay keeps the wolf from the door."

"We'll get by," Mama said in her calmest voice. "To make it in America, the children must speak and read English. They need an education."

"You know how tight things are," Papa said. Ryker heard the frustration rising in his voice. "Norwegian is the language of our people. It's good enough."

"Of course," Mama said. "But we're Americans now." More rustling and squeaking. "I'll help with the haying."

"But the barley is heading out," Papa said. "Damn blackbirds will take the crop without the children chasing them away."

"I've done it before."

"I hope they appreciate all you do for them."

"And you," she said. "How hard you work." Elsa cried out in her sleep, and Ryker reached over to pat her back. The smells of the night pot filled the room, and Sven snored softly beside him. Smoke from the smudges burning in front of the door and window drifted in. Without the smudges, the mosquitoes ate them alive. He strained to hear.

"All right, then," Papa said. "Until the barley ripens. Just the boys. We can't spare Klara, especially if you work in the fields." More shuffling on the cornhusks. "Girls don't need learning. The boys will do chores in the morning and after school."

"Maybe Klara could go on her birthday as a special treat," Mama said in a low voice. "We have nothing for a gift, no flour or sugar for a cake."

Ryker grinned in the darkness.

"And the Red Men?" Mama said.

"I told you," Papa said, and his voice sharpened. "The Sioux know better than cause trouble so close to the fort."

"But you know how they've been treated." Mama sniffed. "Shameful. Terrible. And now their payments are late again."

"I shouldn't have told you," Papa said. His voice softened. "Governor Ramsey and Abe Lincoln will work it out."

Quiet then, but Ryker lay awake long into the night. He was sure that Mr. Tingvold said Minnesota would pay the price if the Sioux didn't get their treaty payments. Ryker wondered what that price might be.

CHAPTER 7

Ryker wiggled on the hard stump used for a stool, peering over the shoulder of his teacher toward the bright sky. Flies buzzed around the stalls. It smelled of old hay and cow manure. A bead of sweat rolled down his back, reminding him of the hot barley field waiting after school.

"Pay attention," Mrs. Tingvold said in a crabby voice. Though she spoke American, she sounded as much Norwegian as the Landstad family. She wore an ugly brown dress and tied her hair in a kerchief like Mama, only one so old and faded it was hard to tell what color it once might have been. Her crumpled mouth reminded Ryker of a rotting apple with its cracks and dents, and she lacked most of her teeth.

Mama said they were lucky Mrs. Tingvold knew enough book learning to teach them a little reading, writing, and arithmetic— even if the Tingvold barn must serve as a makeshift school. The few neighborhood children gathered on stumps and rocks, balancing slates and sharing books. With Martin and Frank gone, Ryker was the oldest boy.

"Take it back," Sven, demanded from his seat near the door. He was always arguing with Johnny. "You're a liar."

"Boys!" Mrs. Tingvold said from the front of the room, picking up the willow rod she used for a pointer as if she were ready to thrash the both of them. She bristled like a broody hen. "What's the trouble?"

"He's lying," Sven said, balling his fists and glaring at Johnny.

"Pa says Martin's dead," Johnny said. He wore store-bought trousers and bright-red suspenders. His dark hair stood out in cowlicks, and freckles dotted his face. "Missing means dead in the army."

"It does not!" Sven said.

Klara moved closer on the stump she shared with Sven and popped her thumb in her mouth. Klara had been allowed to go to school before Elsa learned to walk. But now, Mama couldn't keep watch over Elsa and do all the chores as well. The twins sat together to share a slate.

Ryker didn't know whether to join in the fight or stop the argument. Clippings from the Tingvolds' newspaper told about the battle, casualty lists, and prisoner exchanges. The battle, now called Shiloh, killed thousands of soldiers on both sides. Ryker brought the clippings home to read to his parents. Mrs. Tingvold was nice sometimes.

"Enough of such talk," Mrs. Tingvold said. "No one knows for sure." She glared at Johnny until he squirmed in his seat. "We must pray for Martin and all our boys fighting in the South."

"And you . . ." She turned her attention to Klara, tapping the willow rod against her leg as she spoke. "Only babies suck their thumbs."

Klara's lips quivered as she stuck her hand in her apron pocket. Last year, for the same infraction, Mrs. Tingvold had struck Klara's hand hard enough to leave a mark. Back then, Martin jumped between the teacher and his little sister, defiantly taking the switches in her stead. Ryker should protect her now, but it was Sven who put his arm around his sister and glared at the teacher.

Gunshots cracked in the distance from the direction of the Schmitz farm. How odd for Mr. Schmitz to be hunting with field work undone. A fly droned around Ryker's face, and he flicked it away. He stretched his neck to look out the window, but the only thing in his line of vision was a sandhill crane standing in the cow yard next to a rock pile.

Mrs. Tingvold should be upset with Johnny, not Klara. Johnny was teacher's pet because his family was better off than the others. The Schmitzes lived in a log home and owned a pair of horses and a cutter. Johnny bragged that his father had earned good money working at the sawmill in Slab Town. They enjoyed flour, even during spring starving time. With two cows, they never watered down their milk. Johnny boasted they would slaughter their shoat as soon as the weather cooled. Ryker couldn't remember the taste of pork.

"Ryker will now report on *Uncle Tom's Cabin,*" Mrs. Tingvold announced to the students, as if to change the subject to something more pleasant. "Harriet Beecher Stowe's book explains why we are fighting this terrible war." She smiled a gap-toothed smile. "It puts a human face on the issues. Fiction tells many truths, and some folks blame Mrs. Stowe for causing this war." She paused and looked at Ryker. "You may begin."

Ryker hunched down and squirmed. "I'm not quite finished," he said. Papa kept him busy until it was too dark to read. More gunshots sounded in the distance. The wind moaned around the eaves of the log barn.

Mrs. Tingvold frowned but did not scold. Instead she lectured about slavery, the secession of southern states that caused the war, and President Lincoln's leadership of the northern army. Ryker counted dust motes floating on the shafts of light. He would rather read about Topsy's woes than listen to Mrs. Tingvold. While reading, he forgot the hard work, war in the South, and his missing brother. A faint smell of smoke wafted through the barn door. Ryker craned his neck to look out the window but saw only the green leaves of the lilac bushes growing next to the barn.

Before he went missing, Martin's last letter said that smoke from cooking fires blanketed the encampments in the Shenandoah Valley like one of Mama's down quilts. He said there were enough trees to fuel a million cook stoves or build a whole city of real houses. His description of the green forest made Mama homesick for the land of her youth. Maybe that was why she clung to the old ways, wearing a kerchief instead of a bonnet, refusing to learn the strange English words, and searching for angels in the clouds.

Martin hadn't left for war because of any of the reasons in Mrs. Tingvold's lecture. Martin wanted excitement. He only left to find adventure—and get away from farm chores.

Absently Ryker fingered a lone whisker on his chin. Papa said some boys developed beards in their early teens. Ryker hoped he was one of them. If he grew whiskers, Papa would surely let him take over the scythe.

"Hurry home, now," Mrs. Tingvold said. "School is in recess until after the harvest."

A whoop went up from the other students, but Ryker didn't join the celebration. He gathered his slate and *Uncle Tom's Cabin*. He wanted to know more about Topsy, the girl with skin the color of soot.

Mrs. Tingvold had loaned him the book after she learned of Martin's disappearance. "Reading will help your English," she had said while handing him the book wrapped in a cotton cloth to keep it clean. She wasn't always crabby.

Ryker painstakingly translated each word into Norwegian so he could understand what the story was about. It took a long time. The night before he had come to the exciting part where Topsy ran away from the overseer. He hated to return the book before the end of the story.

He handed the book to Mrs. Tingvold, but she pushed it back into his hands.

"You may keep it a while longer," she said with a gentle smile. "It's good to understand why your brother fights with the Union."

A grin stretched Ryker's face. She said fight instead of fought, meaning she thought him alive. Maybe Mama would allow a candle to read a few pages before bed. *"Mange takk,"* he said. Harvest wouldn't be so bad if the book waited at the end of each day. "Many thanks. I'll be careful with it."

"You'll guard it with your life," Mrs. Tingvold said with a laugh, shooing him off with a wave of her hands. "Now hurry. You've work to do."

CHAPTER 8

Ryker tucked the book under his arm and stepped out into the sunlight. Other students scattered towards their homes, but the twins waited in the shade of the barn with Johnny. A meat cleaver and ax wedged into the flat surface of the blood-stained stump used for dressing meat. Next to the stump sat a foot-powered grinder for sharpening knives, scythes, and plow shares.

Klara sucked her thumb, Sven rubbed the edge of a home-made knife against the grinding stone, and Johnny pedaled. A sunbeam bounced off Sven's white hair. Mama said the twins took after her side of the family, with their fair skin and blue eyes, while Ryker looked more like his father's side with dark hair and brown eyes. "Black Norwegians," she had called them, always laughing and teasing with a decided twinkle in her eye.

Mama hadn't laughed since Martin went missing.

"For shame, Klara!" Ryker said with a disapproving frown.

Klara pulled the thumb out of her mouth. Her sunbonnet dangled down her back by its strings, and she wore a faded calico dress far too short for her gangly legs.

"Leave her be," Sven said. "You're not the boss of us."

Martin always kept the younger children in line. Ryker sighed. He wished Martin were here now.

"Hurry," Ryker said. "Papa needs us at home for the harvest."

"We're going over to Johnny's first," Sven said.

"Ma baked molasses cookies," Johnny said. They seemed to have forgotten their argument. "And I caught a baby fox."

"Not today," Ryker said. The thought of cookies weakened his knees. Lately their table had been bountiful with prairie chickens, milk, and eggs. But they hadn't seen bread for months, and no sugar since Christmas. Even so, Ryker knew Papa would keep them chained to the barley field, birthday or not.

"It's our birthday," Sven said.

Ryker didn't want to work in the fields either. He wanted to finish his book.

"Forget it," Ryker said. He felt as crabby as Mrs. Tingvold.

The smell of smoke grew stronger. Ryker shielded his eyes against the noonday sun and watched a plume of smoke rise above the Schmitz farm to the east of the Tingvold place, just beyond a swell in the prairie.

"Pa's burning the slough," Johnny said. "I'd best get home." Johnny trotted toward the east along the well-worn path snaking through the prairie.

Sven whined about the lack of cookies on his birthday. Instead, he chewed handfuls of wild rose petals plucked from bushes growing alongside the path. Ryker gathered rose petals, too. They puckered his lips but tasted almost sweet. Klara dawdled. The prairie looked flat as a pancake, but it dipped and swelled with rises and gullies. They walked through an ancient buffalo wallow toward their farm.

Overhead a cloudless sky. Songs of wren and meadowlarks added to the music of rustling grass and gentle breeze. Klara gathered a dried stalk with a cluster of leaves like a head of yellow hair. She cradled it in her arms, crooning as if to a baby. Sven caught a snake and chased after Klara until she screamed.

"Get that nasty thing away from us," Klara said, pulling the makeshift doll close against her body to shield it. "Ryker, make him stop."

Ryker sometimes imagined how different everything would be had his sisters survived the smallpox. Sissel and Bertina would be tall girls now, with blond hair tied back with ribbons. They would care for Elsa and help their mother with the endless household chores. They would milk the cow and make butter and cheese. Then he imagined Martin coming home to pick up the rake and work the harvest.

That was what was wrong with their family. People were missing. Bertina had been a shy girl, with large teeth and a gentle smile; Sissel with blond hair like Elsa's.

"Last one home is a rotten egg," he said. They sprinted down the path and veered off across the prairie toward home.

The Landstads' sod house nestled into the side of a low hill. Papa chose the site because of a small cluster of willow trees growing along the edge of a slough. Some of their neighbors enjoyed cabins with logs hauled from Fort Abercrombie's sawmill. Logs cost money. Papa said they charged fifteen dollars per hundred board feet—unheard of prices, but, then, the prairie had no trees. It would take a long while to save enough to build a house. They'd be in the soddy for a while yet.

Ryker watched the hot August wind ripple across the tops of the prairie grass. Plowing virgin prairie, even with two oxen and a sharpened plow, tried the strength of grown men. Martin had the muscles to do it, but Ryker's arms and legs turned to jelly after only a few minutes at the task.

Papa planned to break sod on the westernmost end of their property. He said they would plant more corn next year and that Ryker would help with the plowing. The thought sickened Ryker. He couldn't yet measure up to his brother's strength, but Martin would be surprised to find more land under tillage. His brother would look at Ryker with admiration and tease him about his bulging muscles.

They neared the homestead from the north, coming up to the soddy along the edge of the barley field. His father wasn't in sight.

"Here, Beller," Sven called, but their dog did not bound out of the grass with his usual welcome. "Come, boy!"

"Off hunting rabbits," Klara said. "He'll be back." She stopped to gather a handful of yellow daisies peeking through the tall grass. "Aren't these pretty?"

Fire and Brimstone's pen stood empty with the gate open. Papa had talked about moving them to the west pasture after they finished harvesting the barley, but the barley waved in the breeze, the heads hanging low and full. Loose oxen would destroy standing grain. Ryker shielded his eyes but saw only grass.

In front of the door lay the dead gander, its wingtips smeared with blood, its naked rump showing shadows of new growth. Beside it lay the goose and rooster. Ryker's heart thumped. He stepped over the birds and pushed into the dugout with a lump in his throat the size of Brimstone's choking turnip. He called for his mother.

No one answered.

Mama's collection of feathers fluttered in the air. Broken dishes littered the floor. Eggs splattered against the dirt walls. Someone had overturned Mama's crock of dills. The room reeked of vinegar. No sign of Baby Elsa or his parents. Only the green vines grew undisturbed on the walls.

Sven and Klara stared in disbelief, holding hands and staying close to Ryker.

"What happened?" Sven said.

"Hush," Ryker hissed.

The rifle pegs over the door stood empty. Ryker swallowed hard, remembering the gunshots and the smoky smells. He ran outside with the twins close behind him and searched behind the barn. Near the outhouse, Papa lay crumpled in the weeds, still holding his rifle. An arrow stuck in his chest. Sven knelt beside him, calling his name. Klara stood as if in shock, sucking her thumb and staring. Blood covered Papa's shirt, his skin as white as their mother's linen tablecloth.

Ryker froze, afraid to touch him, as a wave of nausea roiled his belly. He had never seen a dead person except those laid out in wooden coffins. Papa fluttered his eyelids, clutched the rifle, and groaned.

Papa lived. Thank God.

"What happened?" Ryker said. "Where's Mama and Elsa?"

Papa mumbled, and Ryker fell to his knees to hear the words. "Indians took them," Papa said. He dropped his hand to the arrow in his chest. "Couldn't stop."

Ryker's mind whirled in confusion. They had no argument with Indians. Mama always gave them bread.

"I took the gun for prairie chickens . . . for birthday supper." Papa struggled to sit up, but fell back with a gasp of pain. "Beller barked . . . and then screams." His eyelids fluttered. "Run," he said, and it seemed to take all his wind to speak. "Hide. All of you. Root cellar."

"Don't talk," Ryker said. "Save your strength."

Voices sounded beyond the slough. Indians!

"Hurry," Sven said. "Help Papa to the root cellar."

Sven and Ryker half carried, half dragged Papa to the willow tree. Klara lugged Papa's rifle and opened the trap door. Ryker brushed away the tracks in the dirt leading to the door of the root cellar hidden beneath the branches of the willow tree and scrambled in behind them. Darkness closed around them like a grave. Klara closed the door, as a blood-curdling scream bristled the hair on Ryker's neck. They huddled closer. Klara's small hand touched his, as small as a baby rabbit.

"I'm scared," Klara whispered. "Where's Mama?"

"Something's burning," Sven whispered.

Smoke filtered around the door frame. Angry shouts sounded from outside. Near at first, and then farther away.

"The haystacks," Ryker said with a groan. "All that raking for nothing."

They huddled in the darkness, listening to their father's moans. Ryker lifted Papa's head to his lap. Ryker's mind swirled in confusion, trying to make sense of what was happening. Soon the bad dream would be over. He tried to shake himself awake, but the smell of blood and touch of Klara's hand convinced him that it was really happening. His father had been shot with an arrow, his mother and sister taken by the Sioux. They were in mortal danger.

Klara sniffled, and Ryker pulled her close.

"What will happen to us?" she whispered in the darkness. "Where's Mama?"

"Have to find them," Papa said with a fierceness that frightened Ryker. Papa's breath came in gasping shudders, and he grasped Ryker's arm and pulled him closer until Ryker's ear was in front of Papa's mouth. Papa smelled of blood and sweat, his voice barely a whisper. "New baby coming."

His mother had been tired lately, and thicker around the middle, but Ryker hadn't known of another baby. His cheeks burned, and he was glad for the darkness. Such things weren't talked about, and the news made him feel very grown up, at least as old as Martin. The knowledge felt heavy as a stone.

Once he had read a story about a white woman captured by Indians. They forced her to marry a brave. Her children grew up to hate whites. They made war upon their own people. That could not happen to Mama.

"Is there a light?" Papa said.

The earthen walls sucked the strength from his voice. Ryker brushed a spider web away from his face, as Sven struck a lucifer and lit a candle stub. Sven held the candle high, and a feeble ray of light fell over them.

"Stuff that old sack under the door, so they won't see the

light," Ryker said to Sven.

"Help me." Papa grasped the shaft of arrow in his chest and pulled. Nothing budged. Papa's hands trembled violently. "Ryker, pull it out. I don't have the strength."

Ryker did not know how to obey his father. Just looking at the arrow imbedded in his father's chest caused dark spots to float before his eyes. Ryker grasped the end of the arrow. Papa cried out in pain, and Ryker let go.

"*Nei*," Papa said. "Just do it. Pull. Pull harder."

Ryker grasped the arrow shaft with both hands. He braced his feet and pulled with all his might. The arrowhead moved a little, causing Papa to cry out with pain.

"Don't stop," Papa said. "I can take it."

Ryker yanked with all his might. The arrow moved about an inch. Papa screamed and then swooned. Ryker listened for signs the Indians had heard. Nothing but silence.

"You killed him," Sven said. He held the light closer to Papa's white face.

Ryker shook him, calling his name, but Papa didn't respond. It smelled musty as a tomb. Klara kept close to the light, sucking her thumb.

"He's only sleeping," Sven said with a sigh of relief. "Pull it out before he wakes up."

Ryker grasped the arrow again with both hands and pulled as hard as he could. The shaft broke off in his hand, leaving the arrowhead in Papa's body.

Sven pushed Ryker aside and retrieved the folding knife from Papa's pocket. He opened it and wiped the blade across his pant leg. "Here," Sven said, handing Ryker the knife.

It would be scarier to cut out the arrow than it had been to push the knife into Brimstone's side to cure the bloat. He couldn't do it.

Sven handed the candle to his sister and bent low with the

knife. He inserted the blade into the wound, scraping it against the rocky edges of the arrowhead.

"It's not too deep," Sven said. "I think I can get it." Another twist of the blade and he was able to grasp the sharp stone. He pulled it out with a cry of triumph. "Here. I got it."

Sven laid the arrowhead in Klara's hand. Ryker bent to staunch the flow of blood seeping around the wound, tearing Papa's shirttail for a bandage. There was a lot of blood. It soaked through the bandage, and Ryker added another strip of cloth from Papa's shirt.

"What do we do now?" Klara said in a whisper.

Ryker could only shrug his shoulders and shake his head.

CHAPTER 9

They waited for Papa to wake up.

Klara held Papa's hand and kissed it. "We need you, Papa," she said. "You have to live."

Sven scavenged for a ragged gunny sack to use as a blanket. He shook the dust out of it and draped it over his father's body.

It seemed like forever, just listening to their father's rough breathing and frequent moans.

At last Papa woke and pushed himself to his elbow. He cried out. His eyes widened when he saw the bloody front of his shirt in the candlelight. *"Vonlaus,"* Papa said. The blood stain on his shirt blossomed into a crimson flower. "You'll have to fetch help. I'm not going to make it."

"We'll wait until you're stronger," Ryker said, "and go together."

"Nei," his father gasped and stiffened. "It's a mortal wound. Fetch the money pouch," Papa said. "Gather what is left."

"I can't," Ryker said, choking back tears.

"You can. It's over for me. Go—" Before he could finish his sentence, Papa's voice faded into silence.

"Papa!" Klara said. "He needs a drink of water."

For all Ryker knew, Indians hid in the yard, waiting for them to show themselves. Ryker pushed open the door a crack. It was twilight. His stomach growled, and he remembered the dill pickles lying on the cabin floor. Somewhere the cow waited to be milked. Maybe the Indians had missed the cellar under the

61

kitchen where the milk jug, cheese, and fresh eggs were kept. He must fetch water from the well.

"Wait here," he said to the twins. "I'll be right back."

"No!" Klara said. "Don't leave us."

"I'm here," Sven said. "I'll take care of you."

Ryker crept out of the cellar and breathed the fresh air. He pressed close to the ground and crawled to the outhouse. His heart beat so loudly that he doubted he could hear Indians if they were there. He waited a long moment and peeked around the side, looking toward the front of the soddy. The haystack smoldered into a heap of red charcoal beyond the barn, and the smoky smell lingered over the homestead. *Skraelings*! Dirty Indians. The fire had burned itself out before it reached the garden.

No sign of Indians. Crows stirred with a flurry of black wings when Ryker walked by the dead geese, where they were picking the carcasses. He didn't dare start a fire, even if the meat would spoil. Ryker found three eggs in the nest beside the coop. No sign of Beller, Marigold, the calf, or the ox team. Ryker looked around before he dared enter the soddy. The last thing he needed was to be caught inside. The soddy had only one entrance.

As his eyes adjusted to the darkness, he scooped the pickles scattered on the dirt floor and put them into an empty flour sack hanging behind the door. He gathered a string of dried beans from the wall and opened the trap door to the cellar hole under the kitchen. It held a few garden vegetables. He found a jug of milk and a pat of fresh butter. He added to the sack until it bulged. Tears came when he picked up the block of *gjetost* cheese. There would be no treat for Christmas this year.

He stuffed his mother's comb and matching hand mirror into the sack. He eyed the Norwegian Bible, but it was too heavy to carry.

"Dear God," Ryker said, but no words followed. "Dear God," he said again. Then he gathered the money pouch from the hiding place behind the stove. He hung the strings of the pouch around his neck. It held only a few coins.

He reached for the butcher knife from the high shelf and a quilt from under the bed. He must hurry. Mama's hatpin stuck in a pincushion in her knitting basket. It might come in handy. He grabbed the ball of yarn, and Klara's sweater. Flint for fire. A short length of rope. He grabbed the salt shaker off the window sill and picked up *Uncle Tom's Cabin* off the floor where he had dropped it.

"Dear God," he said again. Then he spied the shoes lined under the bed. He grabbed them and stuffed them into the sack.

He was almost out the door when he spied the tintype of his parents' wedding day. His father scowled into the camera, so young and strong. Swallowing a sob, Ryker pulled the picture off its nail and kissed their young faces. He tucked it into his pocket, wondering if he would ever see his mother again.

Swirling gray clouds gathered on the western horizon. Mama and Elsa would be cold if it rained. Even now slivers of lightning sparked in the sky, and the wind rose. Ryker pushed the sack into the hideout and crept back to the well. He prayed as he drew water. He asked God to make the Indians kindly toward Mama and Elsa. They hadn't been kind to his father.

Ryker climbed the willow tree and scanned the flat prairie for their missing animals or signs of Indians. A blanket of yellow flowers covered the prairie. Wisps of smoke from the smoldering haystack stung his eyes. Everything looked the same. He squinted past the endless prairie. Fort Abercrombie should have protected them.

Bitterns and red-winged blackbirds sang from the swamp. A hawk fought the crows for the dead gander. A nighthawk swooped across the darkening sky. The first raindrops splattered on his face, pattering on the green willow branches.

Papa must go along with them. Papa knew what to do. Papa would surely be strong enough to travel by morning. Ryker clambered down the tree as the fat drops turned to drenching sheets of cold rain.

It made no sense to leave during a storm. An unexpected peace settled over him. It wasn't an audible voice, but an inner assurance that made him certain they could wait to leave until morning. He prayed for angels to watch over Mama and Elsa. He prayed for the twins, for Martin, for Papa, and for himself.

He was almost down the tree before he remembered to ask God to keep the new baby safe. Maybe a little brother this time.

Ryker crawled back to the root cellar. The candle sizzled. Papa looked as white as death itself. Blood soaked through the bandage on his chest, and Sven insisted on giving him drops of water.

"Mama always makes sick people drink water," Klara said.

They took turns drinking from the milk jug. It felt cold and sweet on his throat. Ryker hoped the Indians hadn't killed Marigold. She was a good cow, beautiful in spite of the blinded eye, always faithful to give milk, and now with a calf. She may have run out into the prairie when the Indians attacked. No sign of her carcass, nor of her calf.

"Papa, do you want a pickle?" Sven said.

"No," Klara said. "Remember when we had measles? Mama said only water."

His father spoke again, his words as quiet as a butterfly's wings. "You're the man of the family now. Find Mama and Elsa and fetch them home."

"Papa," Ryker said as tears sprouted from his eyes, "you'll be better soon."

"The title is free and clear." Papa's voice sounded barely

audible. "The deed in the strong box dug into the wall under the stove." He rasped a shuddering breath. The candle flickered. "Making hay is easier than breaking sod. You'll make enough to support the family if you stick with it."

"Please," Ryker said. "Don't talk that way."

"I'm fading," Papa said. He clutched Ryker's arm until his fingers gouged Ryker's flesh. "Don't be so foolish as to sell out. There are those who would take advantage. Promise me you'll care for the family."

Ryker's dreams of a better life floated before him. A fancy house with books, decorative pheasants, and two milk cows seemed unimportant. He turned away from the dream and promised to care for the family and keep the farm.

Then Papa called for the twins and spoke a word to each, telling them he loved them and that they should take care of their mother. "Mind your brother. He's as good as any man."

The candle fizzled to blackness. "I never planted that lilac bush she wanted," Papa said. He gasped once, and Ryker thought Papa was gone, but his voice came again from the darkness, even fainter and weaker. "Tell Schmitz . . . fetch soldiers."

Klara begged Papa to live.

Papa slept, his ragged breathing the only sign of life.

"Angels will care for us," Klara said in a shaky voice between sniffles. "Mama says we don't need to be afraid." She prayed Mama's favorite nighttime prayer: "Protect us as we stay awake, watch over us as we sleep."

They huddled in the darkness until first Klara, and then Sven drifted into a restless sleep.

Mama or Martin should be here. His older sisters should be in charge. Outside the storm roared its fury. Even though muffled by the earthen walls, the sounds of pouring rain proved louder than his pounding heart.

CHAPTER 10

Ryker knew he should feel something, but a black fog settled over him, as thick as the smoke over the Schmitz farm earlier that day.

Ryker couldn't rest. He couldn't shut down his mind. It was as if he were missing something important. Something nagging just beyond reach. The smoke over the Schmitz farm. The Schmitzes' cabin was built of real logs. Indians had fired the Schmitz cabin. He couldn't go to them for help.

He remembered the gunshots, and a cold shudder went through him. He thought of Johnny running through the tall grass, and how the twins could have been with him, heading into the face of danger. They had been within spitting distance of the Indians. He looked out the crack in the door. The rain had settled into a steady downpour. A gust of wind brought a shiver to his skin.

Ryker closed the door and touched Papa's cold face, like a slab of meat hanging in the woodshed. He jerked his hand away and groped in the darkness for Klara's warm body.

Papa was gone. The ground shifted beneath Ryker's feet, and it was a long moment before he could breathe.

"Protect us as we stay awake," he prayed through chattering teeth. He must be brave. "Watch over us as we sleep."

Ryker stayed awake through the dark night, rousing to peek out the door several times. The rain stopped, and mosquitoes tormented. Klara cried out in her sleep, but Ryker feared a smudge fire would draw the savages. He covered her with her quilt. Then Ryker crawled outside and lay under the drooping willow boughs.

The sky cleared, and a million stars splattered across the floor of the sky. Somewhere Mama and Elsa looked up at the same stars. Maybe Martin viewed them from a rebel prison camp. Or maybe Martin was already with Bertina and Sissel, Papa, and *Bestemor.* He tried to imagine living far above the stars, in heaven with the Triune God and the cherubim and seraphim. Some things were beyond imagination.

Mama and Elsa might be in heaven, too. They might already be orphans. They would be worse off than Jimmy Henderson, who at least had a father. Ryker could not staunch the flow of tears.

"Help us, God," Ryker said. "Watch over us, Papa." His throat thickened until he thought he might suffocate. "Don't leave us."

Ryker cried until his tears ran out. His head ached. Overhead, the shadow of a swooping bat. The whine of mosquitoes and croaking frogs mixed with the haunting howl of a wolf. Or maybe it was an Indian signaling his fellows to attack them again. Maybe the same Indians who had taken Mama and Elsa. Elsa was so small and sometimes had bad dreams in the night. What if she cried out and an Indian hurt her? What if Mama's baby came tonight?

No, he reminded himself. Mama's baby would not come tonight. Mama would keep Elsa safe from the Indians. Ryker would take the twins to the Tingvolds' with morning light. Mr. Tingvold would fetch the soldiers. They would be all right. At least for now. He looked up at the panorama of stars overhead. Mrs. Tingvold named it the Milky Way. He would remember to ask her why it had such a strange name.

Martin knew how to follow a trail by the stars, just like Topsy in *Uncle Tom's Cabin,* but Ryker knew only how to get lost. The memories of trips to Fort Abercrombie swirled in his mind. How smothered he had felt while traveling through tall grass. But he knew the trail to the Tingvolds'. He had nothing to worry about.

Ryker crawled back into the cellar, leaving the door open a crack to allow the moonlight to pierce the darkness. For a long while, he watched the twins sleep, Klara with her thumb in her mouth, and Sven with his knife gripped in one hand and his arm thrown protectively around his sister's shoulder. They should have celebrated their birthday with a prairie hen supper, Mama kissing them good night and tucking them into their beds. Ryker should be reading another chapter of *Uncle Tom's Cabin* while Mama knitted. Papa should be adding numbers in his tally book, trying to figure how much hay they must sell to buy a better plow. Instead, their world had fallen apart.

Klara called out for Mama. It seemed the night would never end. Ryker held his breath and listened for sounds of danger.

Nothing but whippoorwills. Frogs in the swamp. The scurry of a mouse through the grass. Ryker could not bear to look toward his father's body. Ryker tried to remember the sound of his voice but, instead, recalled a memory from Norway, how Papa had wept when Sissel and Bertina had died. Papa gathered him onto his lap and buried his face in Ryker's chest, sobbing and crying, and telling Ryker that he must live because losing a son would kill him.

"Oh, Papa," Ryker said softly. He held the memory like a treasure. "Mama said you had a heart of gold." He pulled the quilt away from the twins and covered his father, not wanting the twins to awaken to the sight of their father's corpse. Surely, he did not want to see his father's dead face, but Ryker squared his shoulders, bit his lower lip, and pulled back the quilt. He looked long and hard into his father's face. There was nothing of peace about Papa's face, not like Ryker remembered from his

Bestemor's funeral.

Back then, Mama had forced him to kiss his grandmother's cold cheek. Even in death, Papa's face froze into a grimace of pain and determination. Papa had fought to survive to care for them. He had wanted to find Mama and Elsa.

Ryker had no chance to please his father now. Ryker had secretly hoped to step into Martin's spot of favor after Martin left for war. It hadn't happened. Now it never would. It seemed a waste. This long season of labor and struggle. All for nothing.

He leaned over and kissed his father's forehead.

He needed fresh air. Ryker covered his father's face and returned to his place under the willow branches. Puddles of water pooled in the grass, and far away he heard a rooster crowing. A pinkish orange light showed to the east, and Ryker knew they must leave soon.

He called for the twins, and Sven and Klara lay in the dewy grass beside him, shivering at the touch of wet grass. The twins wondered what had happened to Beller. Klara thought he had followed Mama to take care of her, and Sven thought he was off hunting. Ryker did not voice his fear that Beller had been killed by the Indians. Klara's teeth clattered. Ryker thought of the quilt around their father but made no move to retrieve it.

"Where will we dig his grave?" Sven said. "We don't have a marker."

Ryker reached for a small twig and chewed it into a soft brush to clean his teeth. He needed time to answer his brother. He knew their safety depended on his decision, though it was an intuition deeper than words.

"Indians might see a grave," Ryker said. He hated being in charge. Martin should be making the decisions. "They'll follow if they know we were here."

A long silence broken only by the morning chorus of birds. "Then we'll bury him in the root cellar," Sven said. "We can't just leave him."

Digging a grave would take all day. The floor of the root cellar was rock hard this time of the year. Maybe if it were spring flooding, they could manage. But not now. There was no time. They must fetch help. He had promised Papa, and he must stick to his word.

"We can't take the time," Ryker said softly. It wasn't fair. A choking sob rose in his throat. "We have to think about Mama and Elsa."

"We can't just leave him!" Sven said. "It isn't right."

"Ryker is right," Klara said. "Papa wants us to find Mama and Elsa." She stepped closer to her brother. "Besides, Jesus slept in a tomb," Klara said. "Papa will be safe in our hideout until we can come back."

They had dug the root cellar when they first moved to the prairie. Ryker and Martin hauled buckets of rich soil to the garden spot as fast as Papa shoveled them.

Papa had not known he was digging his own grave.

Ryker remembered how they had lived in the dugout until the first crops were in. Afterwards, they used it for storing potatoes and cabbages. The dugout was prone to spring flooding. Ryker disliked thinking of his father's bones drowning every year.

If he lived, he vowed to move Papa's bones to higher land. There was no high land on the prairie, but Ryker would find a place for him, if he had to travel all the way back to Dodge County to do it.

"Not even a prayer?" Klara said.

"I'll fetch the Bible," Sven said.

"Wait," Ryker said, holding him back while he scanned the yard and hayfield. A red fox skittered into the tall grass after a gray rabbit. The rabbit's white tail bounced behind it like a ball of yarn. Indians could be waiting for them to come out. They could be hiding in the tall grass. This might be the last minutes of their lives. His heart raced, and Ryker pushed away a wave of terror.

"I see nothing amiss," Klara said. "I wish Beller were here to warn us."

Ryker took one last look and nodded to Sven. His brother raced to the house and returned, out of breath, carrying the ancient volume from the Old Country.

As Ryker took the family treasure from his brother's hand, he felt the reality of his new position fall upon him. He was the head of the family, at least until Martin came home, or the soldiers found Mama. Ryker squared his shoulders and opened the Bible to Psalm 91, his mother's favorite passage, ending with verse 11, "For he shall give his angels charge over thee, to keep thee in all thy ways."

"Read more," Klara said. She stuck her thumb in her mouth and sniffed back tears. "The part about trouble."

Ryker skipped to the end of the chapter. "He shall call upon me, and I will answer him. I will be with him in trouble; I will deliver him, and honour him."

They prayed the Lord's Prayer together. Mama would want them to be brave.

Prairie nights were cold this time of the year, and he was unsure if the Tingvolds owned extra coverings. Ryker could not bear to look at Papa again but hurriedly pulled away the blanket and covered Papa's face with the piece of burlap sack lying in the potato bin.

It was all he could do. Ryker picked up Papa's rifle but cast it aside when he realized all the bullets were gone.

"I'll put the Bible back in the soddy," Sven said. "Mama will be mad if it gets lost."

"We have to be brave." Ryker stooped down to look first into Klara's eyes and then Sven's. Ryker picked up Papa's folding knife. Klara reached for Ryker's hand. Her fingers felt small, her bones like those of a small bird. Ryker sucked in his breath.

Their father dead. Mama and Elsa stolen by Indians. In this dark moment, even Martin seemed dead.

Papa always said to stand tall and put your back into your work. He said anything was possible if a man trusted in the Good Lord and did his best.

He looked at his small family. Sven tried to be brave. Klara looked up at him with trusting eyes.

"I'm scared," Klara said with a whimper. Fat tears rolled down her cheeks. She stuck her thumb in her mouth.

"We'll be all right," Ryker said. "The angels are with us." He swallowed a few tears of his own and hoped he spoke the truth.

CHAPTER 11

"You're taking all that along?" Sven said. "Better load the ox before you break your back."

But the ox was nowhere in sight. It seemed the Indians had stolen every animal on the farm. Not a single hen scratched in the manure pile.

"Where's the wheelbarrow?" Sven said.

Ryker found it behind the outhouse, loaded with chicken manure for the garden. They dumped the load and placed the bundle of food and supplies inside. Klara could ride if she got tired. Ryker reminded Klara to wear her bonnet so she wouldn't sunburn.

They filled the empty milk jug with well water. Ryker ignored the empty pens, the missing hens. A coyote had scavenged the carcasses of the dead fowl, as evidenced by scattered bones and feather. He chided himself for letting the meat go to waste.

The barley bowed low in the field. A bumper crop wasted. The blackbirds feasted. Could it have been only yesterday that he dreaded working the harvest? Now he would give anything to work next to his father, while his mother hung washing on the bushes and the little ones argued about chores.

Mr. Tingvold would know what to do. He would fetch help from the fort, and Mrs. Tingvold would fix a hot meal.

Just then, Beller leapt out of the tall grass, his black coat matted with cockleburs. He wagged his tail and jumped up on their chests, breathing foul breath into their faces. Beller always did a lot of jumping when he was glad to see someone. Ryker dropped the handles of the wheelbarrow.

"Oh, Beller." Sven threw his arms around the dog and nuzzled his neck. "I thought the *skraelings* got you, for sure."

A single bark might give them away. Ryker faced a hard decision. "He can't go with us," he said.

"Why not?" Sven buried his face in the dog's mangy coat. When he looked up, he showed tears streaking down his face. "You're mean," Sven said. "Martin would let him go along." He positioned his body between Ryker and Beller, as if to protect the family pet. "Mama says he's a good dog."

Klara stood beside her twin. "He's going along," she said. "He's family."

Ryker weighed the decision. They were only going a short distance. Once there, they could chain him in the Tingvold barn. The twins had lost their father, and who knows when they would find their mother. Ryker swallowed a sob. They had lost too much. Maybe Beller would warn them of danger and help rather than hinder.

"All right," Ryker said. "Beller can go."

The twins hugged the dog and squealed in delight.

"But keep him close." Ryker said. He knelt and petted the dog, too. Beller stank like dead fish and skunk. "You'll be a good dog, won't you?" Beller wagged his crooked tail and licked Ryker's face.

CHAPTER 12

They started east, avoiding the main trail and snaking through the tall grass near the edge of the slough. Unexpectedly, Beller pulled away and looked westward with bared teeth. He growled a deep, menacing warning. The hair on the back of his neck stood on end.

"Indians," Sven said in a whisper.

Ryker fought a wave of panic. They had to hide. His father had told him to take care of the twins. Where could they go?

"Here, boy!" Sven grabbed Beller by the scruff of his neck and dragged him toward the slough. "Quiet."

Klara followed close behind, their splashing feet sounding as loud as the school bell calling them to class. Surely the Indians would hear and be upon them, brandishing their scalping knives.

Ryker forced himself to action, though his brain refused to work, and panic scrambled his thoughts. He pushed the wheelbarrow into the mucky water, each step an eternity, and his heart beating like a hammer. The swamp stank of decayed earth and dead fish, and mosquitoes tormented in enormous, whining clouds. For once, Ryker gave thanks for the tall grass that hid them from view.

Beller growled and strained to pull away, but Sven knelt behind a cluster of cattails, gripping Beller's snout with both hands. Klara's face drained of color.

"Hush now," Ryker whispered. "Klara, fetch yarn out of the bundle."

Klara fumbled for their mother's ball of yarn. She unwound a length and bit it with her teeth. Ryker bound the yarn around Beller's snout and tied it into a knot. The dog whined but did not fight the muzzle.

Sven knotted the short rope around Beller's neck for a leash. "That ought to do," he whispered. He wound the end of the cord around his hand and gripped it so tightly that his skin blanched white between the thin ropes.

They held Beller with the combined weight of their bodies. Ryker thought he heard Klara's heart beating but then realized it was his own banging against his ribs. They hid like rabbits, listening and waiting for the Indians to burst upon them. A horse whinnied. Beller bristled, but they somehow kept him down. An Indian burped. The others laughed and spoke in their language.

Ryker strained his ears for anything that might indicate his mother and sister were with the Indians. He heard only guttural language, horses, and an occasional laugh. The Indians continued on their way toward the east. The children remained hidden.

After what seemed like eternity, Klara whispered in Ryker's ear, "You're hurting Beller."

Ryker and Sven released the dog from their stranglehold. Sven held tightly to the rope around his neck. The dog shook muddy water, splattering the children.

"They're gone," Sven said. "See, I told you Beller wouldn't be any trouble."

"We should have left him behind," Ryker said. "He almost gave us away."

"No," Klara said. "Beller warned us to hide." She put both arms around the dog's muddy neck and kissed the tip of his muzzled nose. "Good boy."

Ryker had to admit that she was right.

"Let's go," Sven said with a determined look on his dirty face. Mosquito bites welted across his face and arms. He scratched the back of his neck. "We have to find Mama and Elsa."

Ryker forced his brain to think. They were well hidden in the slough, but they could not find their mother in the swamp. Mr. Tingvold would know what to do. They had to find Mama.

Sven removed Beller's muzzle and allowed him to drink. When Beller finished, Sven replaced the muzzle and kept a firm hold on the leash.

They climbed out of the swamp and peered in all directions, shaking gobs of wet mud off their clothing. Ryker slapped wet muck on the mosquito bites covering Klara's arms and face. No sign of Redskins. Ryker pushed the wheelbarrow toward the Tingvold farm. They would avoid the path in hopes no Indians would find them.

The wheelbarrow tangled in the tall grass. Ryker's muscles bulged with the effort. His arms and shoulders ached, and he paused to wipe his sweaty face.

"Oh, no," Sven said. He climbed on top of a massive rock and looked back over their trail. "Look."

Ryker climbed the rock, too, and looked back in horror. A long winding swath cut through the waving grass. The wheelbarrow left a trail as plain as an arrow pointing their way.

Sven's face looked crestfallen. "It was a dumb idea."

"No," Klara said, always in defense of her twin. "It's not your fault the ground is soft."

Beller lurched against the leash after a gopher skittering through the grass.

"Hang onto him." Ryker lunged to grab hold of Beller's rope. "That scallywag will get us killed." He jerked the rope until Beller wheezed in protest.

"You're hurting him," Sven said. "He's hungry."

"We should leave him tied to the rock," Ryker said. "Dumb, worthless dog."

The angry words soured in his mouth. He sounded like his father. Sven's shoulders heaved, and tears filled his sister's eyes.

"Klara's right. The wheelbarrow was a good idea," Ryker said.

Beller wagged his tail.

"Apologize," Klara said. "Say you're sorry."

"You're right," Ryker said. He reached out to pat the dog's head. "I'm sorry, Beller. You're a good dog."

"And promise you won't say mean things again," Klara persisted.

"No," Ryker said. "I will say nothing bad about Beller." He unpacked the wheelbarrow and hoisted the pack to his back. "But he must be muzzled until we get to the Tingvold place."

Klara overturned the wheelbarrow into the grass. "Papa wouldn't like us leaving the wheelbarrow." She wiped tears with the back of her hand.

The dog whined, as Sven rewound the yarn around his snout.

"We'll fetch it later," Ryker said. "It won't go anywhere."

"Too heavy," Klara said, hefting the sack.

"Wear what you can to lighten my load." Ryker pulled shoes and clothing out of the pack.

"Funny to wear shoes in the summer," Klara said, as she slipped them on her feet. "Papa won't—" She didn't finish the sentence. Her thin shoulders shook with silent sobs. She tied her sweater around her waist and popped her thumb in her mouth. She huddled close to Sven and patted Beller's head.

Mrs. Tingvold would feed them, Ryker knew, but he could not waste their few remaining supplies. They would need every bit to get through the winter. If only they might yet salvage part of the harvest. His brain scrambled to figure out what to do.

They stepped away from the wheelbarrow trail, careful to leave no footprints as they traveled through tall prairie grass. When they came over the edge of the rise next to the Tingvold farm, they knelt by the edge of the harvested fields. A rising wind rustled the turkey-foot grasses surrounding the homestead, the tops showing a purple tinge, a sure reminder that autumn was on its way.

"What are we waiting for?" Klara said. "I'm thirsty."

"Hush." Something cautioned Ryker. The Indians had traveled in this direction. Ryker saw Mr. Tingvold tying grain in the field west of the house. Sheaves scattered across the naked fields. Mrs. Tingvold gathered eggs in the barnyard. Nothing out of the ordinary. Ryker blew out his breath. The Tingvolds would help them.

"All right," Ryker said. He rose to his feet and gathered their pack, as Sven unwound Beller's muzzle. Beller growled toward the corn field on the south side of the cabin.

"Wait!" Ryker dropped to the ground, gripping Beller's snout and holding the leash. Horses snorted, beads rattled, and the slide of metal against metal sounded in the stillness.

"Indians!" Ryker said. They edged back into the tall grass and lay flat. Overhead puffs of clouds dotted a sapphire sky. Flies buzzed, and cicadas droned around them. A bumblebee landed on a purple coneflower, bending the tender stalk under its weight.

Beller lunged away from them. He streaked across the field toward the house, the leash dragging behind him in the stubble.

Sven tried to follow, but Ryker pulled him back.

"No," Ryker said. "Stay down." He craned his neck to see through the grass. A painted Indian wearing a white feather in his hair held the halter of a black pony, also painted in red, and gestured toward Mr. Tingvold in the field. Mrs. Tingvold's white

79

apron bunched around her waist as she filled it with eggs from the haystack. The apron ties fluttered behind her in the prairie wind.

Beller streaked toward Mrs. Tingvold. Ryker's warning turned to dust in his throat. Any sound might draw unwanted attention. They could do nothing to stop what was about to happen.

It couldn't be real. Any minute he would wake up and find it was all a dream. Mama would laugh when he told her about his preposterous dream where she and Elsa were taken by hostile Indians, and Papa lay entombed in the root cellar.

Mrs. Tingvold backed away from the barking dog as if afraid. Beller turned toward the Indians with his back toward Mrs. Tingvold, his ferocious barking protective and threatening. But, surely, Beller was no match for the raiders.

Ryker searched for something, anything, to alter what was about to happen, but he could think of nothing. If he had his father's rifle with bullets. If the soldiers would come charging through the tall grass.

He should do something. Mrs. Tingvold had loaned him the Topsy book and showed kindness about Martin's capture. Last year she sent a loaf of fresh bread for *Jul*, Christmas. How good it tasted. Mr. Tingvold showed Papa how to build the soddy that first difficult year on the prairie. They deserved to be rescued.

Ryker could only watch the beautiful black horse snort and paw the dirt at the edge of the corn field. Other horses stepped out from between the rows of corn. The Indians climbed onto their horses' backs.

"Don't look," he said to the twins. They buried their faces in their hands, but Ryker could not look away. Beads of sweat stung his eyes, as several of the wild men raced through the barley field toward Mr. Tingvold, their horses raising dust and scattering the haycocks under their hooves. Others headed toward Mrs. Tingvold with shrieks and war whoops.

The hair on Ryker's neck bristled. Klara raised her head, but Ryker pushed her face down into the ground. "Don't look!" Beller streaked into the garden patch, away from the approaching riders. Ryker gripped his brother's arm until his hands ached.

Mrs. Tingvold stared at the approaching riders, as if frozen to the ground. "Arne!" she screamed. "Arne!" She ran towards her husband, flinging her arms wide as an arrow pierced her back. She fell forward. Eggs splattered around her. Ryker watched in horror as an Indian rushed toward her with a raised tomahawk. Another pulled the axe from the chopping block.

Ryker could look no longer. He had seen the elephant. He buried his face in his arms. He couldn't move. He couldn't pray. He couldn't think. Martin must feel like this. Ryker hoped a sudden, fierce hope that Martin had survived Shiloh, that he had hidden himself as they were hiding and lived to return home. If only they would all survive: Martin, Mama, Elsa, he and the twins, and the new baby. Too late for Papa.

Ryker jerked his head at the crash of breaking glass. Plumes of black smoke boiled against the blue sky. Flames licked from the windows and doors of the log barn. Their precious school and teacher gone forever.

Indians poured out of the cabin dragging all kinds of things. One twirled Mrs. Tingvold's petticoat over his head and tied it around his shoulders as a cape. Another placed her bonnet over his dark hair. They dumped food stores into the dirt and laughed when flour drifted through the air like snow. A short Indian smashed the cabin window with the splitting maul and held a burning piece of stove wood against the kitchen curtain. Flames curled through the broken glass.

Ryker's brain thawed. "We have to leave. Have to get away," he said. "They'll find us."

"Wait," Sven said. "We can't leave Beller."

"Look," Klara said. She pointed toward a cluster of people on the western edge of the farthest field. "They're white people."

Ryker searched the group for a glimpse of his mother. Women slumped to the ground. Others huddled with children. He had never seen such a dejected looking lot. An Indian stood guard. One kerchief showed among the sunbonnets. The woman might have been their mother, but she faced the opposite direction and wasn't holding a baby. Something about her stance looked unfamiliar. They were too far away to know for sure.

Ryker's eyes had always been sharper than Sven's, though Papa predicted reading would ruin them. A boy stood to his feet, and Ryker recognized Johnny Schmitz's red suspenders.

"It's Johnny Schmitz," Ryker said. He wouldn't mention their mother until he knew for sure. The Indians herded the captives into the tall grass. Johnny edged toward the path, as if planning escape. The Indian struck Johnny, sending him sprawling on the ground. Then the Indian kicked Johnny's back and beat him about his head with a heavy stick. Johnny shielded his head with both arms until the Indian jerked him to his feet and pushed him into the tall grass out of sight.

"What's happening?" Sven said. "I can't see."

"Nothing," Ryker said. His mouth turned dry as powder. Johnny Schmitz, a brat by any estimation, did not deserve such treatment. Ryker must protect his brother and sister.

Sven pulled his knife and started toward the captives.

"No," Ryker said. He grabbed his brother's shoulder and pulled him back into the grass. The Indian on the black horse turned away from the smoking cabin and rode in their direction carrying a lighted torch.

★ ★ ★ ★ ★

"Quiet!" Ryker said. The Indian must have seen them. Overhead puffs of clouds dotted a blue sky. Buzzing flies and droning cicadas sounded around them. It was as if the *skraeling* knew where the children were hiding and came right toward them.

They flattened in the grass. Surely their lives were over. No one would be left to rescue Mama and Elsa. The new baby would be raised as an Indian and never know how hard they had tried to save him. Ryker clutched Klara's hand, fingering her soggy and wrinkled thumb.

The Indian pulled his horse to a stop in the middle of the open field. He waved the burning torch, threw back his head, and uttered a war cry so terrible that Ryker's muscles weakened. The horse reared back on its hind legs. Ryker braced himself. Surely they would all be killed.

There was no place to go. They pressed their bodies into the earth and tried to turn invisible. Klara's ragged breathing sounded next to Ryker's ear, and she clung trembling to his arm. A fly crawled into Ryker's nose, but he didn't dare reach up to brush it away.

He wasn't ready to die. His whole life lay ahead of him. It couldn't end this way. Ryker prayed for forgiveness. He promised God that he would do anything if only they were spared.

Beller shot out of the corn field and nipped the horse's hind hooves. The horse snorted and kicked at the growling dog and rounded to bite him. The Indian raised the burning torch and yelled in an angry voice, then swatted at Beller with it. Sven's gasp of horror was drowned by Beller's ferocious barking. Beller turned and hightailed it back into the corn field, away from the children, still dragging the rope behind him.

The Indian loped past Mr. Tingvold's body, which lay in the

field like a pile of old rags. With a triumphant cry, he leaned over and fired a sheaf of dried grain next to the body.

Flames whooshed upward, the grain as dry as tinder. With another war cry, the brave threw the torch into the standing grain on the far side of the field. The westerly wind licked the flames and blew them across the barley field. The Indian rode around the west edge of the field, away from the growing flames, and set fire to Mr. Tingvold's haystack. The flames shot upwards in orange and yellow tongues.

"They're getting away," Sven said. "Taking Johnny with them."

The Indians melted into the tall grass on the northwest corner of Mr. Tingvold's property. They were taking the path to Fort Abercrombie.

Bright flames danced across the stubble, driven by the west wind. The heat of the fire, even though it traveled away from them, sucked the breath from Ryker's lungs. Nothing burned hotter than dry straw.

Ryker waited, just breathing, trying to make sense of what had happened. Smoke and flames filled the open field. He tasted dirt and felt grit on his sweaty skin. His stomach clenched, and he discovered that he had wet himself.

The fire danced toward the east, leaving behind a blackened prairie. Soon the fire showed only a smoky ridge, like storm clouds on the horizon. Sven let out his breath in a gasp. Klara sobbed.

"What do we do now?" Klara said. She put her thumb in her mouth, shoulders heaving.

CHAPTER 13

Beller rejoined the children still hiding in the grass, his tongue hanging out and his coat scorched and covered with chaff. He laid his head on Sven's leg.

"Bad boy," Sven said. "You could have been killed."

"No," Ryker said. "Beller drew the Indians' attention away from us."

"I'm scared." Klara said. "I want Mama."

Ryker didn't know how to answer. Their neighbors could not help them. They would have to find Mama and Elsa on their own. He looked in the direction where the Indians had gone. He saw only waving grass and a flock of blackbirds crowding around the ruined sheaves of grain. He tried to look away from the bodies lying where they had fallen.

"We'll rest a little," Ryker said. "And make sure the Indians are gone."

They wouldn't be so foolish as to show themselves until he was sure the Indians were really gone. They couldn't take the direct path to Fort Abercrombie as the Indians had taken. It was too dangerous, though the way much shorter. They must go south to Whiskey Creek.

Once they reached Whiskey Creek, they need only follow its banks to Fort Abercrombie. The fort stood on the convergence of the Red River of the North and Whiskey Creek.

Ryker had visited Fort Abercrombie with his father, but he had not paid attention to landmarks or distance. Regret choked his throat. It was too late to ask questions . . . to learn from his father.

Ryker scanned the horizon for landmarks. He fixed his eyes on a small cluster of willow trees to the south. His father always chose a landmark to keep on course and followed the position of the sun and stars for guidance.

Tall grass made it difficult to keep an eye on landmarks, but Ryker would do the best he could. At least at night the stars would be overhead. Sometime tomorrow they should see trees growing along Whiskey Creek. After they reached the creek, it was only a long day's journey to Fort Abercrombie.

Soldiers would find his mother and sister. He would do as his father had instructed. He had no other choice. He and the twins stayed hidden in the tall grass at the edge of the barley field.

Klara whimpered. "I'm thirsty."

"Hush, Klara," Ryker said. He handed her the water jug, then a bite of cheese and the last pickle. "We'll be at the fort soon."

Sven emptied the water jug. "I'll fetch more from the well," he said, wiping his mouth on the back of his sleeve.

The Tingvold cabin and barn smoldered. Hot spots glowed in the scorched fields. Indians might yet be lurking, waiting for anyone attempting to bury the bodies. Indians had returned to where their father had fallen, and it only made sense they might return here. Fire had scorched Mr. Tingvold, lying in the field. Mrs. Tingvold's clothing had turned to blackened ruin on her fallen body. To leave them unburied was surely a mortal sin, but Ryker felt helpless to do anything about it. Besides, he was afraid to touch their bodies.

"No," Ryker said. "We'll find water at the creek. It's not safe to go up to the house."

"Are you crazy?" Sven said. "We need water."

Sven was off and running before Ryker could stop him. Sven sprinted toward the well, with the empty water jug banging against his leg. Beller ran ahead. He looked back at Sven with a lolling tongue and a happy dog smile. Their feet stirred black puffs of ashes and dust. Beller lapped the broken eggs by Mrs. Tingvold's body.

A brave with a bow and arrow might shoot his brother before his very eyes. An Indian seeing Sven and Beller might come looking for Ryker and Klara. Sweat gathered on Ryker's neck and forehead. He wanted to live, not die.

"How can he be so brave?" Klara said. "Just like Martin."

Sven struggled with the winch, filled the empty jug, and let Beller drink from the bucket. It seemed they were gone for an hour, but it was only a few minutes until they raced back across the field.

"Now we can go," Sven said, gasping to catch his breath. He placed the filled jug on the ground next to Klara. "Heavy when it's full."

They must lighten the pack. Ryker emptied everything out on the grass. He placed the nail into the money pouch around his neck. After checking for holes, he poured the salt into his pocket next to the tintype of their parents' wedding. He discarded the empty shaker into the weeds along with Mama's mirror. He placed the comb into the bundle holding their food and quilt.

"Mama won't like losing her mirror," Klara said. "It was from Auntie Beret."

"We'll come back for them when we collect the wheelbarrow," Ryker said. "After we find Mama." He fastened Klara's torn skirt with their mother's hatpin. Mrs. Tingvold's copy of *Uncle Tom's Cabin* lay on the grass. It made sense to leave it behind. They had a long walk ahead of them.

"I'll carry the water jug," Sven said. He picked up the book and handed it to Ryker.

"We'll take turns," Ryker said. He tucked the book into the front of his overalls. He would carry it for a while.

The sun stood straight overhead. The sooner they left, the sooner they would arrive at Whiskey Creek. The blue sky above them gave no indication of the violence he had just witnessed. The pack cut into his shoulders. The grief and distress of the last two days far overpowered the little ache in his back. Ryker turned until the west wind touched his right cheek.

Beller ran ahead, raising rabbits and gophers, chasing a fox and a prairie hen. Sven protested when Ryker suggested they tie Beller with a rope to keep him out of trouble.

"He's hungry," Sven said. "Can't we let him loose for a while? Just long enough that he can catch some dinner?"

Ryker sighed. That dog was trouble. But they couldn't keep him muzzled and tied forever.

"All right. Just for a little while."

Beller yipped a grateful bark and ran into the grass. He returned with a striped gopher tail sticking out of his mouth.

They hiked until dusk, but Whiskey Creek was nowhere in sight. They sought refuge behind a clump of bushes at the edge of a small ravine. Night birds stirred, and small animals scurried in the grass. The smell of skunk wafted through the damp air. Wolves howled in the distance, and Beller growled. Though it was still August, a nip of chill reminded them fall would soon be there. Ryker huddled with the twins under the quilt, but in spite of feeling exhausted, he could not sleep.

"I'm scared," Klara whispered. "Indians might be nearby."

Ryker looked around, almost expecting the Indian brave in war paint and feathers to step from the grass. "Shhh," he whispered. "Go to sleep."

" 'Fraidy cat. Aren't the angels with us?" Sven said. His voice shook, and his hands trembled in spite of his brave words. "You don't have to worry."

The prairie sky stretched overhead, and the stars showed one by one like jewels in the darkening sky. A shooting star sped across the night and disappeared behind the horizon. Ryker did not voice his skepticism. Surely a guardian angel would have spared Papa, had he been doing his job, and rescued the Tingvolds from the marauders.

Beller whined and wiggled away from Sven's grip. He inched through the grass.

"Keep hold of Beller," Ryker said. "We need to stay together."

Sven grabbed Beller and pulled him to his side.

"Is Papa in heaven?" Klara said. "He said bad words sometimes."

Ryker did not know about such things. He tried to remember the preacher's words at Baby Elsa's baptism, something about the mercy of God more vast than oceans. He remembered the lapping ocean waves stretching as far as the eye could see, as far as the prairie on a clear day. Maybe Papa had entered heaven riding on a ray of light. Or a shooting star.

"Mama said Papa had a sad heart since Sissel and Bertina died," Klara said. "God wouldn't close the door on Papa because he had a sad heart, would he?"

"Papa is in God's hands now," Ryker said. "We're all in God's hands."

"Ryker," Klara said, her voice small in the darkness. "I'm making a knot in my apron string to mark the days. Just like Mama does."

"That's a good idea," Ryker said. "You can tie the knot when we say our nighttime prayers."

Together they recited the ancient words Mama so treasured: "Our Father, Who art in heaven, hallowed be Thy Name." The words surrounded them like a sheltering cloud.

After their amen, Klara added Mama's favorite bedtime prayer.

"Protect us as we stay awake, watch over us as we sleep. That awake, we might keep watch with Christ; and asleep, rest in His peace. Amen."

Somehow the night turned to morning.

Ryker woke as the sun turned the eastern horizon cherry red. They nibbled raw potatoes for breakfast. He scanned the horizon, hoping to see the line of trees growing along Whiskey Creek. He saw only waving grass, gray skies, and the rippling path of prairie winds.

They walked all morning until they came over a short rise.

"Oh no," Ryker said. He could have kicked himself.

"What's wrong?" Klara said.

"We're off course. Too far east of where we wanted to go."

The Jacobs farm lay before them. First a cornfield, then a vegetable patch, next a field of barley, and log cabin and barn. Ryker had been to the farm with his father once when they had traveled to Breckinridge for supplies.

He had added at least an extra day to their journey.

The Jacobs family spoke mostly German. Ryker remembered counting at least nine children when he and his father had been there while on their way to Breckinridge. A crucifix hung over the log door. Ryker remembered a pretty daughter about his age, a laughing girl with a kind smile. The Jacobs family made the sign of the cross when they prayed the blessing and ate stinking plates of sauerkraut. Papa's stern look warned Ryker to eat the strange dish without complaint. Ryker shuddered remembering the slimy mess in his mouth.

They crouched at the edge of the cornfield, holding Beller close with the leash. Ryker crept ahead for a better look. Nothing looked amiss. No sign of Indians. But no sign of the Jacobs family.

"Be still," Ryker said, waving his arm at his little brother to get his attention. "Hold tight to Beller." Ryker returned to the children. "I'm going over for a look." A barrage of gunshots rang out in rapid succession, the hollow sounds far away. "Mr. Jacobs will help us fetch the soldiers."

"We should stay together," Sven said. "We'll all go."

"No," Ryker said. "It's too dangerous." Ryker turned his mouth into a frown and sharpened his voice the way Papa used to do to him when he meant business. "Stay in the cornfield until I get back."

Klara stuck her thumb into her mouth and looked at Ryker with solemn eyes. "Then what should we do if the Indians get you?" she asked, moving her thumb just enough to lisp the words.

"Don't be silly. I'll be right back." Ryker pulled a stray blade of grass from her yellow braid and cupped her small face in his hand. "Be quiet as a field mouse."

"You're making a mistake," Sven said. "Those are gunshots." Ryker noticed a slight tremble in his brother's lip. "We should stay together."

"I said, stay here," Ryker said, leading them into the corn field. "No matter what." Beller whined. "Keep hold of Beller."

Ryker crept to the end of the row of corn and crawled through a barley field. The blackbirds sang as if the world hadn't changed, as if the world were the same as it had been yesterday. He imagined the simple beauty of before: Papa sharpening the corn knife; Mama making soap over the outside fire. Even the never ending task of raking hay took on a loving and homey memory.

He crawled out into the weeds, making his way toward the barn and keeping out of sight.

Ryker's breath came in shallow gasps, his heart pounding and his throat dry. He wanted to run away, but he must go forward. Mr. Jacobs would help them.

He squared his shoulders and took a deep breath. Ryker moved through the edge of the yard. He paused behind a haystack and then crouched behind a woodpile. A black cat zipped beneath a wagon.

Ryker half ran to the cabin and paused at the door. Then he took a breath and entered. His eyes adjusted to the dimness. The single room looked just as he remembered, with its crucifix over the door and the long table lined with benches. Dirty dishes scattered on the table, and a pan of oatmeal lay on the stove. A crock of buttermilk sat next to a heel of rye bread. But there was no sign of the family.

Maybe they had been warned to flee to safety. Ryker wished someone had warned them. But then he remembered Mr. Tingvold's conversation with his father about the Indian danger. They would have had plenty of time to go to Fort Abercrombie back then. Papa would still be alive. Mama and Elsa would be safe.

Ryker shook his head and forced himself back to the present. His stomach rumbled and he dipped a spoonful of cold oatmeal, then wolfed down half the pan. It wasn't exactly stealing. He put the heel of bread into his pocket for the twins. He would repay Mr. Jacobs later. The good man would understand their desperate need and make allowances.

Ryker rummaged in the cupboard. A can of peaches fell off the shelf and onto the floor. It rolled across the uneven boards with a *clink, clink*. He threw it into a flour sack, along with a half-eaten sausage. He would return later and work to repay for the food items.

Ryker threw open the door to the cellar, and his eyes adjusted to the sudden blackness. He grabbed potatoes, a cabbage, and a bucket of eggs. The sack bulged. He must hurry. He drew a bucket of water from the well and poured it into an empty vinegar jug. He was taking too much time. He must hurry.

Ryker slung the sack over his shoulder. He looked for signs of Indians and, not seeing any, slipped into the corn field again, careful to follow the same path back to the twins. He paused to pull ears of corn from the garden patch and a fistful of carrots.

The little ones were not where he expected them to be. At first he thought he entered the wrong field. He whispered their name, then called the dog. No one answered. He called louder. He ran up and down the rows but found only half-eaten ears of corn scattered on the ground. Ryker knelt to examine a scuffled mess of footprints. One showed clearly in an open spot between the rows.

A moccasin. Indians!

CHAPTER 14

He shouldn't have left them alone. His father had left him in charge. Ryker had done a piss-poor job of watching them. A bitter taste filled his mouth.

The thought of Sven and Klara in the hands of savages was more than Ryker could bear. His blood pulsed in the veins on his forehead. He had to find them, by God, if it was the last thing he did. Ryker pulled in his breath, shocked at his language. His mother would wash his mouth with soap if she heard him.

Klara's sweater lay in the weeds about a hundred rods west of the corn field. She would freeze once the sun went down. She had been afraid. He had been too busy worrying to put her mind at ease. Now it was too late. Sven was impetuous. They might hurt him, as they had hurt Johnny.

Ryker paused at the edge of the corn patch for a long moment and gathered courage to step away from the tall stalks, exposing himself to whoever might be watching. Crows squawked and bickered over the field like a gaggle of old women.

He followed the trail of moccasin prints. The path wove north-westward toward the fort. Footprints showed in patches of bare ground. Mingled among the moccasins tracks were Klara's and Sven's small prints. It seemed others walked with them. A larger shoe print might be their mother's. He saw no dog tracks.

Maybe they were friendly Indians who took the children to the fort for safety. But maybe they were the Indians who had killed Papa. Maybe the ones who had so cruelly mistreated Johnny Schmitz. It was Ryker's fault the twins were taken. He should have listened to Sven.

Ryker crouched behind a bush to watch the trail behind him. The grass swayed in the breeze, and meadowlarks sang. Overhead a gray sky threaded with bands of clouds like gray wool. He searched the horizon for any sign of movement. A sudden burst of swallows exploded from a scraggly clump of bushes.

The prairie took on a sinister feel. The air grew hot and steamy. Clouds thickened overhead. It felt like a storm brewing. Klara was afraid of thunder. His arms ached from carrying the heavy pack.

An Indian could be hiding nearby. His legs ached, and he felt the burn of stretched muscles as he searched for higher ground where he might see over the tops of grass. Funny about the prairie that way. Though it looked flat as a pancake, it hid buffalo wallows and small ravines. There were a million places to hide. Maybe the Indians waited in ambush to capture him.

A hawk cried. Flies buzzed and tormented.

Without the sun to guide him, Ryker lost his sense of direction. He kept walking, though he had lost track of the trail and did not know where he was going. Maybe he should stop until sundown. Even clouds could not hide the western sunset. He stopped and drank from the jug.

Without warning, Beller exploded from the grass and planted dirty paws on Ryker's chest, almost knocking him over in his excitement.

"Beller!" he said. A surge of gladness welled in Ryker's chest. "Where have you been?"

A bloody ear dangled from Beller's head by a thread of skin. The rope hung around his neck. His coat was matted with chaff and burrs. Beller smiled his huge dog smile and panted into

Ryker's face.

"Where are they, boy?" Ryker said. "Where are the twins?"

Beller wagged his tail in response.

Hot tears ran down Ryker's face. Beller lived. Ryker pressed his face into Beller's stinky coat. He pulled away and rummaged in the pillow slip for a summer squash found at the abandoned farm.

"It's not much," Ryker said. He tossed it to Beller, who crunched it down in a single gulp and looked expectantly for more. "Sorry, boy," Ryker said. "It's all I can spare." When Beller realized there would be nothing more, he bounded off into the grass.

"Beller," Ryker called. "Come back." Ryker picked up the sack of supplies and raced after the dog, running through the tall grass until he came to an enormous rock. Beller lay in its shadow, eating a baby rabbit.

"Beller," Ryker said. "Don't scare me that way." He leaned back against the cool surface of the rock and caught his breath. His throat parched, and he pushed his hand against a stitch in his side. "We have to stick together until we find the twins."

Beller looked at Ryker with a tilted head, the rabbit skin hanging out of one side of his mouth.

"You're *vonlaus*," Ryker said. Of course he didn't mean it. He bent low and hugged Beller again. Sven was right to insist they bring Beller along. "You're a good boy," Ryker said. They sat for a while, leaning against the rock, until anxiety compelled Ryker to climb the rock and search again for signs of Indians or the twins.

The sun dipped in the western sky, making a low ribbon of light on the horizon. Ryker marked the western edge of the rock with a small stone, scraping an arrow pointing west. He would know the right direction, even if clouds obscured tomorrow's sun.

He saw no sign of Indians, the twins, or trees that would indicate Whiskey Creek. An Indian campfire would show in the night. He would climb the rock later. Until then he must keep hold of the dog lest he escape again. He started to climb down but missed his footing and slipped, banging his shin against a sharp edge.

"Ouch," Ryker said, fighting back tears. He rubbed his leg and wrinkled his nose at the stinging pain. "Darn it!" He could have broken his leg with such foolishness. Who would know or even care if he lay out on the prairie with a broken leg?

Beller licked a bloody drip on Ryker's leg and laid his shaggy head on his lap.

He had never kissed a girl, been to a dance, or satisfied his thirst for knowledge. He wanted to grow up, marry, and have children of his own. He couldn't die now. There was much to learn. Besides, his family needed him. "Beller, we have to find them."

He tried to pray, but the Lord's Prayer tangled in his brain and refused to come to mind. He calmed himself by repeating Jesus's name. He prayed for his father's soul, although he wasn't sure it was right to pray for the dead. The prayer came naturally from his heart, and, if it were wrong, he figured God would understand. Then he prayed for the twins, his mother and Elsa, the new baby in his mother's womb, and lastly for Martin.

A cooling breeze stirred the falling shadows. The butcher knife and quilt had been taken along with the twins. He kicked himself for allowing such important items out of his sight. Maybe Klara was using it to keep warm.

He gnawed an ear of raw corn and tossed the cob to Beller. They huddled for warmth, but Ryker couldn't sleep. He tried to remember one of the poems he had learned back in Dodge County, but the only line he could remember was from Longfellow's *Paul Revere's Ride: Listen my children and you shall hear of the midnight ride of Paul Revere.* He repeated it several times, but it was no use. The words evaporated as surely as his family.

He tried to understand what drove the Indians to attack innocent people. Mrs. Tingvold said America broke the treaty. No one Ryker knew had anything to do with the treaties or breaking of them.

Fears pressed from all directions. Just when Ryker thought the mosquitoes would keep him awake all night, his eyes drifted closed. "Wake me if there's trouble, boy," he said before slipping into a heavy, fretful sleep.

A cold rain woke him in the dark of night, sweeping in from the west with roaring thunder and flashes of lightning. Ryker clung to Beller in the pouring rain, praying that Klara would not be afraid, knowing she would be terrified.

"Protect us Lord, as we stay awake; watch over us, as we sleep," Ryker murmured aloud. Beller whined until Ryker prayed the rest of the prayer. As Ryker said the words, he imagined the faces of Sven and Klara, Mama, and Elsa. He repeated the prayer again for Papa, Mr. and Mrs. Tingvold, and Martin. In spite of the rain, he drifted asleep while praying for all those he loved, both living and dead.

Chapter 15

Beller's whine woke Ryker before dawn. Ryker rubbed sleep
from his eyes and climbed the rock again, careful of the slippery
spot and holding a firm grip on Beller's rope, his clothes still
wet from the rain. He shivered in the cold morning fog that
clung to the prairie in drifts of cloud. Martin had described
how gunpowder left a rolling fog over the field of battle.

Rainwater puddled in the grooves of the rock. Beller drank
his fill as the morning birds sang their first peeping songs. The
rising sun burned off the fog, and the smoke of a distant
campfire glowed on the horizon, maybe where Indians held
Sven and Klara. Then he noticed several more campfires around
him. He wiped a stray tear from his eye and pushed back waves
of panic. He was surrounded.

Beller jerked away, almost pulling Ryker off the rock. The
dog yipped and disappeared into the tall grass.

"Beller!" Ryker said. "Come back."

The idea of wandering alone on the prairie filled Ryker with
such terror that he could do nothing but follow the dog, sling-
ing the sack of food over his back. Beller headed toward the
sunrise, away from Fort Abercrombie. Ryker was losing control,
confused and traveling in the wrong direction, and failing again.
Still he followed Beller as the gloom turned into morning. He
was far from the rock when he realized he had forgotten the
water jug.

A cheerful yip and a child's voice caused Ryker to break into a run. He'd know Sven's voice anywhere.

"Beller!" Sven said. Ryker heard the tears in his brother's throat. "What took you so long?"

Klara curled on Sven's lap in the bottom of a small gulley, asleep. Johnny Schmitz slept in a tangle of arms and legs beside them. Sven kept watch with his knife in hand.

"Thank God," Ryker said. Tears of joy leaked from his eyes. God had answered his prayer.

Klara awoke with empty eyes. Her face was burned red, and blisters showed on her scalp. "I want Mama," she said in a voice barely louder than a whisper. Then she popped her thumb in her mouth.

Ryker broke a hole into the shell of an egg and held it to his sister's mouth. She sucked a bit and then returned to sucking her thumb. Johnny sat up and rubbed his eyes. His face and neck were bruised black and blue, and both eyes puffed red and swollen above a split lip. A large bruise covered his arm.

"I'm thirsty," Johnny said. His words were muffled through swollen lips.

The can of peaches held a little sweet liquid. Sven's knife and a small rock opened the can. They held it first to Klara's lips. She sipped and then put her thumb in her mouth.

"Just a little more," Sven said. "You can do it."

But Klara drooped back on the prairie grass and closed her eyes.

The boys passed the can around, and each took a careful swallow. Sven stopped Johnny from drinking more than his share. Then they fished out the peaches with the tip of the knife and divided them evenly, saving a large piece for Klara. They wiped sticky hands on their clothing. Flies buzzed around the sweetness, and Beller whined for something to eat.

"I'm still hungry," Johnny said. "Do you have anything else?"

"Lots of fish in Whiskey Creek," Ryker said but reluctantly

reached for an egg. He came up with a handful of runny yolks and whites. The eggs had mostly broken during his race across the prairie. He must conserve what few things were left. "We'll have more to eat when we get there."

"Sven," he said in a low voice, "what happened?"

"Told you not to leave us," Sven said in a whisper. "*Skraelings* came right after you left." He pointed at sleeping Klara with a finger before his lips. "We were gathering corn, and Beller growled." Sven clutched Beller's neck. "Don't be mad. He's a good dog. It was your fault for leaving us, not Beller's."

Sven spoke the truth, and Ryker knew it. "Did you see Mama and Elsa?"

"Johnny did." Sven nodded for Johnny to explain.

"The Indians grabbed me on my way home and brought me to your ma and sister, and others." He looked at Ryker with an eager expression. "Have you seen my folks? Do you know where they are?"

Ryker shook his head. He expected they had met the same fate as his father and the Tingvolds. *Todt.*

"I need to go home," Johnny said. His mouth twisted into a knot. "Ma will be worried sick."

"What happened to Mama and Elsa?" Ryker said.

"We were together the first day, but then some of the Indians headed west." Johnny shook his head. "The Sioux who took them wore paint and feathers. The ones with us were mostly old people."

"Where did they go?" Ryker said.

Johnny shrugged his shoulders. "They took your ma and sister along with the Jensen girls from Breckinridge." Johnny paused. "Took all the women."

Ryker recalled the plump, pretty girls who had blushed when Martin complimented their fresh-baked cobbler. He let out a sigh of relief. They were nice girls who would help Mama with

Elsa. At least Mama wasn't alone.

"I think they headed toward the fort," Johnny said. "At least they went in that direction, and one of the Indians said the word *Abercrombie.*"

"The soldiers will rescue them," Sven said with certainty. "We don't have to worry."

Ryker let out a breath. It was unlikely, but the more he thought of the soldiers rescuing them, the more he was sure it would really happen. The children would go to the fort and find their mother and sister safe. It felt better to believe than to worry.

Sven whispered how the Indians had dragged them across the prairie, shooting Beller's ear with an arrow when he tried to protect Klara, who couldn't keep up, and how Beller had yelped as he ran away.

"I didn't know but they had killed poor Beller," Sven said, flinging his arms even tighter around the dog's neck. "They were mean to Klara." His lip quivered, and he clenched his thin fists. "They put a rope around her neck when she couldn't keep up and dragged her behind."

Ryker noticed for the first time the red marks around Klara's neck. A cold fury settled in his gut to think of the Red Men mistreating his little sister.

"They had a bottle," Johnny said. "Started drinking after dark. Got drunk and made a lot of noise. Then they slept like stones."

"It was our chance to get away," Sven said. He told how he had used his knife to cut the binding ropes. They sneaked away under cover of the storm.

"How did you keep your knife?"

"Hid it in my shoe," Sven said. "They didn't look there."

Then Sven reached under his shirt and pulled out *Uncle Tom's Cabin.* "Kept it safe," Sven said with a triumphant grin. "Mrs.

Tingvold wouldn't want it lost." Then as if remembering what had happened to their teacher, Sven hid his face in Beller's neck.

"I'm proud of you." Ryker slipped his arm around his brother's shaking shoulders. "You're smart. I should have listened to you."

Sven lifted his face. How small he looked with his thin face, so filthy and sunburned.

"You're as smart as Martin," Ryker said. "I was wrong to investigate alone."

He showed them the food he had scrounged from the homestead. Johnny wolfed down a raw potato. Sven tried to push a bite of potato into his sister's mouth but soon gave up in defeat. She was asleep.

"I hope they don't come looking for us," Sven said. "The mean ones would never have let us get away alive. But the ones we were with weren't as bad. A nice old lady doctored Klara's rope burns with grease."

Ryker peeped over the edge of the ravine and scanned the horizon. Klara needed rest before they could go on. He would let them sleep for a short while, and then they must be on their way.

"I'll keep watch," Johnny said.

Ryker didn't know if he could trust Johnny or not. Johnny's suspenders were missing, and his trousers hung low around his waist. He was barefooted and blistered from the hard travel. Although he was a larger boy than Sven, he somehow looked younger and more vulnerable.

"Your mother was real good to me," Johnny blurted out. "Held my hand and let me stay right by her when the Indians were mean."

Ryker could remind the boy how he made fun of his mother for being a Norskie square head, and all the hurtful things he had said about her kerchief. But it seemed unimportant after all that had happened. All that mattered now was to get to the fort.

"All right," Ryker said. "Keep watch." Johnny's face turned into a grin. "But call me if you see even a blade of grass moving in an unexpected way."

"I'm thirsty," Klara croaked.

They would have to find Whiskey Creek soon.

"They didn't give us no water, no food, nothing." Sven clenched his fist and fingered his knife. "They pushed us around. I wish the soldiers would come and teach them a lesson."

"Mama says they're just poor folks trying to feed their families," Klara said in sleepy voice.

Her eyes closed, and her breathing slipped into the heavy rhythm of sleep. Sven hugged Beller's neck and scratched his belly. The sun warmed as it climbed the eastern sky. Ryker dozed a little until Sven spoke.

"An old Indian woman let us get away." Sven frowned. "She saw us cutting ourselves free but didn't sound the alarm."

"Maybe she was asleep."

"She was looking at us," Sven said. "Her eyes were open."

Ryker tried to push from his mind the image of the Indian beating Johnny when he tried to escape.

"Maybe the angel made her blind," Sven said.

"Klara saw angels in the clouds," Johnny said from his watchman's perch. He had lost his bravado. "I couldn't see them."

Ryker remembered the cloud bank from the night before, the swirling mountains of black and gray. "How far did you walk?" Ryker said.

"Not sure," Sven said. "Walked all night and didn't dare stop." Sven laid his head on the ground and closed his eyes. "Clouds covered up the stars . . . we just walked."

Sven was asleep before Ryker could ask anything else. Ryker stood watch to let Johnny nap before they started out again. Ryker decided they would leave when the sun stood straight overhead. With luck, they might reach Whiskey Creek by night time. Beller stood guard with him as cicadas zinged by their ears. They were lost. Every direction looked the same, grass and more grass.

He let the children sleep. Though sleep pressed hard upon his eyelids, Ryker didn't allow himself a nap. The Indians might return. He kept watch though the hot sun felt like a cozy blanket. Blackbirds cackled; meadowlarks trilled. A striped gopher peeked at them from the edge of the wallow. Across the prairie sounded the cry of a hawk. Or maybe it was an Indian. Ryker couldn't keep awake. Then he remembered the book.

He read through the morning. Topsy struggled to find her freedom from the wicked overseer. Old Tom suffered and died. Mrs. Tingvold had been right. Reading *Uncle Tom's Cabin* taught Ryker more about the evils of slavery than anything he had learned at school.

He could have read all day, but common sense forced him to action. Ryker tucked the book into the waist of his trousers and shook the children awake.

They scrounged in the sack of supplies for something to eat.

"Nothing for you, boy," Ryker said. He reached out and petted their faithful friend. Beller pawed his injured ear, still dangling by a thread.

Ryker fished Papa's folding knife from his pocket and sliced through the bit of flesh holding Beller's ear. Beller yelped once and then sniffed the ear that Ryker threw into the weeds.

"Yuck," Johnny said as he watched the dog take the ear into his mouth. "Your dog's turned cannibal."

Ryker smiled and then chuckled. Sven joined in until they were all laughing—except Klara. The boys laughed until tears rolled down their cheeks, clutching each other as Klara stared dully at them.

"Just like the heathen in Africa," Johnny said.

"We'll change his name to Cannibal," Sven said. His face contorted with laughter, and saliva dripped onto his chin.

"When you laugh like that," Johnny said, "you look like Mrs. Tingvold, except with teeth."

Sven's laughter turned abruptly to tears. He buried his face in his arms. Sven's shoulders heaved with gulping sobs. Beller crawled over and laid his head on Sven's legs, still clutching the ear between his teeth. Klara put her arm around his neck. They leaned into each other.

It was up to Ryker to cheer them.

"I wonder what Martin is doing today," Ryker said. It wasn't funny anymore. He had to change the subject, had to rally his little family and get them to Fort Abercrombie. "Hot this time of year in that country." Ryker brushed a fly away from his face, then remembered buzzing flies around Papa's wound. Ryker shook himself from the memory. "Martin is learning to play the Jew's harp. Remember? I wish we had a Jew's harp right now, or a mouth organ. I'd play a song for you."

"What song?" Klara said in a small, weak voice. She had barely spoken since being taken by the savages. Ryker's heart leapt in his chest.

"Why, something American," Ryker said, cheered by her interest. "Enough of *Per Spelmann* from the Old Country. I'd play *Rally Round the Flag* or *The Battle Hymn of the Republic*." He could tell Sven was listening by the way he turned his ear toward him. Measles had affected Sven's left ear when he was a little boy, and he cocked his head to the right to hear better.

"Frank plays music, too," Johnny said with a bit of defensiveness in his attitude. "He can do anything your brother can do."

"They make music together." Ryker fabricated a story about

Martin's Jew's harp and his journey home after the war's end. Beller looked at him with interest, as Ryker rolled out the story of music, dancing, and the end of war.

"I'll play the Jew's harp, too," Klara said. She plopped her thumb in her mouth and sucked hard. Then she reached for a cabbage leaf and chewed it slowly. Ryker smiled. Beller swallowed the ear. They wouldn't be lost once they reached Whiskey Creek. The thought of his mother and sister's predicament spurred him to action.

"We have to go," he said. "Mama's waiting."

Ryker took a deep breath and squared his shoulders. He tucked the book into the sack for safekeeping. He took his bearings according to the sun and headed in the direction where he hoped to find Whiskey Creek.

His father had always made Ryker feel safe. Now he had to keep Sven and Klara safe. And Johnny Schmitz, of all people, the boy who had been mean to Mama, and who had bullied the twins at school. Papa had put Ryker in charge, and he would do his best. Everyone counted on him. Besides, he couldn't just leave Johnny out on the prairie to starve. Poor boy had lost his parents, most likely. Ryker tried to muster sympathy for him but failed. He would take care of the boy whether or not he felt sympathy for him. Mama would insist.

Klara said nothing. Her eyes stared ahead, and she kept her thumb in her mouth. Ryker could do nothing but hurry her along with the others. Papa said to concentrate on the task at hand and not borrow trouble for the next day. That's what Ryker would do.

They headed straight south through oceans of grass, or at least south as Ryker figured by the position of the sun overhead. Klara lifted her feet as if she were marching. Johnny dragged behind her, listless and mumbling about his parents being worried. Sven held his knife ready. Beller, tethered by the rope, perked his remaining ear, and followed close beside the ragtag group. They were a small army, but they could do it.

They had no other choice.

CHAPTER 16

They trudged through the hot afternoon. Sven kept a tight hold of Beller's leash to prevent him from running off again. They had to find Whiskey Creek. Every so often, Ryker jumped up, trying to get higher than the grass to see where they were going.

"Climb up on my shoulders, Klara," Ryker said after he discovered he couldn't jump high enough. "Maybe you'll be able to see the trees by Whiskey Creek."

"I'll do it," Johnny said.

"You're too heavy," Ryker said. "Klara weighs the least."

Klara struggled to stand on Ryker's shoulders but couldn't find her balance. "I'm scared," she said. "I can't do it."

"Then you stand on my shoulders, Ryker," Johnny said. "I'm strong enough to hold you."

Ryker mulled over his suggestion. They had no other choice. He climbed up on Johnny's shoulders while Johnny knelt in the grass. Then Klara and Sven held Ryker's hands to steady him as Johnny stood to his feet.

Johnny was as strong as a young bull, and, even though Ryker was older than Johnny, no doubt Johnny outweighed him. Ryker put both arms out to steady himself and then looked all around him over the sea of waving grass.

Nothing. Not a tree. Not a sign of another farm, or a creek or a river. No sign of Indians. No smoke or flames. Only grass. Papa would have been a millionaire had they been able to hay this stretch of prairie and sell it to the army.

The sun drooped in the western sky. They were going in the right direction.

"Enough," Ryker said. "Let me down easy."

He climbed off Johnny's shoulders, surprised at the wobble in his knees. They had to keep going forward, just like Martin's regiment marching to fight the enemy.

They walked about another hour, tired and thirsty. If they didn't find water soon, they would not survive.

Klara was complaining about being tired when Beller strained against his leash. He sharpened his eyes toward the west, his whole being attentive.

"He hears something," Sven said turning his good ear to the sound. "Listen."

Ryker heard only moaning wind and swishing grass. "Probably smells a coyote, or even a deer." Beller sniffed the air and whined, wagging his tail and pulling against the leash. He barked and pulled until Sven was lifted off his feet.

"Sounds like a crying baby," Johnny said.

Klara cocked her head toward where Sven was pointing. "I hear it, too," Klara said, and excitement caused her voice to sharpen. "A baby."

"Might be Indians, for all we know," Ryker said. An Indian baby cried just like a white baby. They might barge into a Sioux camp. They might be the very Indians who had taken the twins. Or even the ones who had taken Mama and Elsa. He had to think. Something felt wrong. It might be a trap. "It's just a catbird." Fatigue rolled over him like a gray shadow. "Or a wounded rabbit." He wanted only to lie down and sleep. His stomach growled, and his throat parched. "Forget it."

"What if it's a baby lost on the prairie?" Sven said, and he knelt to untie the rope holding Beller. Beller barked a frantic bark. Not a warning bark, but more like a welcome.

Klara pulled herself to her feet. "I'll go with you, Sven."

"All right," Ryker said. "We're staying together. Just remember that Mama and Elsa are depending on us. We don't have time to run after every bird call."

Beller, freed from the leash, streaked through the tall grass, and Sven and Klara followed. Johnny helped Ryker gather up the small store of supplies. Ryker followed at a slower pace, his feet hurting and his mind foggy with fatigue.

Sven was right. Sounds of crying drifted through the green jungle of tall grass. It was an angry, desperate cry.

Klara screamed. The baby stopped crying, and Beller quit barking. Ryker pushed through the grass and cried out in surprise.

"Elsa?"

CHAPTER 17

Their little sister's eyes were puffed almost shut from mosquito welts, and her face was blistered from sunburn and crying. Her bare feet showed cuts and scratches, and her dress was ripped almost to shreds. Her blond curls matted and tangled around her red face. She clung to Klara with shoulders heaving and snot dripping down her dirty face.

"Hush now, Sistermine," Klara crooned. "I'll take care of you."

"Mama," Elsa said, pulling on Klara's dress. "Mama."

"Where's Mama?" Ryker said. He tried to take Elsa from Klara's arms, but she refused to leave her older sister. Ryker had been wrong again. He felt ashamed of his stubbornness. If the twins had listened to him, Elsa might have been lost forever.

Ryker had carried the last egg in his pocket to prevent it from breaking. The small brown egg was his hedge against starvation, safe from the twins and Johnny. Thank God he had something to give Elsa. Elsa would die without sustenance. He carefully punched a hole into the rounded tip with the nail, breaking through the inner membrane. He held the egg up to Elsa's lips. When she tasted the thick, runny white, she pulled Ryker's hand closer and sucked greedily. A bit of yellow yolk slipped down her chin. Ryker wiped it with his finger and licked it clean. How good it tasted. Warm and good.

Elsa turned her face away. Ryker noticed a little egg left inside the shell. His stomach clenched with hunger, and he wanted it more than he had ever wanted food in his life, but Klara looked ready to collapse. Ryker knew what he must do. Slowly, he handed the egg to Klara.

"Are you sure?" Klara said, with a new light in her eyes. She eyed it hungrily.

"Mama is nearby," Sven said. "She wouldn't leave the baby."

"Unless Elsa wandered off and got lost," Klara said, licking the inside of the egg shell to get every drop. "You know how she is."

They searched but found no sign of their mother, calling her name as loudly as they dared. "We need a plan," Ryker said. "We risk getting lost ourselves."

"Someone should stay with Elsa, and the others should search." Klara popped her thumb in her mouth.

"No," Johnny said. "You hold the ball of yarn, and Sven and I will tie ourselves to the end. That way we won't get lost."

It was a crazy idea, but it might work. Ryker nodded and tied Johnny's wrist to the end of the yarn. He and Sven disappeared into the tall grass while Ryker unwound the ball of yarn. Klara cuddled Elsa. Ryker reached for a rose growing on a bush nearby. He tucked the pink petals in his mouth, imagining they were his mother's Christmas cookies. Not many roses this time of the year.

They fanned out to search the area, calling as loudly as they dared, but found no trace of their mother. Beller lay next to Elsa and refused to budge. Ryker puzzled over this but decided Beller knew their mother was nowhere around. Besides, they needed someone to keep watch over Elsa lest she get lost again.

The boys returned hot and sweaty. "Useless to keep looking," Sven said. "Mama wouldn't let her out of her sight." He hesitated and spoke again. "Unless something happened to Mama . . ."

His words hung in the air like a bad smell. It couldn't be that they would lose their mother, as well as their father. God wouldn't let them become orphans.

"She was all right the last time I saw her," Johnny said. "Indians split us up one time; maybe they did it again." He scraped crumbs from the bottom of the sack and handed them to Elsa. "My folks will be worried sick. I have to get home."

Ryker didn't know how to tell Johnny that his parents were probably dead. Mama might be dead, too. He swallowed a lump in his throat and reached for Elsa. She turned her face into Klara's shoulder.

"Milk," Elsa said. She pulled on Klara's dress. "Milk."

"She said milk," Klara said. She hugged her little sister tighter. "But I don't have any milk to give you, *stalkers liten.*"

"We need to get to Fort Abercrombie as fast as we can," Ryker said to Johnny. "Your folks will know you had the good sense to seek refuge."

"Do you think so?" Johnny's hopeful face twisted into a look so forlorn that Ryker's heart softened. "Those shots and smoke from our place . . ." He buried his face into the crook of his arm. "They're dead, like the teacher." He looked up and locked eyes with Ryker. "I know it. Tell me the truth."

"It doesn't look good," Ryker said slowly.

"Damn them," Johnny said. He clenched his fists as if ready to fight the Sioux Nation. "Damn the redskins. What did we ever do to them?"

Ryker thought to explain the broken treaty, but he had neither the understanding nor the energy to delve into it. "We'll figure it out at the fort."

Elsa clung to Klara. Ryker shuddered to think what could have happened to his baby sister. She might have been eaten by a wild animal, or drowned in a swamp. She could have starved to death or perished of thirst. It made no sense that she would be out on the prairie by herself. Mama would not have let Elsa out of her sight. Indians sometimes adopted little ones into their tribe. Ryker had read stories about such things. He mentioned it aloud.

"She's trouble," Sven said as he reached over and kissed the top of Elsa's tousled head. "Maybe they left her behind on purpose."

"We have you now, Sistermine," Klara said. "We'll find Mama soon and give you all the milk you can drink." Elsa curled her fingers through Klara's hair. "Look," Klara said, pointing to a mass of white clouds in the sky, "angels were watching over her."

Ryker craned his neck to the skies and saw what might have been a face in the clouds. He couldn't be sure. Then it was gone.

Klara smiled for the first time since their father's death. "We're going to be all right." She kissed Elsa and snuggled her close. "All of us. I know it."

"Look!" Sven pointed toward the horizon.

There stood a line of small green bushes hugging the far lip of the prairie. But they weren't bushes. They were the trees growing alongside Whiskey Creek.

Ryker wasn't sure about angels or miracles, but surely Mama's prayers had been answered. Something stirred within him, something akin to hope.

CHAPTER 18

They trudged toward the tree line, and the promise of water. Distances were deceptive on the prairie, and it proved farther away than expected.

No one complained. Johnny slapped gnats biting around his ears. Klara stumbled with Elsa's extra weight in her arms. Sven held Beller close with the rope leash.

"Come to me," Ryker said and reached for Elsa. "Come ride on my shoulders."

Elsa shook her head and clung to Klara.

"Ride the horsy," Klara said. She looked exhausted and so pale that her freckles stood out like brown seeds on her sunburned face. "Ryker is a nice horsy."

"Milk," Elsa said. She loosened her grip on her sister but still pulled away when Ryker lifted her from Klara's arms. She let out a squeal and stretched both arms toward Klara.

"Come," Ryker said. He hoisted her up on his shoulders. "Ride the horsy." Ryker galloped a few steps, trying to gather enough energy to cheer his baby sister.

Elsa's ragged skirts reeked of urine. They made better time for a while, the green bushes growing into trees. Elsa rested her head on top of his and took a short nap. Then she jabbed her finger into Ryker's ear.

"Ouch," he said. "That hurts."

Elsa bawled a protest, and Klara came close enough to hold Elsa's hand. She quieted and was soon back to sleep.

"No wonder they left her on the prairie," Johnny said. "The Red Men didn't want her telling the whole world where they were."

Ryker bristled. Johnny had no right to complain about his little sister. "Oh, shut up," Ryker said. "We'll leave you behind on the prairie."

Johnny's face crumpled. Ryker knew he shouldn't have told him to shut up. Johnny had most likely lost his parents and had been mistreated by the Sioux. He deserved Ryker's pity more than reprimand.

"We won't leave you," Ryker said, relenting. "We're almost to Whiskey Creek. By tomorrow we'll be at the fort."

"I just meant that she's noisy," Johnny said.

"She's a baby," Ryker said. He paused to readjust the sleeping baby on his back. Her dead weight pushed in all the wrong places. "She can't help it."

"We're getting closer," Klara said. "Let's get to the river before dark."

Klara kept a steady pace and didn't lag behind, though her face looked haggard, and her body had disappeared to skin and bones. It seemed the bit of egg had given Klara renewed strength. Or maybe it was finding Elsa.

"What if Mama was sick and couldn't call out to us?" Sven said. "What if we're leaving her behind?"

"We looked everywhere," Johnny said.

"Beller wouldn't leave Mama on the prairie. He would have found her had she been anywhere nearby," Ryker said. He hoped he sounded more convincing than he felt. He shared the same concern, but he knew Mama would first urge him to bring the little ones to safety before spending more time looking for her. Mama always put her children first.

"You know Mama," he said in a confident voice. "She'll be safe until we get to the fort. She might be waiting for us and

117

worrying herself sick about Elsa."

They speculated on how or why Elsa ended up alone on the prairie. Sven thought another old Indian woman had let her go as a kindness. Klara said an angel set her down on the grass where they were sure to find her.

"I think it was just luck that we found her," Johnny said. He rubbed his bruised chin as he talked. "All that matters is that we found her before the Indians could hurt her."

They trudged through the tall grass as afternoon stretched into evening. Ryker's neck and back ached. Elsa felt heavy as a sack of grain on his back. They couldn't stop, but Ryker didn't know how much longer he could go on. Weakness and a bone-tired weariness gripped until he thought he would faint. He thought of Martin in the war. Soldiers endured many hardships.

"I'll carry her for a while," Johnny said. He was a strong boy and built like a young bull. "You need rest."

Ryker gratefully lifted Elsa onto Johnny's back. Elsa wrapped her arms around his head and fell asleep. Poor thing. She needed water. They all needed water.

A breeze carried the laky smell of the river. "We're almost there," Ryker said. "We made it." The grass gave way to a band of marshy area. They knelt down and washed their faces in the mucky water. Beller drank his fill. Johnny pulled a handful to his mouth.

"Don't drink it," Ryker said. It took all his strength to wait for the clean water of Whiskey Creek. "Slough water will make you sick." Around them, red-winged blackbirds sang in the thrushes. Frogs croaked, and swirling gnats attacked them. They wouldn't have lasted much longer.

"I'm dying of thirst," Johnny said. He slurped large handfuls of water in spite of Ryker's warning.

Sven reached for a drink, too, but Ryker pulled him back.

"No," Ryker said. His throat was so dry that his words came

out in a croaking whisper. "We're almost there. You don't want to get sick now. We need our strength to find Mama."

Johnny followed them toward the river. "I'm not sick," he said. "I feel just fine."

"Better safe than sorry," Ryker said. "Papa wouldn't ever let me drink from standing water. Creek water is safer."

They hurried toward Whiskey Creek. It was a small stream there, but Ryker knew it grew larger closer to Fort Abercrombie. "Wait and see if it's safe," Ryker whispered as Sven ran ahead, pulled by Beller. "Indians travel the rivers."

They crouched in the grass. A cliff swallow returned to its nest in the bank. The river rippled toward the Red River and Fort Abercrombie. Ryker could almost taste the cool water, but still he hesitated. Maybe danger lurked in the welcoming stream.

"Look how tall they are," Sven said in a whisper.

Sven hadn't been to the fort with their father and had not seen trees for several years. "Look how high!" He pointed to the treetops, and Beller pulled free. He charged to the river and splashed into the water with a yip.

Ryker held his breath. The children stared at their pet frolicking in the river, waiting for Indians to burst out of the brambles. Nothing happened. Ryker saw nothing amiss. He nodded, and the children crept to the water, splashing and drinking their fill. A few blackberries hung on low bushes. Klara picked all that she could find and shoved them into Elsa's mouth until her lips and tongue turned blue.

"I'm still hungry," Sven said. "Can't we find something to eat?"

Beller growled and warily approached a small snapping turtle that crawled out of the water.

"Stay back," Sven said and thrust a branch in front of the turtle's mouth for it to latch onto. Sven squealed with joy when it clamped the stick with its fierce jaws. "I got it."

Sven pulled out his knife and sawed its long, rubbery neck, stretched to hold the stick. It took a while, but at last Sven severed the head. Blood spurted onto the grass. Beller snatched the head and ran into the bushes.

"We can't build a fire," Ryker said, with grudging admiration. He would have never thought to catch a turtle.

"Indians eat raw turtle meat," Sven said. "Mrs. Tingvold said they eat raw buffalo livers and hearts, and raw fish."

Ryker sobered at the mention of their teacher's name. Where would they find another teacher like her?

"Wake up!" Sven said. "You didn't hear a word I said."

"I heard you," Ryker said. "You want to eat it raw."

"No, I said I need your help to dress it out." Together they removed the turtle's shell and used it as a dish to hold the meat. Sven's knife blade proved too dull to use, but Ryker's folding knife did the job.

Johnny lifted a piece to his nose and gave a sniff. "Smells like fish," he said. He pushed a small bit of meat into his mouth. "Not real bad," he said.

Sven handed a bit to Klara, but she sucked her thumb harder and looked away. He gave the meat to Ryker.

Not to be outdone by the boys, Ryker popped a piece of turtle into his mouth, almost gagging on the muddy fish taste. He forced himself to chew and swallow, thinking of Mama's *lutefisk* at Christmas, and the taste of peppermint candy from the ox carters who sometimes stopped by their farm.

Ryker dug into the sack and pulled out the sausage and a small ear of raw corn. The silk shriveled around tough kernels. He handed it to his little sisters.

"Eat," Ryker said. "You'll feel better."

His stomach roiled with the raw turtle, not feeling better at all. The taste of blood made him gag, and he lay on the shore and scooped water into his mouth to wash it away. Turtle tasted better cooked into a soup with potatoes and turnips.

Sven called for Beller to come eat the innards. He gulped the bloody mess and looked at Sven with bright eyes.

"That's all you get," Sven said.

Klara stripped Elsa's filthy dress and washed it downstream from where the boys were playing. They washed their faces and bathed in the coolness. Ryker filled the turtle shell and peach can with water.

Ryker had just called the children back to the shoreline when a rustling sound came from the cottonwoods along the opposite bank. Beller lunged toward the sound before Sven could grab hold of him. Ryker raced after Beller and caught the end of the rope around his neck. He half dragged and half carried the dog toward shore.

"What is it?" Sven said. "Indians?"

"Don't know," Ryker whispered. The children huddled behind a fallen log. "Be quiet." Ryker knelt beside Beller and put both hands around his snout. "Hush now." He felt Beller's heart beating like a captured bird. Had they come this far for nothing?

Branches rattled, and a flock of cliff swallows startled up into the air. Maybe the Indian with the black horse would swoop upon them with his hatchet high over his head. Ryker held his breath and struggled to see what was coming. He glanced toward his brother and sisters. Sven gripped his knife in his hand, ready to defend them from attackers.

A dark creature crashed through the underbrush. The falling shadows of evening made it difficult to see. Ryker craned his neck for a better view.

"Look! A *bjorn!*" Sven said.

CHAPTER 19

Ryker followed Sven's pointing finger as a large black bear burst from the bushes under the trees on the opposite bank. It stood on two legs and pawed the air. It growled, rolling its head and gnashing huge teeth. Saliva dripped from its mouth. Ryker pulled back, pushing Klara in his efforts to get behind the log. Ryker had a clear view of the bear through some dead branches.

The bear turned toward the sound, rubbing his snout with his clumsy paws as if to fight anything that might be in his path. It was then that Ryker saw what made the bear so angry. Its mouth and throat bristled with porcupine quills.

"He looks like Mama's pincushion," Sven said.

"Like my father's beard," Johnny said.

The bear swatted at his face as if to fight off a bee. Beller was tied, and Ryker hoped the bear would not smell them. The bear dropped to his four paws and rolled his face in the nettles and leaves covering the ground. It roared in anger, wiping its face as if to wipe the quills away, dipping into the river and rubbing again.

"Mama." Elsa toddled toward the river bank. How did she get away?

Time stopped as the bear turned his head to stare at their baby sister standing on the bank. The bear roared, and Elsa screamed in fear.

Ryker leapt from his place of safety and scooped the baby into his arms just as the bear charged into the creek, rushing toward them. Elsa yelled louder, and Ryker was sure his heart would burst with fear. Ryker ran toward the trees while clutching Elsa to his chest, but the bear was closing in on them.

Ryker hesitated. Should he throw Elsa in the bushes and turn to fight the bear? He had the folding knife in his pocket. Should he fall on the ground and cover Elsa with his body in hopes the bear would go away?

Beller streaked by them. Their faithful dog stood between the children and the bear, ferociously barking and growling, forcing the bear to turn away from the children and face him. Ryker stood long enough to see the bear lunge. A cacophony of barking, yipping, and braying filled the air, as Ryker raced to the trees while holding his baby sister.

"Climb a tree," Ryker yelled to the others. "Go high as you can."

The cottonwoods had tall trunks without lower branches, making them impossible to climb. There were smaller trees but not nearly as tall or sturdy. At least they could get away from the bear. Ryker lifted Elsa up to Johnny's waiting hands and climbed onto the first branch of a straggly oak.

"Sven," Ryker said. "Hurry up!" Sven stood on the edge of the river watching the fight. "Come on."

"No," Sven said. "The bear will kill old Beller."

The bear slapped Beller on his side with a massive blow, sending him flying into the water. The bear dove after him.

"Come," Ryker said. If the dog no longer threatened, the bear might come after them. "Now."

Reluctantly, Sven pulled himself away from the shore as Beller came out of the water for another round with the bear. The bear was winning. Ryker had a sick feeling as the bear swiped another blow.

Sven was crying. "Everyone we love is dying," Sven said.

"Martin and Papa, Mrs. Tingvold, maybe Mama . . . and now Beller."

"Hush now," Ryker said, and put his arm around his brother as they perched on the branch. "We have each other. We'll always be there for each other."

"Be quiet—the bear might back off," Johnny said.

Beller put up a valiant resistance. He charged again and again, nipping and drawing the bear away from the children. But then a mighty swipe of the bear's paw sent Beller flying to the rocks at the edge of the far bank . . . a thud and crunch of bone when Beller landed on the rocks. Beller lay like a sack of rags.

The bear dropped to all fours and shook its massive head. It roared and swiped at the quills on its snout. Then it raised to its hind legs and sniffed the air. It scanned the shore and raised its eyes to the tree. It dropped down and waded toward the children, splashing in the water and sniffing around the base of the scraggly tree.

"Horsy," Elsa said.

The giant beast looked up and fastened beady eyes on the children. It stood on its hind legs and grasped the tree trunk with both paws. Then the bear shook the tree.

"Hang on," Ryker said.

Johnny scrambled higher in the tree, and Sven and Ryker moved to the branch where Johnny had been. Even so, the bear kept shaking the tree. The tree next to them would have been a better choice, because it was a little stouter. He should have planned for such an emergency. Ryker was responsible, but he had not done enough to keep his family safe.

Ryker held onto the tree trunk with one arm and clutched Elsa with the other. Elsa squirmed, and Ryker feared he might drop her. He called up to Sven and passed Elsa to him, but, just before Sven's hands reached the baby, the bear roared and gave a mighty shake to the tree. Ryker caught Elsa in midair before she fell to the ground.

The bear wrapped its arms around the trunk and tried crawling up the tree. Ryker smelled its breath and saw the mass of quills around its mouth. It batted at the quills in its mouth and slipped back down to the ground. Then with a fierce roar, the bear shook the tree trunk again.

Ryker could do nothing but hang on to his perch. They could not climb higher. The tree's upper branches were too small to support their weight. They were scarcely out of the bear's reach. He prayed for a miracle.

"Look!" Sven shouted and pointed to the place where Beller had fallen.

Beller struggled to his feet and shook his head as if to shake sleep away. He tottered on unsteady legs until he regained his balance. He saw the bear at the base of the tree and barked a fierce challenge. Gathering his strength, Beller again charged the bear.

The bear turned to face its attacker and pressed its back against the tree trunk. Beller leapt at the bear, nipping and growling. The bear swiped at the dog and knocked him off his feet. Beller got up again and lunged toward the bear. The bear snapped its jaws and ran toward Beller. Ryker bit his lip until he tasted blood. Klara was crying.

The bear batted Beller into the bushes with a single swipe of its giant paw. Beller yipped and was quiet. Just when they thought he was dead, Beller pulled himself to his feet and approached the bear. Beller barked and retreated a few steps and then turned and barked again. The bear followed.

"He's drawing the bear away from us," Sven said. "That good dog."

He was right. Ryker and the children watched Beller tease and taunt the bear to the other shore of Whiskey Creek, away from them. The bear stepped on the opposite shore and turned back toward the children, as if it would return and finish them off. Beller threw himself at the back of the bear, nipping at its neck.

It was a risk to move to a safer place, but Ryker saw no alternative.

"Get down and climb the next tree," Ryker said in a quiet voice. "Hurry, before the bear comes back."

They scrambled out of the tree and climbed into the next. These branches were sturdier, and the children climbed as high as they could. Ryker passed Elsa to Johnny, who was already at the very top of the tree. "Keep her quiet," Ryker said. "Keep your hand over her mouth if you have to, and grab hold of her as tight as you can."

Beller and the bear snarled and growled. The bear smacked Beller such a blow that Beller howled in agony. The good dog fell to the ground in a heap. The bear ambled over to Beller and gripped the dog's head in its giant mouth. It shook poor Beller like a rag doll, throwing him to the side in a crunch of bones.

The bear dropped down on all fours, its silhouette dark against the white rocks on the shore. With low growling and whimpers of pain, the bear lumbered toward the tall grass. It soon disappeared out of sight.

"It's running across the prairie," Johnny said from his high perch. "I can see it running away."

Elsa let out a howl as Johnny released his grip on her mouth.

"Keep Elsa quiet," Sven said. "That bear might come back." Sven scrambled down the tree.

"Wait!" Ryker said. "It's not safe."

Sven paid no attention but splashed across the river and ran to Beller lying on the ground. Johnny and Klara followed, leaving Elsa with Ryker.

"Is he alive?" Ryker called.

"Ya," Johnny said. "He's breathing."

Ryker scanned the banks and surrounding area. No sign of bears or Indians. He put Elsa on his back and climbed down the tree, careful to hang onto her legs lest she topple over and break her neck.

Klara fetched a handful of water and held it for Beller to lap. Beller looked at them with dull eyes and made strange whimpering sounds from time to time. A huge gash on his head dripped red blood until his brown spots looked as black as the rest of him. Johnny ripped the hem off his shirt for a bandage. Sven gathered the faithful dog's head onto his lap.

"You shouldn't have let him go," Klara said with an accusing stare.

"Hush," Ryker said. "Would you rather it were Elsa lying here?"

"I'm sorry, old boy," Sven said. He brushed flies away from Beller's face. "I didn't know what else to do."

They held the dog as twilight changed to night. A chill settled, and Elsa huddled closer to Ryker to keep warm. Klara tied another knot in her apron string. The odor of skunk wafted on the damp air. Wolves howled in the distance. Clouds of mosquitoes descended, and they huddled beneath the blanket to hide from them. Sven refused to leave Beller's side.

Beller died as the moon rose over the trees.

They wept for their faithful friend. Elsa joined the weeping when she saw the others crying. Red marks across her mouth showed Johnny's grip to keep her quiet. Sven could not be consoled.

"It's my fault," Sven said over and over, even though they all assured him that he had done the right thing.

"Beller saved us," Klara said. "He was our angel watching over us."

It grew darker. Klara shivered and hugged Elsa to her chest to keep her warm.

They discussed burying old Beller, but Ryker refused. He felt mean, but he had no choice.

The children's outcry was immediate, but Ryker stood firm explaining that a grave would tell the Indians they were here.

"Let Beller rest where he lies," Ryker said. "He'll understand."

CHAPTER 20

They camped that night in a thicket away from the riverbank. Sven felt smothered by the trees and insisted on sleeping out on the prairie. He refused to talk to Ryker, still angry about Beller's grave. Ryker didn't blame his brother. He would do as his father and older brother would have done. He would take his family to Fort Abercrombie and find help for his mother. They weren't lost anymore. It wasn't far.

"A fire would be cheerful," Johnny said.

"Sorry," Ryker said with a shake of his head. "It's a cold camp tonight."

Ryker held Elsa close to his side. They listened to the mournful sounds of wolves howling in the distance.

"Indians imitate wolves sometimes," Sven said in a whisper when Ryker thought everyone asleep. "Might be Redskins creeping in. Beller always stood guard."

"Mama says the angels take care of us while we sleep," Klara said as she tied another knot on her apron string to mark the days.

"I don't like trees," Sven said. "They close in on a person."

"You've turned into a plainsman," Ryker said. He was glad that Sven was speaking to him again. "Happier under open skies. *Bestefar* said the same about being a seaman, said that some sailors felt uneasy on land after months on the ocean."

An owl hooted. "Do you remember our grandfather? He told tales of his fishing days on the North Sea through the long,

129

dark Norwegian winter."

"He smelled like tobacco," Klara said. "And he kept peppermints in his pockets." She quieted and then said, "I can't remember his face."

"You were little," Ryker said. "You can't expect to remember."

Ryker fished the tintype of his parents from his pocket. It was too dark to see the images, but its touch was a comfort in the darkness. "Mama said that Papa looked just like his father. Martin favored Mama's side."

"Who do you look like?" Klara said.

"Mama says I take after Papa while the rest of you take after Mama's people," Ryker said. Ryker told stories about the Old Country, Mama's brothers and Papa's sister as then, one by one, they fell asleep. Only Ryker stayed awake to hear wolf calls, whining mosquitoes, and hooting owls. He was afraid to sleep without Beller standing guard. A shiver ran down his spine when he thought how close he had come to dropping Elsa into the clutches of the bear. Surely Mama's prayers were answered today.

A small brown squirrel scampered across their camping spot. A field mouse nosed the ground. Something splashed in Whiskey Creek. Maybe the bear coming back for them. The children slept peacefully. Ryker would not wake them without reason. He would go back to the creek and make sure all was well before he allowed himself to sleep.

He crawled toward the creek bank. Overhead the sky was peppered with a million stars. The moon balanced like a sliver of light in the darkness. He wondered if his father looked down from beyond the sky. The banks of Whiskey Creek hid in the shadows. Then a doe glided out of the bushes on the other side of the creek. It stepped to the edge of the water with long, thin legs. The doe raised its head and sniffed before dipping its muzzle in the cool, flowing water.

No deer would be near the water if Indians or bears were nearby.

Ryker sneezed, and the deer startled and ran into the woods, its graceful legs lifting off the ground and jumping through the trees, waving the white flag of tail. Ryker leaned over the water and drank a cool draught. Then he washed the day's grime from his face, swirling his hands in the gently flowing water.

A turkey buzzard picked Beller's bones. Ryker threw a stone to drive it away from their precious pet. He sat listening at the edge of the thicket late into the night. When he could no longer keep his eyes open, Ryker crept back to the campsite and snuggled next to Klara and Elsa.

Ryker woke up just as the sun peeped over the horizon. Morning birds sang from the trees of Whiskey Creek. A coyote yipped from the tree line. Ryker crept to the shore to make sure they were still alone.

The air felt soft and moist, and a gentle breeze rippled the leaves of the trees. A sumac bush already showed red, another sign that autumn was on its way. The dewy grass dampened his knees, and the wet fabric chafed his skin. The fragrance of damp earth filled his nostrils. How beautiful the morning.

A stealthy movement caught his eye.

Ryker looked back to make sure the children were asleep. Elsa slept beside Klara. The last thing they needed was for the baby to sound an alarm.

An Indian brave waded along the bank, following the bear tracks in the mud. He was dressed in buckskins, without war paint. He was hunting, proven by the way he held an arrow loosely hooked into his bowstring. He paused to examine the place where the bear had tangled with Beller and stopped by Beller's body.

There was something familiar about the man. Ryker drew in his breath. It was Finds the Knife, the brave who found Papa's missing knife in the bottom of the slough.

The Indian knelt by Beller's body and touched his damaged ear. Then he scanned the shoreline in all directions. Ryker should have wiped away the tracks, camped farther away from the creek, and known the danger.

Ryker heard a tiny splash as the Indian stepped back into the water. He sniffed the air and paused to listen. Ryker thanked God that he had not allowed the children a fire last night or let them bury the dog. The Indian followed the bear tracks toward the trees where they had hidden from the bear. Ryker held his breath, keeping as quiet as possible while the man examined the marks on the tree trunk, the tracks around the shoreline, and the broken branches littered around the ground. The man paused as if thinking, then stepped back into the water and crossed to the other side. Ryker watched from his hiding place as the Indian melted into the trees on the opposite bank.

Beller would have warned them about Finds the Knife creeping along the creek. It would be harder to get to the fort safely without his protection. But a barking dog might have given them away, as well. Probably better to be without Beller. Ryker looked toward Beller lying on the sand. He was a good dog. He saved them from the bear. Ryker wiped tears off his cheeks and started back to the camp. They had to hurry. If they left right away, they could be at the fort by nightfall.

Ryker counted slowly to one thousand before he dared move. Then he scurried back to where the children slept.

"Wake up," Ryker said. "It's not safe here."

"I dreamed about the bear," Johnny said while rubbing his eyes. "It ate Klara."

"Quiet," Ryker said when Klara raised a protest over Johnny's dream. "Indians. We've got to head to the fort right away."

Ryker crawled to the river alone and looked up and down the winding creek. He strained to hear a telling splash that might signal a canoe. Everything looked normal, as if nothing had happened out of the ordinary, as if Papa wasn't dead or Mama kidnapped. As if they hadn't seen the Tingvolds killed and watched Beller fight the bear. As if the angels hadn't brought them to find Elsa wandering alone on the prairie. Ryker sighed and motioned for the others to join him.

Sven held sleepy Elsa by the hand. Elsa made small, whimpering sounds, like a baby bunny taken from its nest.

"Milk," Elsa said. "Mama."

"We'll see Mama soon," Ryker said although he was far from certain they would find their mother at the fort. "Drink," Ryker said. "Wash your faces." He filled the empty peach can to carry with them. He reached into the bag for the last piece of cabbage and gave a leaf to each of the children. It felt like a holy moment, almost like breaking bread in church.

He tried to pray, but the words stuck in his throat. They were out of food. There was no milk for Elsa. Their father was dead, Martin missing, their crops wasted in the field, and they had no family in America where they could turn. The neighbors who might have helped them were dead. Maybe Mama would never come back; maybe she was dead. Ryker turned his thoughts from tomorrow and concentrated on the present moment.

They had found Elsa. It was a miracle. Beller had saved them from the bear. The Indian on the horse had not seen them hiding in the grass. Sven and Klara had escaped their captors. Johnny saw their mother taken away by another band of Indians.

Mama always said to trust a loving God who cared for His children. Though accusing doubts flooded his troubled mind, Ryker prayed for protection.

"How far is it?" Johnny said, his face smeared with dirt. It didn't help that the Indians had stolen his suspenders, and his trousers draped around his hips.

Ryker found the nail in the pouch around his neck. He had

almost forgotten about it. Ryker gave the nail to Johnny, who pushed it through the cloth on his waist and cinched his pants tighter.

"Much better," Johnny said. "You're lucky to have shoes." He stared at Ryker's feet as if measuring them. "This prairie grass is hard on the feet."

Ryker's feet were much smaller than Johnny's, though Johnny was younger. Not that Ryker would have parted with his shoes, but it made it easier to ignore Johnny's hint.

"Not far now," Ryker said. He remembered camping by the river that night on the trail, the way his father had whittled by the campfire. His father's hands never idled. He remembered then that his father had been whittling the handle for the butcher knife, the one stolen by the Indians when the twins were taken.

"A good handle lasts forever," Papa had said, holding it up with a look of satisfaction.

"I should have listened," Ryker said to his brother. "I shouldn't have left you in the corn field when I went to the farmstead."

"But you would have been taken with us, had we stayed together," Sven said. "You found extra food, and kept the folding knife because you left us in the corn field." Sven shifted the weight of the pack to his other shoulder. "You were there to help Beller find us. You were right, after all." Sven's voice cracked at the mention of Beller's name. Klara put her arm around his shoulder.

"Good old Beller," Klara said.

A load of guilt slipped off Ryker's shoulders. Following Beller to the escaped children led to finding Elsa on the prairie. A barking dog earlier that morning might have meant their death at the hands of the Indian brave hunting along Whiskey Creek. Beller might have given them away had he lived. It didn't seem like a blessing. None of it seemed like blessing.

"Beller protected us to the end," Ryker said.

CHAPTER 21

They would follow the creek north, longer with its windy banks and curves, and stay close to water and shelter. More dangerous because Indians traveled by canoes, but wiser—Ryker wouldn't risk getting lost again. He counted the days since his mother's disappearance. If the Sioux had taken her far out on the plains, Ryker knew the chances of finding her were slim. She would be lost to them. His new baby brother or sister would grow up Sioux. He didn't know what would happen to them. He didn't know if he would be able to provide for his younger siblings on his own. The haystack had burned; the crops were lost. Ryker did not know how they would survive without Papa. Mama would know a way.

He had to find her.

Keep calm and keep moving, his father had always said. Ryker intended to do just that.

Mrs. Tingvold said the Otter Tail and Bois de Sioux Rivers converged near Breckinridge to create the Red River of the North. Ryker scrambled to remember the map she had painted on the wall of the barn. Whiskey Creek emptied into the Red River north of Breckinridge, by Fort Abercrombie. The lazy river meandered north through the bottomlands of the Red River valley—not much of a valley really, as the water flowed too slowly to cut a gorge. The Red River widened the closer it got to Canada. The river overflowed during spring flooding, sometimes damaging houses of those who built too close to its banks. Riverboats had been navigating the Red River for a number of years. Ryker wished a desperate wish that a riverboat would be at the fort to rescue them.

"Mark my words," Mrs. Tingvold had said. "The Red River valley will someday be a thriving farming area."

Immigrants from all over the world were settling the United States little by little. Mrs. Tingvold said westward expansion pressured the Indian tribes already living on the land desired by settlers. Papa had predicted there would be a lot of soldiers looking for farmland after the Rebs were licked. Papa said they were lucky to settle land ahead of the crowds.

"What side of Whiskey Creek should we travel?" Sven said. "Whiskey Creek grows wider as it joins the Red."

Ryker couldn't recall where Papa had crossed over. That journey scrambled in his mind—Papa's laughter when Martin tripped in a gopher hole, smells of sauerkraut, and the soldiers at the fort. Martin had been most intrigued by the horse soldiers and their blue uniforms.

"Best way to get to the fort from this direction is through Slabtown," Johnny said. "We should cross Whiskey Creek now."

"I'm scared," Klara said, while bouncing Elsa on her hip. Elsa pushed her finger up Klara's nose and whined for her mama. Klara turned her face out of the baby's reach and shifted Elsa to her other hip. "The bear and the Indian are on the other side."

"Whiskey Creek won't hinder bears or Indians," Ryker said. "Best to cross over like Johnny said."

"What if the Indians won't let us into the fort?" Sven said.

"Milk," Elsa said, reaching again for Klara's nose. "Mama."

"We'll find Mama," Ryker said. He didn't know what they would do if Indians were at the fort. It might not be a widespread Indian war, maybe just a renegade party on the loose. They might get to the fort and find everything as usual.

But deep down, Ryker remembered the ominous conversation with Mr. Tingvold. He sighed and turned his focus on surviving until they arrived at the fort. It was their only hope. They couldn't be out on their own while Indians were on the warpath.

"We'll do it somehow," Ryker said. Indians might be there, and they might not. "Papa said Indians fear the soldiers."

"I forgot," Sven said. "You're right. The soldiers will take care of the Indians."

Elsa's face welted with mosquito bites, and Klara pulled a fat tick out of her hair. Elsa kept her eyes closed, although Ryker suspected she was awake. She reeked of urine.

"What's the matter?" Sven said with a worried look. "Is she sick?"

Elsa's eyelids fluttered. "Milk," she whispered. She stared with dull eyes.

Mama would insist someone comb Elsa's hair. Mama's comb and mirror had been left behind.

"It won't be long now," Ryker said. "We'll be there today if we hurry."

They traveled in the shade of cottonwoods along the riverbank, heading northwest toward Fort Abercrombie. It would have been faster and easier to wade in the shallow water, but Ryker thought it too dangerous. A passing Indian might catch them in the open. Though traveling along the banks of Whiskey Creek was buggier and harder walking, it would be easier to hide if need be.

Whiskey Creek meandered through the prairie, bending and snaking through the tall grass. Its banks were smothered with tangled brush and trees, deadfalls, and tumbled rocks. Overhead, a cloudless, blue sky. They had not gone far when muffled sounds of laughter caused them to dive into a thicket.

"What is it?" Klara said.

Elsa whimpered and clung to Ryker's leg. He grabbed hold

of his baby sister and held her so she couldn't escape and cause trouble. "Mama," she said. He clamped his hand over her mouth.

"Do you see anything?" Ryker whispered, peering through the dense foliage. Elsa bit his thumb with her sharp little teeth. "Ouch!" He gave his sister a shake and held her mouth even tighter.

"Indians," Sven said. "Get down."

Through a screen of leaves, Ryker watched three canoes paddle past them. The Indians sounded as boisterous and braggadocios as Mr. Tingvold. Their canoes were filled with blankets, cooking pots, petticoats, and a spinning wheel. One wore a red dress tied around his waist, with the lace collar hanging over his breechcloth. Their faces were painted with bright colors.

"Did they kill people to steal those things?" Klara whispered at his side.

"Hush," Ryker said. Elsa squirmed and grunted. Ryker tightened his grip on her mouth and held her closer. He kept his hold until the canoe traveled around a bend in the creek and paddled out of sight.

"They don't act afraid," Johnny whispered.

The Indians acted like conquerors celebrating a tremendous victory, not Indians cowering before the army. Ryker crept down to the water's edge and listened for a long moment.

A blue heron settled on the water, graceful wings rippling the current. A pair of swans floated in the bend of the creek. Frogs croaked, and a turtle sunned itself on a rock. A meadowlark warbled from the prairie, and an eagle swooped down and grasped a fish with its talons. It flapped massive wings to rise again into the sky, leaving a shadow on the water in the shape of a cross. Overhead white clouds rolled across blue sky. How could their situation be so hopeless, and yet the world remained beautiful and untouched?

Ryker fetched the turtle off the rock and brought it back to the children waiting on the shoreline. "Put it in the sack," Ryker said, "for later."

They trudged northwestward toward Fort Abercrombie, staying in sight of Whiskey Creek so they wouldn't get lost again. Johnny insisted on carrying Elsa to give Klara a much needed break. Ryker grudgingly admitted that Johnny was more of a help than a hindrance. Mama liked Johnny, and Mama was seldom wrong about people.

A hawk snatched a rabbit from the prairie grass. Its squeal of terror echoed across the prairie.

"Poor thing," Klara said. "That's how I felt when the Indians grabbed us."

"Wish I had that rabbit," Sven said. "Rabbit stew is better than turtle any day."

"We'll be at the fort by nightfall, if we hurry," Ryker said. "We'll eat our fill when we get there."

"Where have Mama's angels gone?" Klara said in a mournful tone. "We need them more than ever, and yet they haven't shown up since we found Elsa on the prairie."

"Don't worry," Sven said. "Angels stay with us, even when we can't see them. That's what Mama says."

"Mama," Elsa muttered from her perch on Johnny's shoulder. "Milk."

CHAPTER 22

Johnny liked turtle meat. At least he ate most of it. Sven ate a little. Ryker gagged on the stringy meat but managed to swallow it down. The girls refused to touch it.

"Aren't you hungry?" Johnny said.

"Not that hungry," Klara said. She and Elsa drank water and sucked their thumbs.

Ryker had almost decided to open the remaining can of baked beans from the Jacobs's family when he spied a path leading away from Whiskey Creek. Above the prairie grass flocked blackbirds circling and diving.

"It might be a homestead," Sven said. "Looks like birds stripping a field."

A farmer would be vigilant to keep the blackbirds out of his crops, but there was an outside chance there might be someone left to help them. Maybe water. Ryker decided it was worth a try, but he wouldn't go beyond sight of Whiskey Creek.

They soon came upon a corn patch. The children chased away the blackbirds and scavenged the few remaining ears. It wasn't exactly stealing. The log house next to the field had been ransacked, and mostly burned. They rummaged through the fallen timbers but found only charred furniture and half-burned clothing. They found nothing to eat, though Johnny thought they might find a trapdoor into a cellar if they moved the debris from the cabin floor.

"We don't have time," Ryker said. "We need to be on our way."

The cabin had nestled against a small rise. Wild flowers surrounded what remained of a barn and hen house. Prairie grass had been scythed for hay, as evidenced by the charred remains of a stack and a stretch of shorter grass. A snake hissed next to a gopher hole. A bobolink sang. How peaceful it looked—except for the destroyed buildings and broken dreams of whomever had lived there.

Johnny spied the remains of a vegetable garden behind the outhouse. Klara set Elsa under a shady bush and searched the rows for vegetables missed by the scavengers. Sven found an overgrown cucumber and a handful of carrots. Johnny pulled a huge beet out of the soil and took a bite, grinning with purple lips and teeth. The potato patch remained undisturbed.

"What do you think happened to the people?" Johnny said, as he stuffed a tomato into his mouth. Johnny was always hungry. He picked another tomato off the ground and pinched off a spoiled part, fed the good piece to Elsa, and ate the rotten part himself. Elsa made a face but swallowed. Then she lay in the shade and dozed.

"Maybe they went to the fort," Sven said.

"I hope they are safe," Klara said. She found a wooden doll on the ground beside the potato patch. "There were children." Her mouth crimped, and her voice lowered to a whisper. The doll wore a carved face with lips stained red, and a cloth dress and bonnet. Klara handed the doll to Elsa, who grasped it with her little hand but did not raise her head.

"You hold the dolly for now," Klara said, "but we'll give it back to the little girl who it belongs to when we get to the fort."

Sven retrieved an old spade with a broken handle from behind the outhouse. He dug huge shovelfuls of earth around the wilted potato plants, while the others lifted the spuds hidden in the soil. They sifted through the dirt with their fingers to find as many possible. They scrambled to fill their sack. Klara wiped a potato with her skirt and took a bite. Then she woke Elsa and held the potato to Elsa's mouth. Elsa took one lick and turned her face away with a scowl.

"Milk," Elsa said, her fussing turning into full-fledged crying. "Mama."

"Taste, Sistermine," Klara said. "It's good. You have to eat something."

"No!" Elsa said. She hid her face under her arm.

"Can't you do something to keep her quiet?" Ryker said in alarm. "Any Indian within ten miles will hear her caterwauling."

"She's tired and hungry," Klara said. "She wants milk. She doesn't know any better."

Klara chewed a bite of potato and smeared the chewed mess into Elsa's mouth. Elsa sucked Klara's fingers and reached for more.

"Hurry," Ryker said. He glanced at the sun and figured it was almost noon. The sooner they got to the fort, the sooner Elsa would have milk. "We have to leave."

"She'll get sick without something in her stomach." Klara glared at her brother. "And I can't chew any faster."

In the end, they worked together, chewing mouthfuls of raw potato and spitting into the empty peach can. The baby ate as fast as Klara could spoon the chewed potatoes into her mouth. Then, when Elsa had enough, she dozed.

"Can we go now?" Ryker said, impatient with his sister. He was hungry, too, and tired to the point of exhaustion. The fort was not far away. "Or do you have something else you need to do first?"

Sven stepped over to her side as if to fight for his sister if needed.

"Don't be mean. I want Mama, too," Klara said. "And I miss Papa."

Of course she did. They all did. Ryker didn't know how to take care of the family. He didn't know the way to Fort Abercrombie, and he didn't know how to protect them from the Indians. He had failed at everything Papa had asked of him.

"Look," Johnny pointed to the sky.

It might have been an angel. Ryker looked at the clouds surrounding a patch of blue sky. The blue held the shape of a bird, or maybe a parasol. Maybe there were wings.

"I see it," Sven said. "Look, Klara. Everything is going to be all right."

Klara smiled through her tears and wiped her face with the back of her hand. She collected the wooden doll from where Elsa dropped it and stood to leave. Johnny hefted the sleeping baby onto his back. She rested her head against the back of Johnny's head and slept. Ryker hosted the sack of potatoes over his shoulder. Sven filled the empty can with well water. Then they were on their way again.

They traveled alongside Whiskey Creek through the heat of the day, struggling against flies and fatigue, footsore and weary beyond description. Johnny stubbed his toe on a stob sticking out of the ground, stumbling, cursing, and almost dropping Elsa. She jolted awake with a howl. He dropped beside her and bent to suck his bleeding toe.

"You are lucky to have shoes," he said after spitting blood to the side. "I might get blood poisoning." He sucked again.

Klara ripped a strip of fabric from her petticoat and wrapped Johnny's toe. "Don't be a baby. You'll be all right," she said. "You can soak it in vinegar when we get to the fort."

"It's hopeless," Johnny said. "We might as well give up now. Every Indian we've seen was heading toward Fort Abercrombie," Johnny said. He rubbed his aching toe through the bandage. "Everyone there is already killed."

"I'll fight you for saying that," Sven said. "My mama is not dead." He leaned toward Johnny and jabbed a clenched fist under his nose. "Take it back, or you'll wish you had."

"No fighting," Ryker said. "We have to stick together."

Though the fort might be a false hope, it was their only hope. He didn't know where else to go. No settlers remained on their homesteads. Walking to Breckinridge would be impossible for the smaller children. Elsa needed milk. Klara disappeared a little more every day. His own clothes hung on him until he felt like a scarecrow. Even Breckinridge might be under attack by the Sioux.

Unless they were discovered by soldiers or ox carters, picked up by the stagecoach or caught a ride on a riverboat, they had no recourse but Fort Abercrombie.

Ryker had promised his father that he would report his mother's kidnapping—this he must do. If Mama was at the fort, she would be worried. If she was not at the fort, they must send someone to rescue her. Everything hinged on the fort. Surely the Indians were no match for the howitzers and cannon.

"A short rest," Ryker said. He had to turn things around. They couldn't give up. "You can stay here if you want, Johnny, but we're going to the fort."

"No," Johnny said hurriedly. "I don't want to be out here alone."

"Good," Ryker said. "We need your help." Whiskey Creek grew increasingly wider as they neared the fort. It would mean a hard swim to cross now; good thing Ryker had listened to Johnny about crossing the river where it was shallower. How much harder it would have been to come this far without him. "We'd miss you if you stayed back."

"I didn't mean anything," Johnny said. "Just letting off steam." He looked at the ground and then into Ryker's eyes. "If my folks didn't make it," he sniffed and gulped hard, "I was hoping I could stay with you." Small drops gathered in his eyes, and he blinked several times before continuing. "Just until my brother . . . our brothers," he corrected himself hurriedly, "get back from the war." He gulped again, and his voice strained. "I don't have no one else."

"Don't worry," Ryker said. "We can do anything if we stick together."

"Your mother was good to me," Johnny said. "She couldn't speak American, but she kept me beside her that first night when it was so scary." Johnny pulled off his bandage and soaked his feet in Whiskey Creek. "I couldn't understand the words, but she prayed that night."

Ryker's heart swelled. "Mama ends every day with prayer. No redskin could stop her."

"Think how happy Mama will be to see Elsa again," Klara said.

Mama would be overjoyed to see them, if she were at the fort as they hoped. But Ryker faced another, most unpleasant task. He must tell Mama about Papa's death. He imagined the way her face would crumple, remembering how she had screamed when learning that Martin was missing. Hopeless. He couldn't imagine her reaction now. He must confess how he had left Papa in the root cellar without a decent burial. She wouldn't like it.

No, Mama wouldn't like it at all.

CHAPTER 23

Klara slouched on a mossy rock near Whiskey Creek. She folded her knees until her feet were flat on the rock. Then she laid her head on her knees. "I have to rest," she said. "Can't go any farther." Her thin shoulders shook, and she let out a wail. "I miss good old Beller."

Her face looked thinner than ever, and her small shoulders drooped.

"We're almost there," Ryker said. "Let's push on and get there as soon as possible."

Ryker had been thinking of a good meal, a soft bed, and finding his mother. He rehearsed words to tell of Papa's death. He must remember to tell her how he had planned to ask Mr. Tingvold to bury Papa's body, but the Indians messed up his plans. There hadn't been time to dig a grave. Surely she would understand.

Elsa joined her sister in loud crying.

A heavy layer of gloom settled over them. They were alone, worn out, and done in. Ryker had to do something to cheer them. They were so close. He pulled the can of baked beans from the bottom of the sack.

"We won't be needing this," he said. "We'll be at the fort by dark." He doubted they would be there by dark, but he needed to cheer them. He jabbed the folding knife into the lid and pried it open. Then he used the knife blade to divide the beans so each had a portion. They tasted sweet and good. Elsa gobbled them in her mouth, smearing her face with sticky fingers and cooing in delight. Klara said she was too tired to eat, but Sven coaxed her into eating her share, whispering that Johnny would get them. Johnny inhaled his beans and licked the can, careful to avoid cutting his tongue on the sharp edge. Ryker finished his portion and ate a small potato. Johnny ate two.

They washed grimy hands in Whiskey Creek. Klara lay in the shade behind some bushes, and Elsa used Klara's stomach as a pillow. They sucked their thumbs and fell asleep at once. The boys crept behind the brush, while Ryker tidied the shoreline of any trace of their presence. Then he pulled dead branches around him, as he leaned against the trunk of a small oak tree, not wanting to take a chance of being seen by passing Indians. He scoured the shores, looking for any traces of the Sioux. Nothing. The only sound was lapping water and singing birds.

Exhaustion heavied Ryker's eyelids. He would rest his eyes for a minute and then wake the children to be on their way again. He dozed and dreamed of thunderstorms rumbling in from the west. In his dream, Mama's face showed across the skies through lightning flashes and black swirling clouds.

"Guns," Sven said, shaking Ryker awake. "Wake up. Cannon fire."

"Indians attacking Fort Abercrombie?" Ryker said.

"Can't see," Sven said. "But it sounds like just around the next curve in the creek."

CHAPTER 24

Ryker must discover what was happening. He didn't want to stumble into the middle of a shooting war.

He eyed the cottonwoods towering alongside Whiskey Creek. It seemed impossible to climb their slippery bark to get high enough to see anything. Their lower branches must have been twenty feet above the ground. Other trees grew along the creek, but only the cottonwoods were tall enough to see over the trees and brush ahead of them.

Perhaps they would have a better view if they traveled a little farther west. Ryker crept closer to the water's edge and peered in both directions. No sign of Indians.

"Come," he said and motioned to the others to join him. "We'll wade in the creek to save time."

"What about Indians?" Sven said with a suspicious expression on his face.

"We'll be seen for sure," Johnny said.

Ryker's heart raced, and he struggled to catch his breath. Things were happening too fast. He hadn't thought it through. Panic rose up within his throat.

Ryker forced himself to slow down, to take a breath, to think. They might be hit by the soldier's guns unless they used common sense. Not to mention the Sioux.

"Look," Sven said, pointing to a deadfall leaning against a tall cottonwood. "That dead tree is a ladder reaching the crotch of the taller tree next to it."

Ryker looked at a deadfall hooked into the crotch of a towering cottonwood growing on the edge of Whiskey Creek. The dead tree had grown so close to Whiskey Creek that its roots had pulled out in a storm. It lay like a narrow bridge to the cottonwood branches. The cottonwood had no branches for the first twenty feet. Once in the crook, it would be possible for a climber to scale to the top of the giant tree, surely an eagle-eye view of Fort Abercrombie.

"The lumberjacks called them widow makers," Ryker said. "Said gusts of wind blow them loose. Anyone unlucky enough to be underneath leaves a widow."

The top of the tree latched onto the lowest branch of the cottonwood. It might hold. It also might give way with his weight. He would be clearly visible to any passing Indian as he scaled the long trunk of the pine. Ryker imagined the zing of an arrow and how it might feel to fall to his death. The deadfall stretched partly over a sharp curve in Whiskey Creek, hanging over the water. Rocks and ragged tree stumps covered the shoreline.

Too many things might go wrong. It was too risky to consider. There must be a better way to discover what was happening at the fort.

"I'm going to the fort," Ryker said. "It's too dangerous to bring Elsa. You wait here until I get back."

A ferocious volley of shots rang out closer to the fort. They ducked behind the roots of a fallen tree, huddling together and trying to shush Elsa, who feared the noise.

"I'll sneak close enough to see what's going on and be right back."

"No," Sven said. He folded his arms in front of his chest and pinched his lips into a thin line. He looked like Papa, with such a grimace. "Not this time. We stay together, no matter what."

"Papa is dead. Mama and Martin are missing," Klara said.

"We can't risk losing you."

"I'll climb the tree for a look," Sven said. "I'm not scared."

Ryker squinted toward the top of the tree, calculating how far it was to the ground if Sven fell. "I'm the oldest." He squinted again, as a gust of wind caused the deadfall to sway. "I'm not sure it will hold my weight."

"I'm smaller," Sven said. "Let me do it."

"Mama wouldn't like it," Ryker said. He had enough to explain to Mama without adding a dead brother to his list.

"I'll do it," Johnny said. He squared his shoulders and stuck out his lower lip. "You have to find your mother."

The sun hung halfway down the afternoon sky. Gunpowder hazed over the tree line where the shots had sounded earlier. A ribbon of gray cloud rippled overhead like a roiling snake. Ryker couldn't imagine Johnny scaling the deadfall, clumsy as he was, and with a sore toe. He shook his head.

Ryker thought hard. He had left them before, and things had turned out badly. It would be impossible to sneak all five of them safely into the fort, especially under fire. But maybe Indians were only on one side of the fort. Maybe there was a way for them to cross in spite of the Indians. He had to see what was going on before he risked their lives.

Papa always accused Ryker of not listening, of having his head in his hinder, thinking of something other than the task at hand. Papa had been right. Ryker had always been preoccupied with his own thoughts.

Something had changed during this long journey. He had more to learn. Listening to Sven when he insisted on fetching water from the Tingvold well allowed them to survive. Listening to Johnny about crossing the river made it possible for them to get this far. Listening to Klara when she had insisted on following the baby's cry on the prairie had saved Elsa's life. He needed to listen again. He would weigh all the options.

A pair of swans paddled upstream, rippling the water of Whiskey Creek. It smelled of drying leaves and fish. Ryker wiped his face with the back of his hand. It was a risk. He might make the wrong decision and cause the death or capture of his family.

What should he do?

CHAPTER 25

"I've decided," Ryker said. He hoped he sounded more confident than he felt. "We'll stay together. I'll scale the tree to see what lies ahead."

Ryker slipped out of his shoes and rolled up his sleeves. "If I fall . . . or something bad happens," he said quietly, "you'll be in charge, Sven."

"You're not going to fall," Sven said. "Let me do it. The girls need you more than they need me."

"That's a lie," Klara said. She handed Elsa to Johnny and hugged her twin around the neck. "I couldn't bear to lose you . . . or any brother."

It seemed Martin filled everyone's thoughts. Klara sniffled, and Sven looked away with a hiccough.

"Martin and Frank will both come home," Johnny said. His lower lip quivered. "I know they will."

"I've made up my mind," Ryker said hurriedly. He had to act before he chickened out. "If something goes wrong, stay hidden until the fighting stops. You'll have water and enough potatoes for a few days. Maybe you'll catch a fish or another turtle."

"What then?" Johnny said. "We won't know if it's safe to go to the fort."

"Then, Johnny," Ryker said slowly, "it will be up to you to sneak forward and figure it out. The rest of you must wait here until he gets back."

"Tell the soldiers that our mother is missing, and ask them to come back for the children. Fix landmarks in your mind so you can tell them where they are."

"And if the Indians win?" Johnny said. "What do we do then?"

Ryker didn't know what to say. "Papa left me in charge. I've made up my mind."

Klara grabbed him around the waist and hugged him tightly. "I love you, Brother," Klara said. "I'll pray for angels to keep you safe."

"I should do it," Sven said, with a pout. "I'm a better climber."

Sven had shown good sense all throughout their ordeal, but Ryker stood his ground. He was the oldest. It was his responsibility.

"Ryker is right," Klara said. "Papa named him in charge."

"All right," Sven said with a pout. "But I don't like it."

"I'll do as you say," Johnny said.

"All right, then," Ryker said. "I'll give it a try." He looked up where the fallen tree hooked on the lower branch of the cottonwood. It was hard to judge how tall the tree was, but Ryker guessed at least forty feet. It was a long way to the top. The deadfall linked the lower branches of the ancient cottonwood like a steep staircase. It would carry Ryker to the lower branches of the cottonwood where he could climb the sturdy branches of the larger, older tree. He would be as high as an eagle. "Papa and Mama would be proud of you all." He picked up Elsa and kissed her sweaty face. "Be good now," he said. "Stay out of trouble."

He tucked his shoes out of sight and gave instructions for Johnny to hide the sack of potatoes behind the brush.

His first steps on the fallen tree rattled the leaves and caused the branches to shift under his weight. "Stay back in case it pulls loose," Ryker called out to the others. "Keep Elsa close."

Ryker thought for sure he would crash to the earth. He held his breath, steadied himself, and continued climbing. He wrapped his legs around the trunk and clutched the trunk with both hands to pull himself upward. Sticky sap clung to his fingers and toes. A westerly breeze smelled of gunpowder and damp earth.

Ryker must concentrate. Don't think about anything except inching forward. Don't look down. Keep your eyes on the crotch of the cottonwood tree.

More gunshots sounded from the fort. Ryker was higher than the ridgepole on their barn, higher than the sailor in the ship's crow's nest during their ocean voyage, higher than the time he climbed a grain bin in Dodge County.

His head spun, and he felt a little giddy. He clutched the tree with his knees and wrapped his arms around the trunk, resting until his head cleared. A paralyzing fear gripped him. He wouldn't look down again no matter what happened. He would creep forward, even if only an inch at a time. It didn't matter if it took all day to reach the cottonwood. It only mattered that he reached it.

A flock of pelicans flew at eye level, landing with a splash in Whiskey Creek. Ryker did not look down. A pesky fly buzzed around his nose. Ryker wrinkled his nose but did not swat it away. He concentrated on the rough bark, the tree trunk, the sticky sap, and his goal.

He grasped the leafy branches, breathing easier with the branches in his clutching hands. He moved slowly, pushing his feet from branch to branch, inching forward, feeling the rub of bark on his bare feet, feeling the cloth of his shirt tear when it caught on a broken branch.

Another blast sounded from the direction of the fort. Smoke billowed beyond a small rise where Slabtown lay. He could see where the waters of Whiskey Creek flowed into the Red River. He could see men in Slabtown. Red men.

Three Indians chased a gray horse toward them. Paint

splashed across their faces. The horse wore a saddle, and the stirrups flapped as it veered away from the painted men. The Indians paused, bending over to catch their breath and clutching their sides. One pointed toward the river. They quit chasing the horse and jogged instead toward Whiskey Creek. Another volley of shooting sounded from the direction of Fort Abercrombie.

Ryker looked down. The children had left the hideout in the tumble of fallen trees and were standing on the edge of Whiskey Creek, in plain sight. Ryker waved frantically, motioning them to hide. They gazed toward the sound of the guns and didn't see him. Elsa toddled alongside the bank, chasing butterflies. Would it all be for nothing? All this struggling only to be discovered just as they reached the fort.

Ryker didn't dare call out. The Indians were too close. In another minute they would be within view of the children. Ryker prayed a desperate prayer and broke the nearest tree branch. He threw it at the children, but it fell short and landed in the rocks. He broke another, pulled back his arm, and the tree lurched.

Ryker squelched a rising wave of terror. He clung to the tree until it steadied. Then he gathered his courage, pulled back his arm, and threw with all his strength. He had to warn the children. Even if he were discovered, they might still hide in the brush undetected.

The branch sailed through the air and plopped in the creek near the children with a splash.

Sven looked up. Ryker motioned again. Sven understood. Sven jabbed Johnny and snatched Elsa into his arms. They crawled into the thicket, just as the Indians came to the water's edge about twenty rods downstream.

Ryker clutched the tree trunk, as still as a stone, praying they would not look up. The Indians drank from the creek, babbling in their language, laughing, and grunting. One spoke a few words, and the others hooted in laughter. A fox streaked through the underbrush. Ryker watched Sven clamp his hand over Elsa's mouth. An eagle skimmed over the water.

The Indians stopped to watch the eagle's flight. They took dried leaves out of small bags hanging around their necks and tossed the dried leaves to the eagle. It seemed they were praying, but it was hard to tell. They never looked his way, only returned to the prairie from where they came, breaking into a loping run toward the fort.

They disappeared into the tall grass.

Ryker rested his head on the tree trunk and let out a long breath. One thing troubled him. The Indians showed no fear of the soldiers. They had joked, laughed, and been at ease, even though close to the firing guns.

Below him, he saw the children hiding in the thicket. He motioned for them to stay there. He could not be worrying about them. He must concentrate on climbing the rest of the way.

Ryker inched his way toward the cottonwood. The trunk of the deadfall grew thinner the farther he climbed. A pleasant breeze cooled his sweaty face. He disturbed a crow's nest, close enough to see the fledglings learning to fly.

At long last he reached the cottonwood. The fallen tree shuddered and quaked but held firm. Ryker pulled himself into the cottonwood crotch, gasping, stepping across to the cottonwood with rubbery limbs and pounding heart. He had made it.

He had to rest before going on. If only he had a flask of water. His throat parched, and his shirt stuck to his back with sweat. He breathed and tried to be positive. Few people had been this high. It would be an adventure to write about some day. An adventure as exciting as *Uncle Tom's Cabin*.

A white tailed deer slept in a blackberry bramble not ten rods from where the children were hiding. An eagle soared from its nest and dived into Whiskey Creek, then came up with a fish in its mouth. Ryker wiped his sweaty face with hands sticky with sap. He took a deep breath, prayed for strength, and climbed higher.

The cottonwood tree felt as solid as a rock, unlike the widow maker. When he had climbed as high as he dared, he braced himself against the trunk of the ancient tree and turned to face the west. Whiskey Creek joined the Red River of the North around the bend and beyond a line of leafy trees.

Ahead sprawled Fort Abercrombie.

CHAPTER 26

It was like watching a dream unfold.

Fort Abercrombie wasn't much of a fort. It consisted of six main buildings and a scattering of outbuildings, a few haystacks next to a log barn. Horses and cattle were penned next to the barns. Dots of blue jackets huddled around the perimeter of the fort behind barricades of firewood or barrels. No walls surrounded the buildings, as in some forts. Ryker had known this before but saw it plainly from his perch: the lay of the land, the way the Red River flowed as a graceful *S* alongside the buildings, and the bustle of men and animals.

Ryker shielded his eyes from the dipping sun. A number of women gathered around an open fire in the center of the fort, shielded by a cluster of outbuildings. The cooking fire whirled a black smudge overhead. None resembled his mother, but it was hard to tell so far away.

A woman crawled from one small band of soldiers to another, dragging a sack behind her. At each stop she doled out supplies, maybe food or ammunition. How courageous she was to venture into the open. She wore a sunbonnet. It wasn't Mama.

To the south of the fort's main entrance, Indians clustered in Slabtown, out of sight of the soldiers. He watched tipis going up, saw their ponies tethered near the river. More Indian camps showed beyond a small rise to the north. His heart sank. The Indians planned to stay. Sneaking into Fort Abercrombie through Slabtown would be impossible for them to do without

159

being seen by the Indians.

Perhaps the fighting was over.

A brown line of Indians stood up from the tall grass near Slabtown. They whooped horrible cries and rushed the fort. The soldiers turned their guns on the attacking Sioux. Other blue coats rushed to stop the attack from Slabtown. Ryker watched as the howitzers opened up on the screaming Indians. The brown men dropped to the ground like hay before Papa's cradle.

Martin's letters mentioned fierce battles, but it was one thing to read about a battle in a letter or newspaper. It was quite another thing to see the elephant for himself.

Ryker's belly clenched as he realized the dangers Martin faced in the War of Rebellion. The howitzers rained bullets not just shot them. There was no escape. He imagined Martin reloading the heavy artillery pieces, as was his job. In Martin's war, the howitzers fired both ways. No one could survive such an onslaught.

Clouds of gunpowder covered the fort like fog, and even from that distance the pungent odor drifted in the air. Slabtown trees snapped in two with each round of artillery fire, until the beautiful trees became jagged stumps and fallen branches.

Sioux braves shrieked wild yells and rushed again. A haystack by the barn, on the other side of the fort, burst into bright flame. Other Indians crept toward the barn and remaining haystacks with lighted torches. They would set the buildings ablaze before the soldiers realized what was happening.

Ryker watched, mesmerized by the brilliance of the Sioux's plan. The soldiers were too busy fighting the Slabtown Indians to notice what was going on at the barns. The torch bearers neared the other haystacks. Soon it would be too late to stop them.

If only Ryker could warn them. Without the sturdy barns,

fodder for their animals, and the cover of the outbuildings, the soldiers would be vulnerable to even deadlier attacks. He felt helpless, sick to his stomach with the knowledge of what was happening.

A bugle sounded. Soldiers turned their guns on the Indians heading toward the barns. They had been seen. Blue coats hurried toward the barns, some dragging an artillery piece and positioning it to fire in the other direction.

Just then, a soldier rushed out into the open and fired at the Indian brave creeping toward a haystack. A small puff of smoke showed before Ryker heard the shot. The Indian crumpled flat and lay still. A small circle of fire burned next to him from the fallen torch. The soldier stomped the flames out with his boots, brandishing his pistol and shooting at other Indians. Ryker could have cheered.

Ryker's fingers itched for a weapon to help the brave soldier.

He could not understand how a treaty, even if it were broken, could be the cause of such carnage. They had never hurt the Indians.

But the attackers persisted. An Indian brave crawled unseen toward the cattle pen. The cattle burst out of the flung-open gates, stampeding out onto the prairie, followed by screaming Indians waving strips of cloth. The cattle charged over the fallen Indian, racing away from the burning haystack and melting into the prairie.

Soldiers made only futile efforts to stop them. Clumps of Indians hid in the prairie grass beyond view, waiting to kill any soldier foolish enough to leave the safety of the fort.

The battle ended as abruptly as it had started. Even if the Sioux had not overtaken the fort, they had succeeded in destroying one haystack, stampeding the cattle, and doing much damage.

From his high perch, Ryker watched the fort resume a more

normal routine. Sentries guarded all sides of the fort. Civilians in regular clothes gave aid to the fallen. Some soldiers lay their heads down to rest, while others cleaned their rifles. More than one relieved themselves behind the barn.

Women crowded around a man lying on the ground near the cook fire. This must be how God feels, Ryker thought. To look down on all of us and see everything going on, nothing hidden, nothing out of sight.

Indians surrounded the fort on all sides. Their fires added wispy smoke to the settling gunpowder. They posted guards, too. Beyond site of the fort, and out of range of the artillery, Indian women butchered stolen cattle. The Indians would feast while the soldiers and civilians at Fort Abercrombie kept watch. It wasn't fair.

The hopelessness of their situation almost paralyzed Ryker. *Vonlaus.* They needed to get into the fort, but the fort was surrounded. Ryker's only plan had been to get to the fort. He and the children might hide for a while, but they had little food and couldn't stay hidden forever. Nothing hindered a wandering Indian from stumbling across their hiding place.

Ryker scanned the women within the confines of the fort. He was too far away to see faces, but Mama wore a gray dress the morning she was taken. Most of the women wore gray dresses. Ryker saw only sunbonnets.

Ryker studied the lay of the land. Their only possibility of entering the fort was by the river winding alongside the cluster of buildings. A strong swimmer might sneak into the fort under cover of darkness. None of them were strong swimmers. They were in the middle of a hornet's nest, as surely as Martin had been at Shiloh.

What they needed was a cave, or another root cellar, someplace safe where they could hide until Ryker figured out what to do.

"Are you going to stay up there forever?" Sven called from the base of the tree. "What's happening? Do you see Mama?"

"Be quiet!" Ryker called down. "I'm coming down."

He looked down. The dizzy feeling returned, but he couldn't put it off any longer. He considered how best to place his hands and feet. His muscles cramped from clinging to the branches. He looked up into a clear blue sky without even a wisp of cloud.

As he turned to back down the branches, he caught a glimpse of blue next to the river. At first he thought it a bird of some kind and squinted his eyes against the bright afternoon sun. He couldn't be sure, but it seemed to be a soldier hiding in the tall grass. Maybe an Indian wearing a soldier's jacket, or a stray jacket dropped by someone in a hurry.

He kept the blue splotch in view as he climbed down the cottonwood tree. The sturdy branches made for an easy climb until he reached the crotch where the deadfall intersected with the cottonwood. He pushed away the fear that a blue-jacketed Sioux might be waiting to ambush him when he stepped away from the tree. He must focus, or he would fall and break his neck.

Below him, Klara chased after an escaping Elsa. Klara swooped the laughing baby into her arms and stepped back behind the briars. A sudden thanksgiving bubbled in his chest that God had returned their baby sister to them. He would concentrate on the miracle of finding her, and not on the fears that made his legs weak and shaky. The preciousness of family, and even Johnny, filled him. How lucky he was to not be alone in such hard times. He prayed that he would be able to obey his father, rescue the children, and find his mother.

Ryker held onto the sturdy cottonwood as if it were a welcoming friend, reluctant to leave its hospitality. He stretched a foot to the wobbly deadfall. It quivered and bowed. He could not close his eyes, as he wanted. Instead, he looked up into the sky and watched a fluffy cloud float in from the western horizon.

It had a funny shape. It looked like a dog with a long tail and sharp nose. One ear was missing. Beller! He was their angel, after all.

With a new burst of confidence, Ryker put one foot onto the thin upper trunk of the tree and felt for a branch to hold with his left hand. He shifted from the cottonwood to the descending staircase of branches. He felt like the acrobat on the high wire that Mrs. Tingvold had once seen at a circus.

He waited for the tree to fall crashing to the ground, but nothing happened. Beller drifted overhead, riding a prairie breeze. His tongue hung out in the same friendly expression he had always worn. His presence strengthened Ryker's resolve.

Carefully, inch by inch, Ryker backed down the tree trunk, moving first his right foot, and then finding a handhold with his right hand before moving the left foot down to join the right. Beller would protect him.

Ryker reached the lowest branches of the deadfall and paused to steady himself. Next he must leave the safety of the branches and scale down the branchless tree trunk. He wasn't sure how to place his feet to get a sturdy grip. It had been easier climbing upward. He clung to the branches, and looked out to where the blue jacket had been.

It was gone.

The children stood on the edge of Whiskey Creek, shielding their eyes while looking up at him. Klara stood with folded hands, no doubt praying for his safety. How much she was like their mother. He wanted to call out for them to see Beller overhead. It must wait.

He must focus. He could not be thinking of Indians, angels, or his mother. He must move his feet to the slim trunk and find a handhold to guide him backwards down the rough bark. He looked down into the flowing water of Whiskey Creek directly below him. His head swirled. He moved his left foot to the stub of a broken branch.

A loud splintering sound cracked through the air, as the branch gave way. Ryker jolted to one side in a futile attempt to regain his balance. He overcorrected. The widow maker lurched and rolled. Ryker grasped toward the trunk, but it was too late.

The widow maker broke away from the cottonwood. After the first jolt, it slipped into a swishing dream of leaves, branches, and rough bark. Ryker clutched for anything to hang onto but felt himself falling down, down, down.

A hard splash into cold water. Then nothing.

CHAPTER 27

Ryker woke in a panic, clawing and struggling to breathe. A sunbeam peeked through green leaves. A heavy branch pressed down upon him, and it took him a second to realize that he was trapped underwater by the fallen tree.

He felt himself losing consciousness. He refused to breathe, though his lungs nearly burst with the need for air.

A strange roaring sounded in his ears, and he felt himself being pulled to another world. His lungs exploded. Would this be his end? He had promised his father to care for the family. They needed him. He had to survive.

With his last bit of strength, Ryker pushed away from the tree and bobbed above the water, coughing and gasping for breath. He heard, as from a far distance, Klara's scream. He reached out and clasped a handful of leaves. It slipped through his fingers. Water filled his mouth and blinded his eyes.

He sank beneath the cold, murky water. It wasn't fair that Mama should lose another child. He wanted to tell her about learning to listen to other people. That was the kind of thing she would understand. And he had wanted her to hear of his father's death from him. It would be easier if he were the one to tell her.

But it was not meant to be. He faced eternal judgment and realized with a sinking dread that he had nothing to offer to God when they met on the other side. He asked God to forgive him for all his failings and braced himself for the end.

But just when he thought it over, a strong arm hooked his shoulder and dragged him to the surface of Whiskey Creek.

Ryker splashed and kicked, coughing and sputtering, aware of a terrific pain in his head. His thoughts jumbled. Where was he? What happened?

Beller! Ryker had seen one of Mama's angels. Then he remembered falling.

The same strong arm dragged him out of the creek and hoisted him onto the bank. Klara, Sven, and Johnny gathered around as he lay, struggling for breath. Elsa put her face next to his and stuck her finger up his nose. He pushed Elsa's hand away and tried to sit up. Weakness forced him to lie back on the grass.

"Are you dead?" someone said in a nasally whisper. The voice sounded familiar. "That was quite a fall."

Ryker's heart thumped. His mind scrambled. It must be the person who rescued him. His head whirled, and he couldn't think straight. He moved his arms and legs. Everything worked except his brain. He had fallen. He remembered the panicky feeling of falling, and falling. He should be dead. Ryker raised himself to his elbows.

The young soldier Mama had talked out of deserting sat beside him on a rock, wearing a blue jacket. He was the soldier Ryker had seen from the treetop.

"Hannibal?" Ryker shook the cobwebs out of his brain. "What are you doing here?"

CHAPTER 28

"I spied you climbing down the tree, and watched you splash in the river," Hannibal said. Hannibal was breathing hard, and water dripped down his hair. A faint shadow of a mustache bristled his upper lip. "Thought you were killed."

"I'm alive," Ryker said. "At least I think I'm alive." He pushed himself to a sitting position, but a wave of dizziness forced him to lay his head on his knees. "Thanks." A knife-like pain pierced through his temples. He lay back and rested his eyes. "Thought I was a goner."

"We need shelter," Hannibal said, scanning the trees on both sides of the creek. "Indians thick as thieves all around this country."

Ryker listened as from a distance, too dizzy to answer. Sven pointed out the thick briars where they had been hiding. "There's an open spot in the middle. Not very big, but no one will see us unless they're looking."

"Hurry," Hannibal said. "Indians might come this way."

Klara and the baby disappeared into the thicket. Ryker tried to stand, but his legs refused to work. His body felt numb, like it belonged to someone else. He suspected he would soon be black and blue from head to toe, as dark as Topsy in *Uncle Tom's Cabin*.

Johnny and Sven half carried and half dragged Ryker to the thicket.

"Where's Hannibal?" Ryker whispered.

"He's sweeping our tracks from the creek bank with a broken pine bough," Sven said.

Ryker opened his eyes and saw two Svens instead of one. His brain was playing tricks with him. He squinted until two brothers became one again.

"Water," Ryker said. "Fill the cans." At least his brain was working a little. "Where's the supply sack?"

"It's here," Klara said as Sven collected the empty cans, left the thicket, and came back with a supply of drinking water.

Klara pulled the tintype of their parents' wedding day from where she had tucked it into *Uncle Tom's Cabin* for safety. She stared at it for a long time, then showed it to Elsa. "Look," Klara said. "Mama and Papa."

"Milk!" Elsa said with a loud wail. "Mama!"

Her cries pierced into Ryker's brain like an Indian's scalping knife. "Quiet," Ryker said, holding his hands over his ears. He saw two Klaras and two Elsas.

Johnny swooped Elsa into his arms and bounced her until her wailing turned to giggles. Johnny reached into the prickly brambles and pulled out fat blackberries. He popped one into Elsa's mouth. Then another.

"The Sioux need water for their campsites," Hannibal said when he returned from the creek bank. "I covered our tracks as best I could." He rubbed his forehead. "I have to find out what's going on at the fort," Hannibal said. "I don't know if I should stay here or try to get into the fort."

"I saw it from the treetop," Ryker said. "The whole battle. Haystack burned. Cattle stampeded." He rubbed his forehead. "Howitzers kept them at bay, but it was a close one."

"We'll sneak into the fort by Slabtown," Johnny said. "It's the easiest crossing."

"Not a chance," Ryker said. "That's where the Sioux are the thickest."

They sat in silence for a long time. Elsa dozed in Johnny's lap. Ryker sipped tepid creek water, shuddering to remember the horrid suffocation of being trapped beneath the creek's surface.

"What are you doing out here alone?" Johnny said.

Ryker saw two hazy soldiers and two Johnnies. He closed his eyes and waited for a long minute. When he opened them, there were only one of each. He sighed in relief.

Klara handed Hannibal a potato, and he took a bite as if it were an apple. He told how he had been sent to bring settlers into the fort. He had been chased by hostiles and lost his horse and his rifle. "Only one bullet left in my pistol," Hannibal said. "I'm in tough shape."

"Did you go out our way?" Ryker asked.

"Most settlers came in when the warning went out," Hannibal said. "But no one from your neck of the woods." He chomped another bite, potato juice dripping down his chin. "Three of us were sent to bring 'em in. We didn't want folks caught flat-footed."

"Did you see my folks?" Johnny said, with a catch in his voice. "We live just north of the Landstads' place."

"Log cabin?" Hannibal said. "Burned to the ground." Even through his grogginess, Ryker noticed the sadness in his eyes. "Nobody . . ." Hannibal shook his head and didn't finish his sentence.

"Maybe they're at the fort," Johnny said. He spoke as if trying to convince himself. "I'm sure of it."

"They weren't there yesterday," Hannibal said slowly. "Might have come after I left . . ."

"And our mother?" Sven said. "Was she at the fort?"

Hannibal shook his head.

Sven told Hannibal about their father. "They killed him,"

170

Sven said. He balled his fists and squared his jaw. "Stole Mama and Elsa."

"We heard a baby crying out on the prairie," Klara said. Her eyes filled with a strange light. "An angel brought her to us."

"I'm feeling sick," Johnny said as he rubbed his belly with a rueful expression on his face. "Shouldn't have drunk water from the slough."

"I saw Beller," Ryker said. He could rest. He would leave all the worrying and watching to Hannibal. As he drifted off, he whispered, "I saw Mama's angels."

CHAPTER 29

Ryker slept like a stone.

Klara shook him awake when the evening gloom was turning to the dark of night. "I was scared," she whispered. "You looked dead."

Dense fog settled like a heavy quilt over Whiskey Creek. The tops of the trees showed above the thick cloud. Overhead the first stars poked through the canopy of sky. An owl hooted in the shadows, and a night bird rustled in the treetops. The temperature dropped, and they huddled together for warmth. Hannibal reeked of sweat and stale smoke. Johnny groaned with bellyache.

"I'm better," Ryker said. He rubbed a tender spot on his head and stretched his neck. "Don't worry. I'm all right." He muttered something about Beller protecting him. He realized he was not making sense but could not stop himself from rambling about angels and poems and Mama. The dream he had been having seemed real.

Ryker drifted off to sleep listening to the twins tell Hannibal about Beller's heroic death. If Hannibal answered, Ryker did not hear it.

Ryker dreamed that Mama fried side pork for Christmas Day. In his dream, his father was laughing and welcoming Martin home from the war. It was a good dream, and Ryker left it with reluctance when Hannibal shook his arm and whispered frantically in his ear.

"Quiet!" Hannibal said. "Indians."

Ryker raised to one elbow and tried to understand what was happening.

Voices sounded from the creek through veils of heavy fog. They could see nothing. It sounded like children playing, and a woman's voice.

Ryker looked to make sure the twins and Baby Elsa slept. The twins cuddled like puppies. Klara sucked her thumb, and Sven had his arm around Elsa. Johnny lay off to the side in a tangle of arms and legs.

An autumn-like coolness made Ryker shiver. Smoke from a campfire curled through the tree roots, and smells of cooking meat made his tummy rumble. They spoke a strange language, not American or Norwegian. Neither was it German. Ryker knew enough to recognize those languages. Hannibal was right.

Indians.

Ryker's head ached, and his limbs ached like he had been hit by a locomotive. He moved one leg, and then the other. To his relief, his eyesight had returned to normal. He saw only one of everything.

"Quiet now," Hannibal said in a nasally whisper. "There's an Injun woman and her two children setting up camp on Whiskey Creek."

Ryker's heart sank. They would be heard if they tried to leave the hideout. There was no way to move through the deadfalls without making noise. Even if they did manage to sneak away, where would they go? They had to use their heads.

The rising sun cast an eerie glow through the fog. Crickets droned a happy chorus. The sounds of loons and calling geese mingled with the splashing sound of children playing in Whiskey Creek. The children did not seem to mind the cold weather.

"No braves," Hannibal whispered. "But you know they're close by."

They watched and waited as the sun burned off the fog, and the morning settled over Whiskey Creek. Chains of pink tinged clouds blistered overhead. Ryker and Hannibal watched a woman putting up a tipi just outside their hideout. She had long black hair pulled into braids and wore a leather dress. Moccasins wrapped her feet and lower legs. She worked quietly, calling out now and again to the children splashing in the creek. A birch bark canoe lay overturned on the bank.

"Darn," Hannibal said in a whisper. "Why couldn't she go downstream a ways?"

A small animal roasted in her cooking fire. The woman left the tipi to stir something in an iron kettle. The smells tantalized the hungry boys. The woman turned the meat; a drop of fat sizzled in the flames. She looked familiar, but Ryker's fuzzy brain couldn't remember where he had seen her before.

"Wonder if her man will come when the meat is ready," Hannibal whispered. "We need to get out of here." He wiped his sweaty face on the back of his sleeve. "Trouble is coming, and no doubt about it."

Ryker pondered how to escape with the young ones, especially Elsa, in tow. If it were just the twins, they might manage to get away, but Johnny was as clumsy and noisy as an ox in the underbrush, and Elsa was always finding trouble.

"They might capture you," Hannibal said, "but this blue uniform means they'll skin me alive." He brooded for a long while. "We should wake—" Hannibal started to say, when Elsa screamed.

"Owie!" She rubbed her cheek. "Mama." She slapped her neck and screamed again.

Ryker lunged toward the crying baby, but it was too late.

"What's wrong?" Klara woke up with a squeal. "Yellow jackets!" She jumped to her feet and grabbed her sister, brushing them away while wrapping the howling baby in the quilt for protection against the angry insects.

Sven slapped at yellow jackets and cried out. Johnny sat up, rubbing his eyes, banging his head on a deadfall. Johnny swore, and Elsa hollered even louder.

Three brown faces peered through the tangled roots of downed trees, a woman and two children.

Ryker remembered where he had seen them before.

CHAPTER 30

Good Person had been the one to fish his father's folding knife from the slough and had received the gift of Mama's bread. Her man had hunted along Whiskey Creek the morning after Beller tangled with the bear. The woman did not look happy to see them.

She scowled and pulled Klara out of the hiding place by her arm. Elsa screamed and clung to her older sister so hard that Ryker feared she would choke her older sister to death. Ryker and the others followed Klara.

"Where's Hannibal?" Johnny whispered.

Hannibal was nowhere to be seen. Ryker tried to remember. They were talking, and then Elsa woke up. Hannibal must have sneaked away during the fuss. Some soldier he was. He could have at least tried to protect them.

Johnny seemed content with Ryker's whispered answer that Hannibal had returned to the fort. Even though Ryker was disappointed with the young soldier for deserting them, he bore Hannibal no ill will. Hannibal had a better chance of getting away without them. Maybe he would return with soldiers to rescue them.

"Mama," Elsa said in a hoarse whisper.

She lay limp as a sack on Klara's neck, the apples of her cheeks replaced by hollows, her blue eyes, always so bright, dull and empty. She looked spent. He tried to remember when she had last eaten.

Good Person had helped him before, but she showed no signs of helpfulness now. Mama said she was just honest folk trying to feed her family. Ryker hoped Mama was right.

"Look," Ryker said while pointing at the sobbing baby. The welts blossomed across her face, and she screamed when Ryker grasped one of the stingers. He took Elsa into his arms. Klara rubbed her neck in relief. Ryker pointed toward the bank and slowly walked to the creek, half expecting something terrible to happen, like an arrow zinging from the brush, or a war whoop sounding over the water. He knelt and gathered handfuls of cool mud from the creek bank, daubing Elsa's welts while speaking soothing words.

"Come," he said in a low tone to the twins. Good Person stood on the bank as if trying to make up her mind what to do with them. He doubted they would still be alive if an Indian brave had found them hiding in the thicket. "Plaster mud on your stings. And drink all the water you can hold." He looked up and down the creek, but the sharp turns and bends made it impossible to see more than a short ways. Gunshots sounded from the direction of the fort. "Be ready to run when I give the word."

"Milk," Elsa said. Her lips chapped and cracked. "Mama."

He cupped handfuls of water for Elsa to drink. She choked and spilled it down the front of her tattered dress. "Milk," she said.

The Indian boys had followed Ryker to the creek. Laughing Boy was taller since Ryker had last seen him, and his teeth had grown in. He wore only a loin cloth tied around his middle. It almost covered his private parts. Little Dog wore nothing at all.

Ryker tried not to stare. Their eyes shone like black stones, and their brown skin glistened from swimming. Laughing Boy carried a small bow and a quiver of arrows. Good Person spoke, and Laughing Boy threaded an arrow from his quiver into the bowstring. Though the boy held the arrow pointed downward, Ryker had the feeling he would not hesitate to aim and shoot.

"What do we do now?" Sven whispered. "Are we captives?"

A knife lay on a stone next to the cook fire. Good Person placed the knife into her belt when she noticed Ryker looking at it. She nodded toward Ryker and the twins. She paused when she looked at Johnny but didn't nod.

"Let's make a run for it," Johnny said as he eyed the creek. Not too unexpected, after what he had experienced at the hands of the Sioux.

Ryker didn't know what to say. They might barge into a hostile war party. They might run into the Indian on the painted horse, the one who had murdered Mr. and Mrs. Tingvold. But they couldn't stay. Who knew what might happen when the Indian men returned. "We know her," Ryker said after a long pause. "It's Good Person; remember how Mama helped her?"

"She doesn't act like she knows us," Klara said. "Are you sure it's the same woman?"

Ryker pushed Elsa into Klara's arms and stood to his feet. He cleared his throat and faced the woman. He made a motion of unfolding and jabbing a knife. The woman looked at him blankly. Then Ryker mooed like a cow and went through the stabbing motion again.

A glint of recognition flashed across her face, but she did not smile. The little boys laughed and held their noses as if remembering the terrible stink from the foundered animal. They remembered.

Ryker patted his chest and pointed to the twins and Elsa. The woman nodded and seemed a little friendlier. She patted her tummy and made a motion of eating. At first Ryker thought she was asking if he was hungry. But then the woman pantomimed how she had received food from someone with hair like Klara and Elsa. She touched her own black braids and then touched

Elsa's hair. Then she patted her tummy again, gestured toward her boys, and measured out a woman's silhouette.

She was telling how their mother gave food to them.

A lump rose in Ryker's throat. Mama said a kindness was always returned in the end. It was as if Mama were with them, taking care of them through this dark time.

The woman then pointed to the fire and the twins. She motioned giving them food. She did not include Johnny. The woman motioned them to the cook fire.

"Looks like she's going to feed us," Sven said.

"Good," Johnny said. His round face had thinned down during their days on the prairie, and he was as pale as new snow. He reached toward the food. "Maybe I'll feel better after I eat."

But Good Person pushed Johnny away from the food. She pantomimed for him to gather firewood. He stood helplessly, as the woman handed the others small portions of meat served on pieces of bark. It was only a small amount, but it was the first hot food they had eaten in days. Ryker wasn't sure what exactly they were eating—something dark and stringy with a wild flavor. It tasted so good that tears came to his eyes as he chewed and swallowed. He tried to count the days since Mama had been taken, but all of them blurred into one nightmare of misery. He must ask Klara how many knots she had tied in her apron string.

Johnny reached again toward the meat. Good Person shoved him hard enough to send him sprawling on the ground. She jerked her thumb toward the thicket and motioned again for him to gather wood.

"What did I do wrong?" Johnny said in disbelief.

"Just do what she says," Ryker said.

"I'll share," Sven started to give him a bite of meat, but Ryker stopped him.

"Not now," Ryker said. "Save it for later, and give it to him when she's not watching." No telling what might happen if they made the woman angry. "Do what she says."

Johnny trudged to the trees and untangled a branch from the mess of fallen trees. Ryker saw a branch zing against Johnny's face, causing a rising welt across his eyes. Johnny tossed the branch carelessly by the fire and slouched on a rock, rubbing his sore forehead and cursing his bad luck.

Good Person flew into a rage, beating Johnny's back with a stick of firewood and yelling in her language. Her boys laughed and giggled, as Johnny shielded his face with both arms and scrambled to obey her wishes.

Johnny dragged more dead branches toward the fire. His expression looked so downcast that Ryker tucked part of his meat into his pocket for Johnny.

Klara removed a bit of chewed meat from her mouth and smeared it into Elsa's mouth. The baby made a terrible face and turned away. Her eyes looked dull, and her head drooped.

When everyone had eaten, Good Person motioned for Johnny to scrape the pot. Her eyes looked hard, and she jerked her chin toward the cooking pot as if angry.

Johnny fell upon the meager bits of food, gnawing a bone and licking grease from his fingers. "I didn't do nothing to hurt her," he mumbled. "Why does she hate me?"

"Smile!" Ryker said. "Act as if nothing is wrong." Ryker smiled and nodded toward the Indian woman, though he spoke to the others. "Be as pleasant and natural as if visiting your relatives."

A soft mewling came from the tipi, and Good Person spoke a command to Laughing Boy, who fetched the baby in his cradleboard. Good Person and Little Dog stood as if on guard.

Good Person unlaced the ties holding the baby flat against the board. His chubby lips smacked, and he reached for his mother's bosom as soon as his hands were free. The woman smiled at the baby and rubbed her cheek against his. She didn't look as scary when she smiled at the baby, more like any mother. Then she sat against a tree stump and gave him her breast. The baby sucked greedily, patting her chest with his plump hand.

Ryker and the boys looked away. A woman nursing a baby was nothing new, and certainly nothing to be ashamed of, but they were of the age when a woman's body embarrassed them.

"Now is the time," Johnny whispered. "Get away while she's busy."

Elsa stared at Good Person and pointed to the nursing baby. "Mama." Elsa crawled over and pulled at the woman's dress, her small face covered with mud splotches, pathetic in her pleading. "Milk," she whispered in a croaking voice.

"Come, Sistermine," Klara said. "It's not for you." Elsa whimpered and stretched small hands toward the Indian woman in a gesture of desperation.

They were all hungry, but Elsa had not learned to eat regular food.

Elsa tugged the woman's dress. "Milk." She wailed a weak and desperate cry. "Mama."

"Please," Klara said to the woman. She pointed to Elsa, and then to the woman's chest. "Please."

Ryker held his breath, half expecting the woman to beat Elsa with a piece of firewood, too. Good Person clucked her tongue in an irritated manner but motioned for Elsa to climb up on her lap. Elsa sank into the crook of the woman's arm and began to suck. She sucked until her cheeks collapsed, and tears rolled down her thin cheeks. She sucked too hard and choked on the milk. Then she settled into a more normal feeding, closing her eyes in bliss. Elsa's white skin contrasted with the woman's brown.

"Thank you," Klara said. Ryker saw tears in Klara's eyes as she spoke. "I wish I knew the Sioux word for thank you."

Good Person concentrated on her baby with hardly a glance

at Elsa. Ryker got the feeling she wasn't happy about the arrangement.

"What would Papa say?" Sven whispered.

"Don't care what Papa would say," Klara said. "Mama would be glad. She'd call her an angel of mercy."

"It's like a bear suckling a pig," Johnny said, "or a goat suckling a calf." He stared at the bared chest and nursing babies. "It's not natural."

"We give cow's milk to orphan lambs." Sven was usually contrary to whatever Johnny said. "It's none of your beeswax what kind of milk Elsa drinks."

"But an Injun," Johnny said in a dark tone. "Think what they've done."

"Haven't you heard of a wet nurse?" Ryker said. "Milk is milk. Now be quiet about it."

"Didn't mean nothing," Johnny mumbled. "Just seems odd to me."

The woman gestured toward the fire, the trees, and back to the fire.

"Gather more firewood," Ryker said. The woman held their lives in her hands. They must keep on her good side. "We'll help you."

Ryker, Johnny, and the twins gathered firewood into a nice pile. The woman nodded in approval. They stood awkwardly by, waiting instructions. The woman motioned them to gather hazelnuts growing along the bank of Whiskey Creek.

Elsa had drifted off to sleep. When the woman saw that she slept, she tried to set her down. Elsa woke and cried to nurse again. The woman frowned, but let her feed some more. When she had enough, Elsa pulled away with a loud burp. Bubbles of white milk showed on her lips and dripped down her chin.

The Indian boys giggled and pointed to her milky mouth. Elsa smiled and patted her hands together as if applauding. It was her happiest smile since they had found her on the prairie.

Klara scooped Elsa up into her arms. Ryker saw Klara lick the milk from Elsa's chin when she thought no one was looking.

They dared not ask for more food. All they could do was try to be helpful and hope food would be offered.

"Why does she pick on me?" Johnny said.

"Mama gave them food," Klara said. "She's repaying the favor. She knows you're not part of our family."

Good Person pantomimed again, a taller figure and a shorter, pointing to the children, and then pantomiming a taller and shorter person again. She was asking about their parents.

Ryker answered by pantomiming a taller and shorter person, and then the taller one. He hated sharing the grim news. He mimed an arrow in his heart and fell to the ground with his eyes closed.

Good Person's eyes clouded. She understood. Then she pantomimed the shorter figure with a questioning look.

Ryker pondered how to explain. He grabbed Sven by the arm and pretended to drag him away from the campsite. Good Person nodded gravely. She understood.

Ryker tried to pantomime how they were looking for her. He mounded his belly to show that his mother was expecting another baby. He was unsure if she understood.

If only Good Person would help them find their mother.

CHAPTER 31

Elsa napped for a short while that morning and nursed again when she woke up. She seemed more like her old self, demanding and spoiled. Her eyes looked brighter, and she laughed aloud while playing in the sand by the creek bank.

At another time and place, they could have been on a picnic alongside the rippling creek in the shadow of the beautiful trees . . . except for an occasional gunshot heard from the direction of the fort, and the anxiety of not knowing what would happen next.

Each gunshot caused Good Person to look up and down Whiskey Creek, as if she expected trouble. She must be afraid of the soldiers. Ryker knew she had to nothing to fear from them right now. From his view in the cottonwood, he had seen them under siege. The soldiers were fighting for their lives.

They were safe for the moment with this Indian woman, but Ryker knew others would not look upon them so kindly.

Elsa woke from her nap and immediately went to the Indian woman and pulled on her skirt. "Milk," she said. "Mama."

Good Person busied with chores around the camp and ignored Elsa's request. Of course she could not waste the whole day nursing Elsa. Even Mama complained when Elsa nursed too often.

"Come Sistermine," Klara said, but Elsa pouted her lip and stomped her feet.

Ryker panicked. Elsa threw fits if she didn't get her way. The

Indian woman wasn't thrilled to have them there. If his sister had a tantrum, she might ruin everything.

The cradleboard was propped against the tree stump. Elsa pinched the sleeping baby's face, causing him to cry. "Milk," she demanded. "Mama."

"Elsa," Ryker said. "Be good." He was almost close enough to pick her up when it happened.

Elsa let out a wail, stomped her feet, and threw herself to the ground, kicking and screaming. "Milk!" She howled as if the yellow jackets were stinging again.

The Indian boys giggled, holding their hands over their mouths and laughing at Elsa's rude behavior. Ryker could have crawled under a rock in embarrassment. Elsa was definitely more like her normal self.

Good Person frowned but gathered Elsa into her lap to nurse. Elsa guzzled like a little pig. Elsa was a baby, not old enough for good manners, but Ryker felt embarrassed at her behavior.

Good Person called out to her boys. Laughing Boy went upstream and Little Dog, downstream. Ryker suspected she asked them to stand guard.

Little Dog came running back before Elsa had finished nursing, pointing upstream and jabbering in an excited voice. The woman gestured toward the river and made canoeing motions with an imaginary paddle.

"What does she mean?" Klara said.

"Indians," Sven said quietly. "What will we do now?"

The woman pointed to the hideout in the tangled tree roots and made hurrying motions with her hands.

"She wants us to hide?" Sven said.

Ryker saw a hundred things wrong with the idea. How could they hide within spitting distance of Indians on the warpath? A dog or curious child would find them in no time. Elsa might cry out. Maybe the woman would betray them.

"Hurry up," he said. They had no choice but to do what she asked. He reached for Elsa, still nursing. She howled in anger.

"Milk." Elsa clutched the woman. "Mama."

Good Person looked upstream. Sure enough, the bow of a canoe showed coming around the bend of Whiskey Creek. On this stretch of water, the creek angled back and forth in sharp turns. She put Elsa back to her breast and gestured that Elsa should stay with her while the others hid. She issued a sharp command to her son. Little Dog scrambled to sweep the sandy ground with a leafy branch.

Good Person meant to hide them. A wave of relief and gratitude swept over Ryker. But what about Elsa? It was impossible to hide a nursing baby. Her blond hair was a sure sign that Elsa didn't belong with this Sioux family.

Ryker paused as the others scrambled into the tangled roots. Good Person shooed him again and said something in her language. She patted Elsa's head. Ryker understood her promise to care for her.

It felt as if he were throwing Elsa to the wolves. Mama would not like it. Papa would not understand. In a flash of insight, he knew Martin would do exactly what the woman said. They had no other choice. They must trust Good Person until they could escape. Ryker breathed a prayer and crawled into the hideout.

"Stay away from the yellow jackets," he whispered.

"What about Elsa?" Klara said. Tears dripped down her thin cheeks and gathered in the hollow by her lips. "We can't leave her to the Indians."

"Mama is praying for us," Sven said. "The angels will care for Elsa. Remember how they helped us find her in the tall grass?"

"Isn't there something we can do?" Klara said.

"Pray," Ryker said. It was their only hope. "Pray as hard as you can."

CHAPTER 32

The children lay on their bellies looking out of the peephole in the thicket. Sticks and stones poked into Ryker's chest, and he struggled to lie still. The noonday sun baked down upon them. Ryker scanned the skies for signs of angels, maybe another glimpse of Beller watching over them, but saw only clouds linked like chains. Elsa still nursed.

"Five of them," Sven whispered. "Are they good or bad Indians?"

"Injuns are all bad," Johnny said. "They'd just as soon slit our throats as look at us."

"Not all Indians." Klara shied away from a snake slithering under a log. "Good Person's feeding Elsa," she said.

"Hush," Ryker whispered.

Good Person sat nursing Elsa as if it were the most natural thing in the world. Indian braves called a greeting from their canoe. She called to Little Dog, who ran in the direction his brother had gone.

Canoes scraped against the shoreline. Five painted braves stepped into the water and dragged canoes up the bank. They carried bows and spears. One had a rifle slung over his shoulder. Animal skins draped their bodies, and leather moccasins adorned their feet. One brave, taller than the others, wore red paint streaked through his long hair and a woman's blue shawl wrapped around his waist like a belt. The handle of a butcher

187

knife stuck out from the blue cloth near a bloody splatter. Ryker shivered.

A shorter, fatter brave held three dead hens by their feet. He tossed them next to the fire with a grunting command. Another carried a bulging sack. They looked into the empty cook pot with a disappointed expression.

"Look," Johnny whispered. He pointed to a quiet brave who guarded the canoes. The man carried a lance with dangling scalps. One had been taken from a white woman. Another was that of a yellow-haired child.

How easily Elsa's scalp could join his collection.

"I'm scared," Klara whispered. Her teeth chattered, and she buried her face in her arms.

"Still as mice," Ryker whispered.

The woman stood, probably to fix the meat, but Elsa fussed when taken from the breast.

The Indian woman spoke to the braves, patting Elsa on her head in an effort to quiet her. Ryker suspected she explained the presence of a white baby.

The men showed intense interest in Elsa, clucking and chatting among themselves, kneeling down to look into her eyes, reaching out to pat her hair and touch her clothes. Elsa pulled away from their probing hands.

"Milk." Elsa said. Her lip pouted, and she stomped her feet. "Mama," she said in a louder voice.

"Oh no, she's going to have a fit," Klara whispered. "Look."

The woman spoke in low tones.

"Milk," Elsa said.

The woman paid her no attention. Elsa threw herself on the ground in an all-out temper tantrum, kicking and screaming as loud as she could. The Indians startled at Elsa's exhibition of bad temper, then acted amused. One imitated her antics, stomping his feet and shaking his fist. The others roared with laughter.

Elsa screamed all the louder. Papa would be appalled. Papa believed that children should be seen and not heard. Elsa was definitely being both seen and heard.

"Someone should smack that girl," Johnny said in a whisper.

"Hush," Ryker said.

The woman walked over to Elsa as if it were the most natural thing and used two fingers to pinch her nose. Elsa screamed, her face turning crimson. She quit yelling in order to breathe. The woman released Elsa's nose. Elsa sniffed, her small body shuddering with quiet sobs. Ryker dared to breathe again.

Just when Ryker thought the danger passed, the tall Indian reached over and prodded Elsa's chest with a pointed finger. The men all seemed fascinated by Elsa's hair. They touched it, pulled it, and the tall man even put her hair in his mouth to taste it. The fat one poked a finger into Elsa's eyes. He pulled his finger back, ready to poke again. Elsa saw the finger coming her way and bit down with a definite chomp.

"Aieee!" The man pulled away his hand, to a chorus of jeers and laughter. He shook his sore finger and glared at Elsa. Ryker knew from firsthand experience how painful those sharp little teeth could be.

As the men taunted and teased, the wounded man stalked to the water's edge and gathered his war club. He brandished it toward Elsa with an angry snarl.

The men turned quiet, and Ryker held his breath. Good Person stepped between Elsa and the warrior and gathered Elsa into her arms. She held the flailing baby under one arm while undoing her baby from his cradleboard with the other. Then she sat beside the stump and calmly settled both babies to her breasts.

The fat man stood holding the club. Ryker thought he might snatch Elsa away from the woman.

Good Person spoke mildly and stroked Elsa's hair. It was as

if she claimed ownership of their baby sister. The man with the shawl barked a command, and the others guffawed. The fat man threw down the war club in disgust. He stalked over to the cooking fire with angry words.

"Elsa always gets her way," Johnny said in a whisper. "No wonder she's spoiled."

"Be quiet," Ryker hissed.

The fat men pulled a loaf of bread from the sack. He tore the loaf with his teeth and stuffed his mouth, glaring back at Elsa with a snarl.

Artillery interrupted from the direction of the fort. An eagle screamed. Sounds of rifle fire mingled with war whoops. The tall man spoke an order. The fat man dropped the remaining bread. In a moment they had gathered their weapons, climbed into their canoes, and paddled toward the battle. Good Person called out to them as they rounded a bend of Whiskey Creek. One of the men answered back. Soon they were out of sight.

Good Person laid the babies aside and gathered a small square of cloth. She put a pinch of tobacco in the center of the square and twisted it into a pouch, then tied it to a string and draped it over a tree branch with a low murmur.

"What's she doing?" Johnny said.

"Praying," Hannibal said in a whisper. "Indians wrap tobacco in cloth for prayers."

"Where did you come from?" Ryker said. "We thought you went back to the fort."

Hannibal looked frazzled and sunburned. Wet patches of sweat showed down his back and under his arms. He smelled even worse than yesterday.

"The fort is surrounded by Sioux," he whispered. "There's no getting in, no matter what we do." He wiped his face with the back of his arm. "Do you have anything to eat?"

CHAPTER 33

Good Person gestured for them to come out.

"Hurry before she comes over here," Hannibal said. "I'm dead meat if she finds me."

More gunshots and artillery shells sounded from the fort, as the children crept out of the hideout. Good Person looked anxiously toward the west. Elsa gnawed the crust of bread the fat Indian had dropped on the ground.

Good Person pointed to the chickens, and then to Johnny and Klara. She pantomimed pulling feathers. Klara stood with a blank stare.

"She wants you to pluck the hens," Sven said. "I'll help you." He reached for the birds, but Good Person stopped him. She pointed toward Klara, and then Johnny. She shook her head toward Sven.

"What's going on?" Sven said.

"She wants Klara and Johnny to do it," Ryker said.

Good Person thrust a chicken into Klara's arms and gestured again for Johnny to pluck feathers. Klara stared without moving. The woman poked Klara's arm and pointed at the bird. Klara nervously dropped the chicken on the ground. Good Person flared in anger.

Johnny started plucking as fast as he could. Feathers fluttered in the air like a small snow storm. The woman grabbed Klara by the arm and roughly pushed her toward the chickens.

"I don't know how to do it," Klara said with a helpless look toward Ryker. Good Person pushed Klara to the ground.

"I'll show you, Klara," Ryker said. "Don't make her mad." He nodded toward the woman and motioned that he would help his sister. Of course, Klara would not know how to pluck a hen. The Landstads needed every hen for eggs. There had been none slaughtered since coming to the frontier. Klara's hands shook, and her freckles stood out like pebbles on a sandy shore.

Good Person was just plain mean. Ryker hid his anger behind a friendly smile and motioned again that he would help his sister. The woman crimped her mouth and nodded.

Ryker sat beside Klara and showed her how to grasp hold of the feathers. He spoke soothing words, trying to reduce his sister's fears. He reminded her how angels hid in the clouds and told about seeing Beller in the clouds.

Klara's hands trembled, but she pulled a hen onto her lap and plucked a feather from the dead bird, wrinkling her nose in disgust.

Both Indian boys came running back into camp, chattering and pointing toward the fort. Good Person shook her head and pursed her lips. She spoke, and her boys took positions on the nearest bends of Whiskey Creek, one upstream and the other downstream.

Good Person turned to Ryker and Sven. She gestured toward the sky and made motions of the moon rising.

"She's talking about tonight," Sven said.

The woman pantomimed more canoes coming to the campsite. She made the motion of a setting sun and rising sun. She thought the men would return in the morning. Many men, by the way she opened and closed her hands to show her fingers. She spoke in her language, and Ryker did not know for sure what she was saying.

Good Person pointed to Ryker and Sven, and then to the fort. She pointed to Elsa and Klara and pointed to the tipi. She pointed to Johnny and made a face. She looked questioningly at Ryker.

She repeated the pantomime. It seemed Good Person wanted Ryker and Sven to go to the fort that night and leave the girls with her. Ryker figured she meant to keep Johnny as a slave.

Good Person pointed again to Ryker and Sven and pantomimed guns and scalping.

"She's saying it isn't safe for us to be here," Ryker said slowly. "But she'll keep the girls with her."

"I'm not leaving them," Sven said. "We stay together."

"She says we must leave," Ryker said. "Says we'll be killed if we stay."

"What about me?" Johnny's fat lips quivered, and his chin wiggled. Good Woman looked at his tears with what seemed to be disgust. She motioned for him to pluck another bird.

Elsa toddled to the water's edge, and the woman called to her in her language. Good Person patted Elsa's hair and said the name several times. Good Person bent down and grasped a cricket with two fingers and said the name. Then she held the cricket toward Elsa and repeated the word.

"She's renaming her Cricket," Sven said. "She doesn't need an Indian name."

Then Good Person pointed to Klara and said another name. She repeated the new names again, each time pointing at the girls in turn. Good Person reached over and dangled her hand in the river and said the word again, pointing at Klara.

Klara's lips wobbled, and tears slid down her cheeks. "I don't want an Indian name. I have a Christian name."

The woman repeated the Indian names for the girls and then patted her chest and pointed to her tipi and to her sons. The woman chattered in her language. She pointed to Elsa and to her breast. She was saying that Elsa must stay because of her milk. She pointed to Klara and Elsa. She wanted the girls to be together. She pointed to the girls again and patted her chest. She was promising to care for them.

"They belong to us," Sven said. He balled his fists and reached for his knife. "She can't have them."

"Let's run away now," Johnny said. "Grab the canoe, and get out of here while we can."

Ryker shook his head. "Not yet," he said. "Tonight. We won't leave you behind. Trust me." He couldn't leave the girls behind. Papa had put him in charge. They must all stay together. He must be very cautious. He could not afford to anger the woman.

Then Good Person motioned toward the hideout. She pointed to Sven and Ryker, indicating they should go into the hideout together. Then she made a sleeping motion with her hands next to her cheeks.

"She wants us to nap," Ryker said.

"Don't leave us," Klara said when they walked past her on the way to the hideout. She and Johnny sat in an ocean of feathers. "You can't leave us behind."

"She wants slaves to do all the work," Johnny said. "I have to get away."

"We won't leave you," Ryker said. "Just act agreeable." Everything in him wanted to fight for his sisters. "Do what she says, just for now."

Klara's shoulders drooped, and streams of tears dripped down her cheeks. The woman ignored Klara's distress. She pointed to the hideout and made again the motions of the sun setting and pointing toward the fort. She pointed to her chest, to Ryker, and then to the fort. She made paddling motions with her arms, then pointed to Ryker and Sven.

A desperate sadness fell upon Ryker. They had come so far together.

Good Person chattered in her language. Ryker stopped her. He pointed to Elsa and said the Sioux word for cricket. Then he pointed to Klara and repeated the name Good Woman had given her. The woman nodded encouragingly. He pointed to the woman with a questioning look. He must at least know her name. If they were to decide to leave the girls with their mother's friend, he must at least know her real name so he could find them again.

She pointed to herself and said a name. Then she pointed to each of her boys and said their names. Ryker repeated the names. She giggled at his pronunciation. The woman repeated the names.

"Remember," Ryker said. He made Johnny and Sven repeat the names several times. "We need to know in case we get separated."

He must trust the Indian woman, the woman who was Mama's friend, the Indian woman he called Good Person, who for some reason was unkind to Klara and hated Johnny.

Elsa woke and toddled to the edge of the water. Good Person called her name sharply. Then she pulled Elsa to where Klara sat in a mound of feathers. She gave Elsa's hand to her sister for safekeeping with a brisk nod. She fetched a basket from the tipi and motioned for Klara to gather the scattered feathers into the basket.

"Some things never change," Klara grumbled. "I get stuck with all the work."

CHAPTER 34

The boys crawled into the hideout, careful to avoid the yellow jackets.

"Watch out," Hannibal whispered, pointing to a hole in the ground near the entrance. "Yellow jackets are meaner than snakes. Especially if their nest is bothered."

"I hate being shut up in the trees this way," Sven said. "If I make it out of here alive, I'll stay in prairie country for the rest of my life. I like to see the sky."

Sven lay on his belly by the peephole where he could see the girls. Ryker crawled next to him. The Indian boys were nowhere to be seen.

"Why do they want the girls?" Sven said.

"Indians adopt babies and children into their tribe," Hannibal said. "Raise them as their own." He paused. "Some girls are taken for wives but others as slaves." He explained that girls, slaves, and women did the work around camp.

"And Johnny?" Sven said. "What will happen to him?"

"He'll be a slave like in *Uncle Tom's Cabin*," Ryker said. He glanced out the peephole to where Klara and Johnny plucked feathers. "The reason for the war in the South."

"Treat them bad and work them to death," Hannibal said with a shake of his head. "The women have it bad, but the slaves have it worse. I've heard stories . . ." His wheezy voice drifted off.

"We can't leave them," Sven said. "Not the girls, not even Johnny."

"Maybe it's better to leave the girls with her," Hannibal said slowly. "She'll keep them safe. Isn't it better for some of us to survive? We need to send help to find your mother."

"I don't trust her," Sven said. "She'll hand us over to the men in spite of her promises."

"She would have betrayed us this morning," Ryker said, "if she were going to do it. Why go to the trouble of taking us to the fort?" Ryker took a breath and tried to focus his mind on what Martin would do in their situation. Everything came into focus as if written on paper. "She owes Mama, and we can trust her."

"How do you know for sure?" Hannibal said.

"I just know," Ryker said. "Mama called her a good person."

Sven urged for immediate escape. "Let's just walk out of here and climb into the canoe and start paddling. She couldn't stop us."

"We have a better chance after dark," Ryker said. "We can't paddle up Whiskey Creek to Fort Abercrombie in broad daylight."

"We're too many for one canoe," Hannibal said. "We have to use common sense."

"We're all going," Sven said.

"We three might disguise ourselves as Indians, if we left Johnny and the girls behind," Hannibal said.

"The soldiers would fire on us if we barged into the fort looking like Indians," Ryker said.

They suggested wild ideas for escape. Sven said they could swim the Red River and sneak into the fort under cover of darkness.

"Except you and the girls don't know how to swim," Ryker

reminded him. "It takes a strong swimmer to manage this current."

The sun turned the hideout into an oven.

"We won't go to the fort." Sven paused for a moment. "We'll head toward Breckinridge. We'll find help there."

"I don't know about that," Hannibal said. "Heard of a massacre at the Breckinridge Hotel. Might still be overrun with hostiles. We'd be in a worse pickle." He described a tunnel built at the fort used to fetch water from the river without being seen by Indians. "A canoe under cover of darkness might get us close enough to sneak into the fort through the tunnel."

Good Person sounded a warning. Ryker looked through the peephole. Two Indian braves walked toward the campfire. They each carried rifles, and fresh scalps dangled from their lances. One brave wore a woman's apron twisted around his head, and the other had a blue dress wrapped around his shoulders. They narrowed their eyes when they noticed the white children picking hazelnuts, with Elsa playing around their feet. They questioned Good Person, never taking their eyes off of the girls.

"No," Sven whispered. He reached into his pocket for his knife. "We've got to save them."

"Quiet!" Ryker hissed.

The men walked toward the children, but Good Person stepped in front of them. She spoke firmly, pointing to first Elsa and then Klara. Then she patted her chest. She claimed them as her own.

The man handed the blue dress to the woman, pointing at Klara.

"He wants Klara," Sven said in a whisper. "Don't let him, Ryker. You can't let him take her."

Good Person shook her head and crossed her arms. They could only trust that she would keep her promise.

The brave yanked the apron from his friend's head and added

it to the dress. Ryker quit breathing. The Indian was raising his bid. The man spoke loudly, almost angrily, shoving the clothing toward the woman and jerking his chin toward Klara. The woman held her ground.

"I've got one bullet," Hannibal whispered. "I might be able to get one of the men, but not both."

Good Person shook her head and moved toward the girls. She gathered Elsa into one arm. She yelled at Klara and Johnny and with her free hand shoved them toward the hazelnut bushes. Klara stood as if in a trance. The woman yelled into Klara's face and shoved her again. Then Good Person picked up a small branch and beat Klara about the head and shoulders, screaming and slapping her. Elsa wailed in terror and reached for her sister.

"What is she doing?" Sven was in tears. "She's hurting her."

Klara cowered before the angry woman, as angry as the yellow jackets had been. The men called out with leering expressions on their faces. Ryker watched in horror as they moved toward his sisters. Just when it seemed all was lost and the men would grab them, Good Person picked up Elsa and grabbed Klara's arm, and dragged them toward the tipi. Johnny gathered hazelnuts as fast as he could, pale with fear.

Good Person shoved Klara into the tipi. She jerked the flap of the tipi, yelling inside as if she were scolding. Then she pushed Elsa in the tipi with her sister and stood in front of the doorway with a defiant look. She faced the men, loudly complaining and motioning toward the tipi.

The men shrugged and pointed at Johnny. They argued with the woman a long while.

"What are they saying?" Sven whispered.

"Quiet," Ryker said.

Good Person shook her head and crossed her arms. The men pointed again at Johnny and handed the clothing items to the woman. She shook her head. The men added a red bandanna handkerchief to the dress and apron. The woman placed the clothing alongside the tipi and returned to standing guard.

One of the braves yelled at Johnny and motioned him to come to them. Johnny shook his head and kept picking hazelnuts. The man walked over and grabbed Johnny by the arm, dragging him back to his companion. "Please," Johnny said, pulling away from the Indian. "Please . . ." He was crying now, digging his bare heels into the ground and blubbering, calling out for Ryker and Hannibal to save him.

Good Person watched without expression. Johnny tried to squirm away, but the man jerked him by the hair and threw him to the ground. He pulled his war club from a leather thong at his waist. He raised it high and struck Johnny hard across the shoulder. Johnny screamed and crawled toward the hideout.

"He's bringing them toward us," Ryker whispered in horror.

"We've got to help him," Sven whispered. "They'll kill him."

But they could not stop the forces already in motion. The Indian laughed and pointed to Johnny crawling toward a fallen tree. He placed an arrow on his bowstring and took aim. He took aim and shot an arrow into Johnny's foot. Johnny screamed but kept crawling away, the arrow showing on both sides of his foot.

The bowman took aim. He shot Johnny in the other foot. The men spoke laughingly to each other, mocking Johnny's tears while setting more arrows.

The next arrow zinged into Johnny's buttock. Then another into the other buttock. The men congratulated each other. Johnny crawled faster, pulling himself by his elbows to get out of range of the deadly arrows. His screams had stopped, but he grunted in pain with every inch forward.

The Indians threw down their bows and drew hunting knives. They walked toward Johnny, still crawling away from them. One grabbed Johnny's leg and dragged him over the rough ground toward the cook fire. He grabbed a protruding arrow and wrenched it free as Johnny screamed in pain.

"Help me!" Johnny screamed. "Why don't you do something?"

Ryker pulled Sven closer and pressed his brother's face into his chest. "Don't watch," he whispered. "Pray. It will be over soon."

But it wasn't.

CHAPTER 35

Johnny's screams continued for what seemed like an eternity, while Good Woman calmly sliced chickens into the stew pot. The Indians tormented poor Johnny like *Katt* played with captured mice.

Little Dog returned to the camp. He watched without expression as the braves tortured poor Johnny. Little Dog soon joined the men, kicking and striking the helpless boy and dropping burning coals onto his face and chest.

"I told you we should have left right away," Sven whispered. "Now it's too late."

"Devils," Hannibal said. "I'd like to get my hands on them for one minute." His voice quivered, and he clenched his fists until his knuckles turned white.

"Can't you do something?" Ryker said.

"I have one bullet left," Hannibal said. "I might kill Johnny and end his misery, but the shot would draw them to us."

"Do it," Sven whispered. "I can't stand to see him suffer."

"He's as good as dead already," Hannibal said. "Throwing our lives away will not change a thing."

The men danced around the fire waving Johnny's bloody scalp, but they danced without enthusiasm. One reached into the pot and pulled out a piece of chicken, far from cooked, and gnawed the bone.

"He's still alive," Sven whispered. He had pulled away from Ryker's chest and was looking toward his friend's body. "I saw

Johnny's foot move."

Ryker heard a groan. Johnny wasn't dead.

Both men ate and belched loudly. Johnny groaned again, and one of the Indians calmly walked over and stabbed him in the chest with his hunting knife.

The groans stopped.

The man walked purposefully toward them, as if he had heard them speak and knew they hid in the dead trees. Sven flinched, and Ryker steeled himself for the worst. Maybe the woman had betrayed them after all. The man tucked his knife back in his loin cloth and relieved himself directly in front of their hiding place, urine splattering through the leaves onto their faces and hands.

Ryker stayed still as a stone, holding Sven close, feeling his little brother's trembling body. Hannibal's raspy breathing sounded in his ears. The smell and touch of urine sickened him, but Ryker did not dare raise his hands to wipe his face.

The Indian turned to leave, and Hannibal reached to wipe his face, bumping one of the branches. It didn't move a lot, just enough to cause the dead leaves to shudder. Hannibal turned white as death.

The Indian brave paused and looked toward the hideout. He pulled his knife.

He directed a question toward Good Person, who shrugged her shoulders as if to say she didn't know. The man came toward the tangled mess of downed trees. Ryker held his breath. Sven held his knife in one hand and a sharp stick in the other. It was over. They would be discovered and killed as poor Johnny had been killed.

The warrior poked around the edge of the deadfalls. He lifted a fallen tree. In another moment they would be exposed. Sven reached out and jabbed his stick into the yellow jacket nest.

Angry insects swarmed toward the place where the fallen tree had been moved and attacked the warrior with a hundred vicious stingers.

"Aieee!" the man cried out. The yellow jackets bit his face and neck. "Aieee!" He charged toward Whiskey Creek. "Aieee!" He dived into the water.

The other brave kept his distance but made fun of his comrade when he came up, spouting water like a giant fish. The man said something to Good Person, and Ryker thought they were making another trade.

The man twisted water from his long hair. Then both men gathered their weapons, and Johnny's scalp, and walked toward Good Person's canoe.

"Oh no," Hannibal muttered. "They're taking her canoe."

Good Person protested loudly. The men shrugged and answered in calm tones. One brave pointed to the clothing lying by the tipi as if that were enough payment. Good Person pointed toward Johnny's body, screeching her protest as the men crawled into the canoe and paddled toward the fort. She called after them, but they kept paddling without a backward glance.

Hannibal let out a whispered string of cuss words that would send Mama running for the soap to wash out his mouth. "The canoe," he said. "Why did they have to take her canoe?"

CHAPTER 36

Good Person lifted the tipi flap and called Klara and Elsa by their Indian names. Klara limped out of the tipi while rubbing a sore spot on her hip from the beating she had received. The woman clucked and fussed over both Klara and Elsa, tenderly treating Klara's wounds with mud and cool water. She led Klara to a shady place and brought her a dish of food.

Klara stared at Johnny's body with blank eyes, holding her dish without eating. The woman smiled into Klara's face, patting her cheek and urging her to eat. The woman fetched a blanket from the tipi and covered Johnny's body with a clucking sound. Then she gently nudged the food toward Klara's mouth.

"She only treated her that way to keep her away from the Sioux," Hannibal said. "She's adopted the girls."

"I don't care," Sven said. "She can't have them. She traded Johnny to the bad Indians without lifting a finger to save him."

"She promised to take care of the girls," Hannibal said. "And she did." He sat up, stretching his limbs before him after being cooped up so long. The sun dipped down the western sky, and Ryker judged it to be mid-afternoon. "We might have a chance for the three of us to sneak into the fort." He waited a long moment. "Better chance without the girls."

Hannibal was right. It would be safer and easier without the girls along. Good Person would care for them, but Ryker knew what his parents would think about leaving them behind, even in the woman's care. And the thought of his sisters being raised by those who had killed their father, stolen their mother, and brutally murdered Johnny and the Tingvolds sickened him.

One thing was certain. They had to find a way to safety. If they remained where they were, they would meet the same fate as Johnny. Losing the canoe meant their bad situation had turned even worse.

Sven cried himself to sleep. From time to time he called out, and Ryker felt ashamed for all the times he had been mean to his brother. He was such a good boy, and now he had lost his father and mother, wandered the prairies, escaped from the Indians, and witnessed his friend's murder. Sven showed more sense than Ryker when it came to surviving. His smart thinking in poking a stick into the yellow jacket nest had saved their bacon. Johnny might be alive if they had left when Sven wanted to leave.

But there was no guarantee any of them would be alive if they had left when Sven first asked. It was bad luck the Indian woman chose this stretch of Whiskey Creek for a campsite. Bad luck was bad luck.

Ryker went over it in his mind again and again, trying to make sense of what had happened. He had been in school, reading *Uncle Tom's Cabin,* dreading the harvest. Then he was in charge, fleeing across the prairie, trying to fetch help for Mama. The brutal scenes he had witnessed flashed repeatedly when he least expected them. Mrs. Tingvold's eggs spilled from her apron as she fell forward. Mr. Tingvold's expression showed disbelief when the Sioux rode toward him with raised clubs. Papa's admonition to find Mama echoed in his thoughts. The brutality and senselessness of it made old troubles seem very small.

While Sven slept, Ryker and Hannibal plotted their escape. A hollow log lay to the side of the bank. They would wait until dark, snatch the girls, and put Klara and Elsa inside the hollow log. They would steal the bandanna handkerchief and gag Elsa's mouth. There was no other way to keep her quiet. Ryker, Sven, and Hannibal must swim alongside to guide the log to the fort. It would be better if Sven could also be inside the log, but Ryker doubted the opening would hold him. Sven could not swim but could hang onto the log for safety. Ryker had learned how to swim in Dodge County but did not consider himself a strong swimmer. He would feel safer with a log close by.

"What if we are spotted?" Hannibal said. "The Indians on the river, and the soldiers at the fort. Either might shoot us."

Ryker shook his head. "I don't know. We can only try. Maybe it will be foggy like this morning."

They looked out the peephole and scanned the short section of sky visible from their hideout. Gray clouds peppered the sky like the dapples on *Bestemor*'s old mare. A cold north wind rippled the water of Whiskey Creek, sending dried leaves and small twigs sailing toward Fort Abercrombie.

"We'll drift down Whiskey Creek until it flows into the Red River," Hannibal said. "Then we'll paddle to the tunnel and crawl into the fort."

Intermittent sounds of fighting came from the fort. Sven slept, though fitfully. Poor Klara busied with chores. When she finished one task, the woman immediately found another. Hannibal assured him that all girls worked around the Indian camps, and it didn't mean that Klara was a slave like Johnny had been.

By the time the sun dipped low in the western horizon, Klara had worked her way next to the hideout. She kept gathering hazelnuts but spoke to them in a low tone as she did. Klara's face was blistered with sunburn, and bug bites peppered her bruised arms and neck. She drooped with fatigue.

"Don't you dare leave us behind," Klara said in a fierce voice. "I hate Good Person for what she did to Johnny."

"She saved your life," Ryker said. "And she feeds Elsa." Elsa nursed alongside the Indian baby. From time to time, Elsa giggled and played with the baby. "She's not all bad."

"I'm afraid." Klara looked over her shoulder. "Did you see poor Johnny? They would have killed me for sure if the woman hadn't pushed me into the tipi."

Ryker hesitated before he spoke. He was in charge. He had to make sure his sister knew the score. "If something happens to us," Ryker said, "if we are taken by Indians or something else terrible"—he took a breath and spoke the hard truth—"then you and Elsa must live with Good Person and do whatever she asks of you."

"I won't," Klara said. "I'll never."

"You will," Ryker said. "She's Mama's friend. She is your only hope for survival if something happens to us." A blue heron landed on Whiskey Creek with a flurry of graceful wings and paddling feet. "Wait for the soldiers to rescue you. Tell them about Mama being taken and Papa killed. Teach Elsa her American name. The farm belongs to our family. You know that Martin will come home after the war. Maybe you can return to it someday, even without us."

"You promised to take us along," Klara said. She sobbed so pathetically that Ryker wanted to take her into his arms, but he couldn't. "Don't leave us."

"Be brave," Ryker said. "We're leaving as soon as it's dark. The woman thinks we're leaving you behind." He told her their plan to hide her and Elsa in the hollow log and paddle to Fort Abercrombie.

"I'm scared," Klara sniffled.

"We're all scared," Hannibal said. "We'll be all right."

"Klara, you have to remember this," Ryker said. "If something goes wrong, remember your Indian name and the name of your Indian mother. Your best bet is to return to her."

The woman called Klara to the tipi.

A wispy fog swirled over the water. An early autumn tang

chilled the air, and the night sounded with crickets and calling owls. The fragrance of burning wood and chicken stew filled their nostrils. The Indian boys returned from standing guard. The woman motioned them to leave the hideout and come to the fire. Ryker and Sven left Hannibal in the thicket.

Good Person first gave food to her boys and then shooed them off to the tipi, probably for bed. Then she doled out small portions to Sven and Ryker. When the boys finished, she handed a smaller portion to Klara.

"What did Johnny do wrong?" Klara whispered as she sat next to her brothers by the fire.

"Nothing," Ryker said. "She's helping us because Mama was kind to her. She felt no obligation to help Johnny."

Elsa toddled over to the fire, and the woman motioned for Klara to tend her sister. Elsa babbled and giggled. Elsa thrived since having regular milk. Maybe there would be another wet nurse at Fort Abercrombie.

Good Person kept glancing up and down Whiskey Creek as if expecting company. Clearly she was saving the food for someone else. It was almost dark, and a layer of fog settled over the water. Ryker caught Sven's eye and nodded.

"Soon as we get a chance," Ryker said in a whisper. "Klara, be ready to grab Elsa and run. Leave everything behind."

The Indian baby sounded from the tipi. When the woman tended him, Ryker filched a piece of meat from the stew pot, ran back, and handed it to Hannibal through the peephole.

"Come, Hannibal," Ryker said. "It's now or never."

CHAPTER 37

Klara scooped Elsa into her arms and headed toward the hollow log. Ryker snatched the red bandanna handkerchief. Hannibal ran from the hideout, stuffing food into his mouth as he came. Ryker tied the bandanna around Elsa's mouth and stuffed her into the log. She squealed in protest, but Klara crawled in after her, making shushing noises to comfort her baby sister. Sven, with a final glance toward his friend's body, hurried to help Ryker drag the log into the water. It was heavier than Ryker had expected, and Ryker was grateful for Hannibal's extra muscle power.

Hannibal shoved his pistol into Klara's hands. "Keep this dry," he said. "Remember, there's only one shot. Use it if it comes to that."

The frigid shock of Whiskey Creek made Ryker's teeth chatter. They pushed out into the middle of the stream, holding onto the log with one hand and paddling with the other. He looked to make sure Sven was holding onto the log. Sven gripped the stub of a branch. He was kicking and paddling for all he was worth.

As they rounded the first bend, Ryker heard one of the Indian boys sound the alarm. It was too late. They were out of sight and on their way to Fort Abercrombie.

"Sven," Hannibal whispered. "No need to wear yourself out. Just hang on."

The fog thickened. From time to time Ryker's feet touched

the bottom of the creek bed. He used this opportunity to push with his legs and move toward the middle of the stream again, letting the current pull them in the right direction. Drums sounded ahead and grew louder with each bend of Whiskey Creek.

"Ryker," Klara said through a knothole in the side of the log. "What's happening?"

"Be quiet," Ryker whispered. "Voices carry over the water."

They drifted around another sharp bend. Campfires glowed through the fog. Drums pounded relentlessly. Ryker pushed harder, forgetting his fatigue, wanting only to get away from this dangerous area of Whiskey Creek. They were almost to the next bend when screeching cries sounded through the night. A break in the fog revealed a huge fire surrounded by dancing Sioux.

Ryker bumped his shins on the creek bed, and the hair on his neck stood up in terror. Elsa mumbled through her gag.

"We're too shallow," Hannibal whispered. "Push out into the middle of the stream."

They managed to maneuver the log into deeper water, and Ryker counted heads to make sure they were still together. Ryker touched Hannibal's arm across from him on the other side of the log. The air felt colder than the water. He pushed his arm under the water.

"Klara," he whispered through the knothole. "Are you all right?"

"Yes," Klara said with chattering teeth.

"Sven," Ryker whispered. Whoops and hollers sounded from the dancers. Maybe Sven had not heard him above the noise. "Sven," he said a little louder.

Nothing.

"Where is he?" Ryker said. Panic rose in his throat. His brother did not know how to swim. He should have tied him to the log somehow, or kept him close enough to keep an eye on him.

"I don't see him," Hannibal whispered.

The fog thickened until they could not see their hands in front of their faces. "Sven," Ryker said again. He and Hannibal felt along both edges of the log. "Sven."

"I'm here," a small, choking voice sounded far away. "Help."

Hannibal swam toward the voice and returned with a near-drowned Sven in tow.

"Climb onto the log," Hannibal whispered. "You're done in."

Sven grunted as he sprawled halfway across the log. "I can't climb up," he whispered, shivering with chattering teeth. "Tired . . ."

Hannibal boosted Sven up on the log.

"Hang on," Ryker said. "We don't want to lose you."

They paddled as hard as they could to put distance between them and the dancing Indians. Hannibal said it was a scalp dance, or a war dance. Whatever kind of dancing it was, the wails and whooping kept up as the little craft continued down Whiskey Creek. Ryker breathed a sigh of relief when they turned a bend. They no longer saw campfires along the shore.

"Are you all right?" Ryker said. "What happened?"

"I slipped under the water," Sven said. "I doggy paddled . . . couldn't see you in the fog. I thought I'd be dead as Johnny."

"You don't know how to doggy paddle," Ryker said. The realization of how close he had been to losing his little brother made him tremble. He couldn't bear to lose anyone else.

"I learned," Sven said, spitting out a stream of water. "Watched the Indian boys."

Whiskey Creek joined the Red River of the North, and the fog lifted enough to reveal glowing lights of Indian campfires.

"Slabtown," Hannibal said grimly. "Injuns here, Fort Abercrombie beyond."

"We're almost there," Ryker said. The current quickened in the bigger river. It made it easier to paddle but also more challenging to steer. The worst thing would be to land on the shore next to the Indians. They had to stay in the middle of the river and aim for Fort Abercrombie. The fog protected them; Ryker was grateful for it, but it also made it difficult to see where they were going.

They would never make it. *Vonlaus.* How could they glide under the noses of hundreds of Indians? Inside the fort waited food and shelter, protection, and Mama. Outside the fort was starvation, exposure, and cruel death at the hands of the Sioux.

Hannibal looped his belt through the knothole. "Hang onto this," he said to Sven. "Don't let go no matter what happens."

"Where is the fort?" Ryker whispered.

"Across the river from Slabtown," Hannibal whispered.

Ryker's legs and feet felt numb. He reached up and patted Sven to make sure he was still safe. Klara whispered the Lord's Prayer.

"Let's go," he said. "We're almost there."

CHAPTER 38

The fog pressed like a layer of smoke. Not a breeze. Every breath moist and cold. Smells of cooking and burning fires drifted over the water, along with laughter and muttered voices. Once they heard a baby crying.

They glided down the river, churning feet beneath the water and passed the noise and lights of Slabtown. A beaver swam alongside of them for about twenty rods, grasping a leafy branch in his mouth.

"There it is," Hannibal said. The relief sounded in his voice. "Fort Abercrombie straight ahead."

A bulky shadow stood in the hazy fog. On the right was the steep bank of Slabtown, and on the left was the fort. Ryker remembered Fort Abercrombie as a scattering of buildings around a parade ground. He had seen from his perch in the cottonwood how the Sioux hid in the tall grass around the fort.

"Where is the tunnel?" Ryker whispered.

"Not too far ahead," Hannibal said. "Hard to tell in this fog."

They paddled toward the fort. A canoe glided toward them out of the fog. It floated not ten yards to the right of their log. Ryker saw it coming, but it was too late to warn the others. He held his breath and prayed for angels to protect them.

One of the Indians muttered a few words, and the other answered with a grunt. At least two Indians, maybe more. Ryker quit paddling, just dangled in the icy water and prayed, as the canoe drifted past.

"Did you see that?" Hannibal whispered. "Too close."

Sven was hanging onto the belt with skinny arms and shaky hands. His teeth chattered. "I bit down to stop the chattering, and I think I broke a tooth."

"We're almost there," Ryker said in a whisper. "You're brave. Just like Martin."

He had to make sure Sven kept awake. He looked ready to topple over. They headed toward the opposite shore, toward safety and warmth.

"It has to be here somewhere," Hannibal said. "Do you see anything?"

They paddled alongside the fort entrance and then turned and paddled back again. Hannibal kept muttering about finding it, that it had to be right in front of them, when a voice sounded through the fog.

"Who goes there?"

"Private Hannibal Mumford bringing settlers into the fort," he said.

"Well, why didn't you say so in the first place?" the soldier said. "I was about ready to open fire on you, Hannibal." He held up a lantern.

A shot rang out in the darkness, and the soldier fell.

"Quick," Hannibal said. He and Ryker pulled the log over to the cave entrance as a shower of bullets thudded around them. Hannibal threw the lantern into the river. They pulled the girls onto the shore. Klara still held Hannibal's pistol. Sven scrambled down from the log. The soldier staggered to his feet.

"Are you all right, Elmer?" Hannibal asked the soldier.

"Just winged," Elmer said. "Follow me." Elmer scrambled into the mouth of the cave, holding his arm and cursing in German.

Hannibal, holding Elsa, plunged after him with Ryker and the twins behind him. The cave was more of a deep trench and

215

was covered with brush and branches. It stank of earth and hay and was as dark and narrow as a grave. A single glimmer of light showed far ahead of them. There was barely enough room to stand, and Sven went ahead in the narrow passage.

Out of the darkness, an Indian war whoop sounded at the cave entrance, directly behind them.

Ryker's heart lurched into his throat. Had they gone through all their ordeal only to die at the very edge of safety? Ryker pulled Klara by the hand, hurrying toward the light. They must outrun the Sioux warrior. They must find Mama.

The Indian yelled another hideous cry. Ryker smelled rancid bear grease. The roof of the cave would burn easily—dried brush and straw, broken branches. He shoved away the image of blazing fire overhead, without anywhere to escape.

Klara stopped and turned toward their attacker. She raised and pointed Hannibal's pistol in the direction of the war whoops. The Indian lunged forward. A ray of light glinted off the blade of his raised knife.

Klara pulled the trigger.

The shot exploded.

Silence.

CHAPTER 39

They stumbled through the cave, tripping over roots and small stones. Ryker heard nothing behind him but felt terrified the Indian might yet attack them. Klara knew nothing about shooting; surely her shot could not have been fatal.

The Sioux seemed invincible. Ryker had seen only white men die at their hands, never the opposite. Certainly not at the hands of a little girl.

"Don't shoot," Hannibal called out. "Coming in with survivors and a wounded soldier."

A young sentry helped them through the cave opening, holding a lantern. Earthworks protected the entrance, shielding them from the view of the Indians. A campfire burned with bright sparks flying up into the night.

Klara still held the empty gun. She looked down at it and threw it in the grass as if it were a snake. Hannibal picked it up and tucked it into his waistband. Sven's eyes swelled almost shut. Their teeth chattered, and the twins clung to each other in a desperate embrace. Sparks scattered from the blazing fire. Nothing seemed real.

Hannibal plopped Elsa into Ryker's arms. Sven pulled his knife out of his shoe and sawed through the fabric around Elsa's mouth. She howled as loud as the Indian's war whoop when free of it. All the while Ryker scanned faces, searching for his mother.

The sentry let out a low whistle. "What do we have here?"

He sent a runner for Captain Vander Horck. "Mumford, you lead a sorry looking bunch."

"You're looking at heroes," Hannibal said with a wheezy snort. He stretched his hands toward the fire, rubbing them together. "They've come through hell to get here and live to tell about it."

Not all of them lived, Ryker wanted to say. Papa and the Tingvolds and Johnny didn't live. He was too tired to form the words. The warmth melted his frozen limbs and made his eyes droop with exhaustion.

"Welcome." Captain Vander Horck hurried toward them. "Quite a speech, Private Mumford. I want to hear more, but first I need reconnaissance information."

Hannibal reported the fires in Slabtown, the war dance by Whiskey Creek, and the burned homesteads on the frontier. A woman bandaged the wounded soldier's arm. She said that his wound was not mortal. The children warmed their hands and then turned and warmed their backsides. It would take a long time for their clothes to dry.

Hannibal spoke to the captain, while two armed soldiers disappeared into the tunnel.

Ryker asked a fat woman wearing an apron if she had seen their mother. She shook her head and didn't answer. Her face showed kind sympathy. Ryker asked again.

"I don't speak no foreign tongue," she said in a loud voice as if Ryker were deaf. "Can't understand you."

Ryker could have kicked himself. He had used Norwegian words. It took a moment for him to remember the American words he needed. When he asked again, he saw her shake her head again. He described Mama as a Norwegian woman wearing a blue kerchief. "She doesn't speak much American. And she's . . ." Words failed him. Such things were not spoken, but he felt desperate. "There will be a baby." Ryker was glad the darkness hid the blush he felt rising on his cheeks.

"Haven't seen her," the woman said, in a gentler tone. "Maybe the captain knows something."

"And the Schmitz family?" Ryker said. "Their son Johnny was with us, but he didn't, he couldn't . . . he didn't make it." The twins held each other with Elsa wedged between them. Klara reached her free hand and gripped his.

The woman draped blankets over their shoulders and gathered Elsa and the twins into her guiding arms. "Let's get you out of those wet clothes."

"Milk," Elsa said with a pitiful wail.

"Poor little thing," the woman said. "Auntie Abigail will find you milk. Don't you worry. You're safe with me."

The twins looked about ready to collapse. The blanket felt like a warm caress around Ryker's shoulders. He was having a hard time keeping his eyes open.

"Thank you, Missus."

"I'm Auntie Abigail. Just call me that. Everybody does." Auntie Abigail hoisted Elsa in her plump arms. Elsa tucked her head under the blanket. A small sliver of light glowed through an open door across the parade grounds. "Think you two will make it on your own steam?"

The twins nodded, barely standing up. How thin and frail they looked. Klara's gaunt face reminded him of a corpse. Her lips showed blue with cold. Sven's clothes hung in rags, and one of his shoes was missing. Still, he had kept his knife through all they had gone through. Ryker's hands were empty. He had lost their quilt, lost Mrs. Tingvold's book, and lost every bit of their supplies. It was a good thing they had not taken the family Bible with them. It would have been lost as well. Then he remembered the coins. He fingered the pouch still hanging around his neck.

At least they had a few pennies. An overwhelming dread fell

upon him. Mama wasn't at the fort. He didn't know how he could take care of his sisters and brother without Mama's help.

Hannibal disappeared with the soldiers. Ryker must thank him later. They would have not survived without him.

"Are you coming?" Auntie Abigail looked over her shoulder toward Ryker. "Soup on the fire."

Ryker nodded. His brain refused to think.

"Stay together, and keep your heads down." She positioned herself in the lead. "If the fog lifts, the savages will be taking potshots again."

"I have a few questions for the young man," Captain Vander Horck said to Auntie Abigail. "Take the little ones. He'll soon join you." He turned his attention to Ryker.

"Now tell me what happened," Captain Vander Horck said. "I understand you are a hero."

The unexpected kindness brought tears to Ryker's eyes, and he struggled to regain his composure. He must deliver his important message.

"The Sioux killed my father." He gulped, choking on the difficult words. He still could not grasp that hard truth. "Stole my mother and baby sister, Elsa." He wiped his nose on his wet sleeve, shivering when the cold cloth touched his face. "We found Elsa on the prairie." The events of recent days swirled in his mind, and it took all his energy to speak sensibly. "Sven saw an angel." The captain wouldn't care about angels. "Sioux killed the Tingvolds, and Johnny Schmitz."

More soldiers gathered around them, eager to hear Ryker's story.

"Before Papa died, he said to fetch soldiers to find Mama." Ryker swallowed hard. "Maybe you already found her?" His voice cracked. It was a long shot, but maybe, just maybe, God had another miracle for them, a miracle as wonderful as finding Elsa on the prairie. "Maybe she found her way to the fort."

"Not that I am aware," Captain Vander Horck said. He asked the soldiers if anyone had seen a lone woman coming into the fort. No one had.

"And your father's name?"

"Johann Landstad," Ryker said. He should have said his father's name at the start.

"I'm sorry for your loss," Captain Vander Horck said. "I remember him well." He adjusted his spectacles, then clamped a strong hand on Ryker's shoulder. "Johann was a good man, as honest as Abe Lincoln himself." The man reeked of pipe tobacco and sweat. "When he said his hay was of good quality, you could believe it. Always kept his word."

They stood in silence for a brief moment. He cleared his throat. "Didn't you have a brother?"

"Martin," Ryker said. "Signed up last year."

"I remember now," Captain Vander Horck said. "Lied about his age."

Captain Vander Horck asked where Martin was fighting and clucked his tongue when he learned that Martin was missing since Shiloh. He slipped into deep thought, rubbing the bridge of his nose with a pointed finger.

"We'll find her, son." He removed his hand from Ryker's shoulder and straightened his back. "We'll whip the Sioux, and then we'll find your mother."

Ryker had done it. Papa told him to get word to the soldiers, and he had done it. Ryker's legs shook so hard that he feared he might fall down. His teeth chattered, and it took all his determination to follow after Auntie Abigail who had gone ahead with his brother and sisters. It was a short walk, and as he crossed the threshold into the warm and lighted building, he heard a sharp command issued from Captain Vander Horck.

"Man your posts," he said. "Expect an attack at first light."

CHAPTER 40

Ryker squinted at the unexpected brightness of a lighted lantern in the blockhouse. The room was crowded with women and children, sprawled on the floor, leaning against the wall, overflowing every bed and cot. It seemed they were making ammunition, or at least handling ammunition. The smell of gunpowder filled his nostrils, along with the pungent smell of sweat and cooked cabbage.

He followed Auntie Abigail toward a long bench along the opposite wall and collapsed in relief. All conversation ceased as Ryker and his family walked into the room. Everyone stared. Ryker searched each face, hoping to find Mama.

"Have you seen my husband," a woman said from the side of the room. "John Millicent, from McCaullyville? He went for supplies. Maybe you saw him?"

"No," Ryker said with a shake of his head.

"Percy Gunderson?" a young girl said. "We had to leave without good-byes. We are to be wed next week."

"No," Ryker said again. "Heard the Jensen girls were taken west along with my mother, but that's all I know."

They pressed in then, all asking questions and wanting news about neighbors and family members. Elsa let out a howl in protest and buried her face in Klara's chest.

"Enough." Auntie Abigail held up her plump hand. "Can't you see they're dead on their feet?" She asked for the loan of dry clothing and ordered a skinny woman to prepare food.

"They'll be ready for your questions tomorrow."

How long had it been since Ryker had been inside a building? Tomorrow he would count the knots on Klara's apron strings.

Mrs. Jacobs and her many children huddled in the opposite corner. Tomorrow Ryker would confess how he had taken food from her home. He didn't know how to repay her, but he would. Like Papa, Ryker would be an honorable man, a man of his word. Right now he was too tired and hungry to explain.

Auntie Abigail scavenged for dry clothing, and a tall woman used a blanket to curtain off a corner where they could change away from inquisitive onlookers.

"It's for a grown woman," Klara said. She held up a woman's party dress that would have fit their mother.

"It's only for tonight," Ryker said. "At least it's dry." He wore a shirt several sizes too small and a pair of ragged trousers large enough to wrap around him twice. Sven wore a night dress. "Our clothes will be dry tomorrow."

They came out in their hodgepodge of rags and finery, at least clean and dry again. Auntie Abigail brought cabbage stew and fresh bread. How good it tasted. Ryker smacked his lips and downed every drop of hot food. Klara held a bit of bread dipped in broth to Elsa's lips, but she turned away and whimpered for milk. Auntie brought another ladle of broth, and more bread, before Ryker could ask.

"Eat up," she said. "You deserve it, after what you've been through."

A buxom woman with dark hair and a tired smile approached them. "I'm Mrs. Kelly. I've extra milk for your baby. Abigail says she asks for milk."

Elsa hesitated to leave Klara's lap, until she realized there was milk. "Mama," she said. Elsa's tiny hands shook as she eagerly accepted the offered breast. She leaned into the woman and nursed blissfully with closed eyes. Auntie Abigail found a pallet on the floor for Elsa and the twins. She covered them with a quilt. "Lie beside them," she said to Ryker. "We'll talk tomorrow."

How good to sleep inside and out of the cold. How wonderful to go to bed with a full stomach, knowing armed soldiers stood guard. The twins already slept, Klara sucking her thumb and snuggling up to her brother. Ryker thought of poor Johnny lying by Whiskey Creek. He hoped the woman had buried him but suspected that she had not. Johnny had done nothing to any of them, nothing at all to deserve such hatred. Like Papa in the root cellar. Before Ryker could think another thought, he fell asleep, too.

War cries and rifle shots startled him from his rest just as a glimmer of dawn showed through the window glass. Women fluttered and scattered like a flock of hens, closing the shutters, counting their children, praying aloud for the safety of the soldiers and the defeat of the Sioux. Some cried. Others covered their heads with their arms and waited for it to be over.

An old woman covered her head with her apron and wailed. "We'll all be killed," she said. "They're coming. We'll all die."

"She's from the Breckinridge massacre," Auntie Abigail said in explanation and hurried to the woman's side. "Now, now, don't scare the children," she said. "Soldiers will take care of us. We're not going to die."

One woman forced her children to sit in the corner farthest from the windows and covered them with heavy quilts in case of stray bullets. They complained of suffocation, but she paid them no mind. "Better stifled than shot," she said, finding yet another blanket to throw over them.

Others tipped heavy tables and huddled behind them. All was confusion. No one knew from which direction the Indians might attack.

"Last time they came from Slabtown," Auntie Abigail said. "Probably will come screeching in from the opposite direction, knowing their heathen ways."

Elsa howled until Mrs. Kelly came to her rescue. Ryker wanted to protect the twins and Elsa, too, but didn't know how to do it. It seemed to him the thick walls of the blockhouse were sufficient protection from small-arms fire, the only fire power of the Sioux.

"I'm scared," Klara said. The look of terror in his sister's eyes was almost more than he could bear. "Are we really going to die?"

"No," Ryker said. "We're safe here." A flutter of worry stirred his gut, and he hoped he spoke the truth. He pulled her closer to his side and tucked his arm around her in a comforting manner. "The Sioux are no match for the howitzers." He told her what he had seen from the top of the cottonwood, how the Indians tried many times to enter the fort, but each time they were repelled by the cannons. "The soldiers will protect us. Don't worry."

The tall woman held a privacy blanket for those who needed to use a night pot. The smells of human waste, sweat, and gunpowder made the blockhouse air a thick, disagreeable stew. There was nowhere to go, nowhere to hide. They could only hunker down and wait for it to be over.

Mrs. Jacobs began praying the Our Father in German, and soon every voice joined in, only in his or her own language. The comforting words fell on the room, soothing the worriers and strengthening the faint hearted. Deliver us from evil. Oh, God. Let it be so.

A short lull in the shooting made them hopeful the fighting had ended. It didn't last.

"I'm a killer," Klara whispered in Ryker's ear. She flinched as the cannon blasted again. "I hated the Indians for Papa, and what they did to poor Johnny." The Gatling gun chattered. "I wanted to kill all of them. Even that woman." She pulled up her knees and hid her face in the folds of the too-large dress. "Mama was wrong. That woman was not a good person. She should have helped Johnny." Her voice was muffled, and Ryker strained to hear her words. "I hated and killed. Now I'll burn in hell."

She lifted her face and looked into Ryker's eyes. "Won't I?"

A loud barrage of rifle fire and Gatling guns sounded outside, giving Ryker a moment to consider his answer. Mama knew words to make Klara feel better. He tried to think of what Papa might say. Once, Martin stole *Bestemor*'s *solia*, the beautiful pin used to hold her shawl in place. Martin was very young and only wanted to play with it. But he dropped it in the haymow, and they never found it. Papa said then that God is a merciful God, the God of second chances. "All we can do is pick ourselves up and begin again," he had said.

Just remembering Papa before he grew so bad tempered brought tears to Ryker's eyes. Papa had not always been mean and strict. He changed after moving out to the prairie, and even more so after Martin signed up. But the real Papa had been different. Captain Vander Horck knew Papa to be a good man, an honest man. Ryker decided to remember Papa the way he used to be.

"Do you think Martin will go to hell for being a soldier?" Ryker said. "He's fighting to free the slaves."

"Of course he won't go to hell," Klara said. "Not Martin."

"You're a soldier, too. Like Martin," Ryker said. "You fought for your family. You saw how they treated Johnny. That might have happened to Elsa or Sven." He took a deep breath. "You had no choice. God understands."

"Are you sure, Ryker?" she said.

Ryker slipped into the Norwegian language of their intimate family. "Love demands action to prevent further harm." Sounds of fighting grew louder again. "Until we find Mama and Martin, we are all that is left of our family. We must care for each other."

Klara raised her thumb to her mouth but stopped herself. She tucked her hand under her leg. "I wish Mama would come," she said.

Elsa finished nursing and toddled over to them. Ryker nodded a thank-you to kind Mrs. Kelly. Elsa burped and clapped her hands. Elsa had grown accustomed to the sound of gunfire. She crawled into Klara's lap and fell asleep.

Mathilde Jacobs kept watch through a crack between the logs and from time to time would call out news of the battle. She was about Ryker's age, a pretty girl with dark hair and eyes, and a crooked smile.

"It's too smoky from the gunpowder to see much," she said. "Smoke hangs like fog over the parade ground."

Ryker crawled to her side to see through the crack, too. Just like when he had watched from the cottonwood, gunpowder hung low over the parade ground. It was a wonder anyone could see anything. How easy it would be for the Sioux to sneak in to the compound, as they had done in the previous battle. Ryker remembered how the Indians had hidden in the tall grass surrounding the fort.

The guns blasted, and Ryker heard a strange cracking sound and then the crash of falling timber.

"The Gatling guns are cutting down the trees across the river where the Indians are hiding," Mathilde said. "Think of the power of those bullets to cut through the tree trunks."

Good thing the army had not turned the guns in his direction while he had been perched in the cottonwood. The guns quieted, and all was still.

Auntie Abigail brought their dry clothing and held up the quilt for them to change.

"Look," Sven said. He pointed at Ryker's ankles. "Your pants are too short. You've grown taller this summer."

"I guess I have," Ryker said. His voice cracked. He lifted a hand to his face and felt a line of fuzz on his upper lip. He wondered if he were tall enough to see over the prairie grass. He must take over the job of scythe-man now that Papa was gone. There was no one else.

Hannibal entered the blockhouse holding his rifle in hand. His pistol stuck out from his waistband. How tired he looked. He brought word from the captain that the soldiers needed food and water.

The women hurriedly gathered a soup pail, spoons, tin cups, and loaves of bread.

"Did you ever figure out how many days you were out on the prairie?" Hannibal said as he waited for the food. His face was smeared with dirt and gunpowder. Gray lines circled his mouth. "Didn't Klara keep track?"

"Nine days," Klara said. "I made a knot every night."

The days blurred into one bad dream in Ryker's mind: Papa's death; the Tingvold massacre; the twins capture and escape with Johnny; finding Elsa on the prairie; Beller's death; their capture by Good Person, and Johnny's death. Then their freezing swim to Fort Abercrombie. Ryker swallowed hard. "Klara feels bad about killing that Indian."

"Then she'll be happy to know she only wounded him." Hannibal grabbed the food and started toward the door. "Sentries saw him limping away."

Klara's grin lit up the morning.

CHAPTER 41

After that, Fort Abercrombie settled into a mind-numbing siege. The Sioux surrounded them, hiding in the grass around the fort, waiting to pounce on anyone so foolish as to show himself.

They didn't attack, but they didn't go away. The soldiers grew testy from constant guard duty. Settlers worried about their homesteads, crops left in the field, and missing family members. Klara cared for Elsa, who was always finding trouble.

Ryker was the oldest boy in the blockhouse. Others his age helped stand guard, care for the few remaining horses, and run errands for the soldiers. Every time Ryker volunteered to help in the defense of the fort, he was turned down. Even the smallest tasks with the soldiers were denied him.

Nathan and William Jacobs were younger than Ryker by a full year, and yet they carried and distributed ammunition to the soldiers, brought them their food, and worked in the horse barn.

Working in the barn would have been welcome relief from the women's work he and Sven were assigned. Their days filled with carrying water, fetching firewood, dumping night pots, emptying slop pails, and helping Auntie Abigail with dirty dishes and laundry.

It wasn't fair. He said as much to Captain Vander Horck after they had been at the fort for a week. "Why are you making me stay with the women?" Ryker said. "Boys my age are in the army."

"Son," Captain Vander Horck said, "I know boys of your age are fighting for Lincoln." He cleared his throat and fingered the bridge of his nose. "I appreciate your offer, but you must stay out of danger to care for your family." He straightened his shoulders and started toward the door. "I owe your father that much."

Ryker glanced over to where the twins played patty-cake with Elsa and little Jane Jacobs. It was true. Without him, his sisters and brothers might end up in an orphanage. Ryker steeled himself to being a house slave for the sake of his family. It wasn't fair.

The days grew shorter, and the temperatures dipped into autumn. After a week of cold and damp, an Indian summer burst upon them. The weather grew hot and sultry as mid-August rather than late September. Everyone scanned the horizon, hoping for reinforcements to arrive from Fort Snelling.

"Will they ever come to rescue us?" Klara said one morning when Ryker felt grouchy and ill-tempered. "I want to go home."

Little Jack Jacobs went sleepwalking in the middle of the previous night and was rescued by the sentry before he could run off and get captured by the Sioux. Bawling babies, snoring old ladies, and general misery kept Ryker awake the rest of the night. He wanted to go home, too.

It was hot as a hayfield in the blockhouse, and Ryker made excuses to get away for some fresh air. He found Hannibal pitching hay to the horses. Ryker picked up another pitchfork to give him a hand.

"Wish we could go swimming in the river," Hannibal said. His wheezy voice made every comment sound like a complaint. "I stink to high heaven."

Ryker reminded him that at least the soldiers slept in the open where they might catch a breeze. "You should try sleeping with a whole room of mothers and children." It felt good to complain.

That night a soldier sneaked away for an evening swim while fetching water. A lurking Sioux shot him in the upper back as the solder crawled out of the water. Hannibal was standing guard and helped the wounded man to the blockhouse and Auntie Abigail's ministrations.

Ryker woke up hearing the commotion.

Auntie Abigail fussed over the young man's wound, ripping cloth into bandages and sending William Jacobs for cow manure to make a compress. "You know better than to expose yourself that way," she scolded and yanked the bandage so tightly that he cried out. "What would your mother say?"

"We're all sick of being forted up," Hannibal said in the soldier's defense. "Stand in the open, and you might take a bullet. Dip in the river, and you feel an arrow. What do they want, anyway?"

A baby cried, and Mrs. Jacobs tied a string around Jack's wrist and hers to prevent him from sleepwalking. Ryker knew what the Sioux wanted. They felt cheated and wanted their land back. Captain Vander Horck said the Sioux were fighting because the treaty payments were late.

"The Sioux want to starve us out, drive us out, and kill all of us," Auntie Abigail said with a determined crimp in her mouth. "You don't have to make it any easier for them."

The next afternoon a northwest wind roared in across the prairie. The hot summer-like air chilled into the sharp sting of autumn. The cookstove belched black smoke into the blockhouse with every downdraft, making Auntie Abigail curse with frustration.

"Pardon my French," she said to no one in particular. "This stove would make a preacher swear."

The wind rattled the doors and windows. Women scurried to

latch the shutters. Mathilde peeked through a crack in the wall, reporting soldiers chasing their caps and shielding their eyes from blowing sand. The wind snatched the outhouse door out of Mrs. Kelly's hands and ripped it off its leather hinges, leaving Mrs. Kelly relieving herself in plain sight of anyone walking by.

Auntie Abigail asked Ryker to fetch clothes off the line before the wind carried them away.

"Such a wind," she said, looking toward the sky. "Have you ever seen the like? A blizzard without snow. Put rocks in your pockets lest you blow clear away."

The wind snatched a clean petticoat from Ryker's hands and blew it across the parade grounds toward the river. Ryker ran after it, noticing how the grass bent almost to the ground. The cloth snagged on a stack of firewood. Ryker peeked around the wood pile, strictly against the rules. Brown bodies hid in the bending and blowing grass, taking advantage of the bad weather to attack the fort.

Ryker ran for the nearest sentry. "Indians sneaking up on the east," he said, trying to catch his breath, embarrassed to be holding a petticoat that waved like a flag of truce in the wind.

The sentry sounded a warning and sent Ryker to fetch Captain Vander Horck. Soldiers rushed to their positions, shirt-tails and caps flying in the wind, squinting into the blowing dirt. The wind gave no sign of letting up. A few shots sounded as the soldiers shot at Indians exposed by the waving grass.

"Hold your fire," Captain Vander Horck said as he came out, holding onto his hat with one hand and jacket with the other. "These devils are smart as foxes," he said with grudging admiration. "They know to use the weather to their advantage."

He motioned other officers toward him, and they stepped into the empty jail house to confer. Even inside they raised their voices just to be heard above the howling wind. Ryker stood with Hannibal outside the door. Ryker stayed quiet, hoping he would not be noticed. He wanted to be in the thick of it, for once, instead of hiding inside like a baby.

"Wind's blowing toward Slabtown," Captain Vander Horck said. A burst of wind muffled their next words. Then their voices became audible again. "We'll chase them back and clean out their cover at the same time."

"He's talking about setting a fire," Hannibal said.

"Makes sense," Ryker said. "The wind would blow it right into their faces." He remembered the fire that raced across the Tingvolds' fields.

"But two can play at that game," Hannibal said. "What's to stop them from setting a fire west of us?"

Ryker sobered. A single firebreak on the west side of the fort wouldn't do a lot to stop a prairie fire. As if reading his mind, one of the officers voiced the same concern.

Captain Vander Horck said it was worth the risk. It would quell the attack, destroy the cover, and minimize raids in days ahead.

"A lone savage could do a lot of damage if he sneaked inside the compound." He ordered a fire just east of the earthworks nearest the Red River.

A barrage of orders sent soldiers scrambling. Hannibal rushed to carry the torch.

The wind blew it out, and Hannibal returned for another light. Then, shielding the small flame with this hand, Hannibal hurried to the earthworks and threw the torch over the top.

The wind did the rest. Flames whooshed in the autumn grasses and roared ahead of the wind, raging toward the river, where it burned itself out. Indians screamed as they clambered to escape the flames.

Soldiers opened fire.

CHAPTER 42

The days passed into weeks. A hard frost killed the grass surrounding the fort, leaving less cover for hiding Sioux warriors from all directions. Supplies grew short, along with tempers. Elsa learned to drink from a cup. Klara and Sven filled out a little, though they were both too skinny.

Ryker struck up a friendship with Mathilde Jacobs, the girl who kept watch during the battle. Mathilde was kind and steady. At least she had acted that way when he told her about taking food from their homestead during their escape across the prairie. She assured him the Indians would have only stolen anything left behind.

Rumors abounded: help was on its way from Fort Snelling; help was not on its way from Fort Snelling; help had started from Fort Snelling, but the reinforcements were slaughtered by the Sioux; Lincoln had won the war in the South, and help was on its way; Lincoln had lost the war in the South, and the Confederates were coming to take over Fort Abercrombie.

Hannibal confided that Captain Vander Horck did not know if reinforcements were coming to their rescue. "Said all of Minnesota may have fallen, and we'd never know."

Every morning some would say help would arrive that day. At night the same folks would promise help would come the next day. Auntie Abigail felt in her bones that Governor Ramsey had everything under control. Mrs. Kelly found a four-leafed clover, which meant good luck coming her way. Mathilde Jacobs said she and her mother were praying a novena to St. Michael for deliverance.

"I'm sick of this," Sven said one day. "I'd rather be raking hay than listening to all these wild stories."

"I know what you mean," Ryker said. "We're not used to being stuck with strangers. I can't wait to be home again."

As he spoke the words, he realized that he was homesick for their prairie home. Homesick, like Mama had been for Norway. He remembered Mama's faraway look in her eyes as she told stories about the *stabbuhrs,* cheeses, and home.

"Let's sneak out," Sven said. "Who would stop us?"

"It's not safe," Ryker said. "We can't risk being killed or stolen. Like it or not, we have to wait until the Sioux are whipped." Ryker wanted very much to return home. "Besides, we have to find Mama."

"Then let's just get away from these people," Sven said. "Please. Just a little peace and quiet. I'm sick of griping women, fighting kids, and stinky soldiers. I've had enough."

Being forted up meant no relief from the constant pressures of people. Ryker knew of a quiet place alongside the horse barn. A guard stood nearby. It should be safe enough, even though it was strictly off limits for civilians. Of course, Captain Vander Horck couldn't risk some child wandering off and being captured. There had been enough death.

Ryker cornered Hannibal when he helped Auntie Abigail carry breakfast to the men. Hannibal said he would be guarding that corner all afternoon, and they were welcome to come if they wanted. "Just keep it to yourself. I don't want to get in trouble," he said.

Ryker told Klara where they were going, but no one else. Then the boys pretended to leave for the privy and followed the inside of the perimeter. No smoke showed over Slabtown. Soldiers kept watch at intervals, shielded by stacks of firewood, barrels, or earthworks.

When the boys reached a place secluded from view, they lay on their backs in the dried grass and studied the clouds. Blue sky and wispy clouds proved much easier on their eyes than a blockhouse filled with crabby refugees and crying babies.

"Did I tell you how Beller watched over me that day I climbed the tree?" Ryker said.

"You mean the day you fell out of that cottonwood?" Sven said with a giggle. "It would have been funny except we were so afraid you would be killed."

"The day I almost broke my neck," Ryker said.

"At least you can write a story about it," Sven said. "Though you haven't talked about writing stories since Papa died."

"Been too busy, I guess," Ryker said. He hadn't thought about writing anything, not a poem or a story or anything. He sighed. Maybe he never would write anything again. Their teacher was dead. No one to teach him how to do it anymore, even if they managed to return to their farm.

"You fell out of that tree like a leaf falling off a branch." Sven's voice grew serious. "We almost died of fright. What would we do without you?"

"You would have figured something out," Ryker said. "You showed better sense than I did during our escape." He took a breath. "Klara shot the Indian before it could hurt us." He watched a stream of clouds move across the sky. "I should have left the woman's camp earlier, like you said. Johnny would be alive if I had listened. Now Johnny is dead, and it's my fault." The clouds scampered like small mice riding the prairie wind.

They talked about Johnny, remembering his clumsy ways, his kind heart toward Elsa, and the way he had changed his opinion of their mother. Ryker would have to tell Frank the sad news of his parents and brother's death. He did not look forward to that.

"Martin says Mama is a saint," Ryker said. "She's good to everyone."

"I wonder where she is," Sven said. "If only she had been with us when we were captured that first time. I would have taken her with us, when we got away."

Sadness welled within Ryker's throat. The baby would be born soon. He hoped it would not be raised as a Sioux.

"Lately I've been counting the miracles we've seen," Sven said. "Klara going to school for our birthday and being gone from home when the Indians attacked."

"She could have been killed, like Papa," Ryker said.

"And finding Elsa on the prairie," Sven said. "A miracle beyond miracles. Do you think an angel dropped her in our path?"

"We were lost," Ryker said, "but maybe we were in exactly the right place." The awe and mystery of the thought sent his mind whirling. "Maybe it was God's plan all along."

A flock of geese honked as they flew south in a jagged arrow shape. More clouds tripped overhead. Ryker had rarely seen the sky so blue, the air so clear.

"And Beller fighting off the bear," Sven said, "and the old Indian woman watching us escape without hindering us."

"I've been thinking about Papa lately," Ryker said. "Mama said Papa wasn't cut out to be a pioneer. She said they would have been better off staying in Norway, where they at least had family support during hard times."

Papa would be alive if they had stayed in Norway. Mama would be baking flatbread. Martin would be a student, not a soldier. How different their lives would be.

"Papa said I didn't listen," Ryker said. "You were smart enough to know how much we needed Beller."

They gazed upward for a long moment without speaking. The blue sky was dotted with clouds like small strokes from a paintbrush, a hundred small wisps, almost like . . .

"Angel wings," Sven said. "Look at them, hundreds of angels." He jumped to his feet and pointed. "It means we're being rescued." He took off running for the blockhouse. "I have to tell Klara."

Ryker tried to imagine what being rescued would feel like. Reinforcements coming from Fort Snelling might mean it would be safe to go home. But how would he ever manage to care for his family alone. He had turned fifteen during his journey to Fort Abercrombie. The haystacks were gone, the cattle taken, their good dog gone forever, and the crop ruined in the field. There might be potatoes in the garden patch, and if they were lucky the deer had left the squash alone. No neighbors would be there to help in times of trouble. No firewood put up for the coming winter. No geese or chickens to give them eggs. The few coins in his pouch would not be enough to buy food for the winter.

He counted the angel wings overhead. At least a hundred, maybe more. They needed every single angel to help them to endure the coming months.

CHAPTER 43

On their way back to the blockhouse, Ryker overheard Hannibal and Elmer talking about the Sioux. It was good news, for a change, and Ryker could hear exultation in their voices.

"They're leaving Slabtown," Elmer said. "Taking down their tipis, loading up the grandmas, and heading out."

"What?" Ryker said. "All of them?"

"Don't know," Hannibal said. "Hope they all go and stay gone."

"They're whipped," Elmer said and patted his arm still in a sling. "And they know it."

Other soldiers commented on hunting season and the need to store provisions for winter. "Might be why they're going," Hannibal said. "But seems odd to leave when they have us pinned to the wall."

"Some heathen trick," Hannibal said. "Give us the idea they're leaving, when in fact they're readying for another attack."

Ryker stretched on tiptoe to see over the barricades. No smoke showed over Slabtown. No sign of the Indians. The sky had cleared leaving only the bluest blue. A cool fall wind came from the northwest, blowing smells from the stable to where he stood by the earthworks. Leaves crunched underfoot.

Maybe it was really over, and they could return home. As wonderful as that sounded, Ryker knew it meant a new level of problems. He must figure out a way to support his family. He was too young to be a man, but he had no choice.

He knew how to make hay. However, it wasn't haying season. Ryker knew how to milk cows, feed pigs, harvest feathers, plant a field, and tend a garden patch. He knew how to go to school, write a poem, and read a book. Somehow he had to corral enough skills to provide for Elsa and the twins. He wouldn't let them starve. He would die rather than see them sent to an orphanage.

By mid-afternoon, the whole fort knew that the Sioux were gone. The rumors changed from talking about why the reinforcements hadn't come to talking about returning to their homesteads. Most were sick of Fort Abercrombie and willing to take the risk.

"No one is allowed to leave until we know what's happening," Captain Vander Horck said. He said the Indians might have left for a pow-wow or some other custom. They might be back the next day. "We've put up with each other this long; we'll see it through to the end."

"But, why did the Sioux leave?" Auntie Abigail called out. "We saw them leave. They wouldn't do it without a reason."

"We'll send out a patrol in the morning," Captain Vander Horck said. "Until we know more, it's business as usual at Fort Abercrombie."

A shout rang out through the fort. "Soldiers coming! Reinforcements on the way!"

The blockhouse emptied out, as everyone rushed to the earthworks for a look. Sure enough, a line of soldiers in blue marched toward the fort on the Abercrombie Trail. Ryker couldn't count them fast enough. It seemed more soldiers were coming than were stationed at Fort Abercrombie.

"See," Sven said. "I told you."

Ryker told Mathilde about the angel wings. Soon everyone in the fort knew about the sign from heaven and of help finally coming. Soldiers fired their weapons, and the bugler sounded a cheery call. Elsa danced and clapped, surely not understanding the commotion but loving the excitement of smiling people. Hannibal put two fingers into his mouth and whistled. Auntie Abigail, who had been as strong as a lion throughout the whole siege, sat on the bench next to the wash stand and wept.

"Don't mind me," she said to anyone who would listen. "I always cry at good news." Tears rolled down the folds of her plump face. "Don't mind me."

A scraggly line of soldiers marched toward them led by a commanding officer riding a horse. Ryker didn't see a single wisp of smoke over Slabtown. No wonder the Sioux had left. They had known about the reinforcements.

They were saved. The siege was over.

Captain Vander Horck ordered a military salute. Hannibal and Elmer were put on guard duty. Captain Vander Horck knew better than to completely trust the Sioux. Someone had to keep watch for a sneak attack.

The civilians were not to be left out. They formed a double line across the parade ground and made ready to welcome their liberators. The soldiers neared—a foot-sore and battle weary lot they were—and straightened their lines. They marched forward with squared shoulders, heads held high.

They were sweaty, dirty, and covered with dust. More than one wore a bandage, proof of injury or attack along the way. Many limped, some holding each other up with clasped arms. It had been a long march across Minnesota. Behind them rolled supply wagons pulled by army mules.

The soldiers marched into the fort as the bugler played "Rally Round the Flag" accompanied by a drummer boy and a young woman on the fiddle. The besieged solders and citizens cheered and sang until they were hoarse.

Yes, we'll rally round the flag boys, we'll rally once again.

The fiddle player played so hard she busted a string.

Sounding the trumpet call of freedom.

Tears dripped down Ryker's cheeks, and he didn't care who saw them. They were saved. The siege was over.

The Union forever, hurrah boys, hurrah!

"They'll bring mail," Sven said. "Maybe news of Martin."

Ryker must write to Martin with the sad news of their parents when they knew where he was. He would write about Mama's kidnapping and their ordeal of escape to Fort Abercrombie. More letters were needed to relatives in Norway and to Papa's cousin in Dodge County. Ryker sighed. His writing days were not quite over.

"They'll bring news about the war," Auntie Abigail said. She stood with the crowd, waving a white handkerchief and yelling until red veins popped alongside her temple. "Maybe I'll hear about Robert," she said. She sprang forward to kiss a grizzly man with a ragged beard. Then she grabbed Captain Vander Horck and kissed him right on the lips.

The captain pulled back in surprise, and Auntie Abigail twirled and danced a jig.

She danced as if the war were over, as if all the boys were coming home. Ryker elbowed Sven in his side and pointed to Auntie Abigail, who had grabbed Captain Vander Horck by his arms and was dancing in time to the music. She whirled and flounced her skirts, her fat cheeks jiggling, as the captain struggled to keep up.

No one had heard how the Union was doing since the Sioux went on the warpath. Ryker half dreaded knowing. It could be bad news. He might learn that Martin had died. That Frank Schmitz had been killed. That the Union had fallen.

But now was time for celebration.

"Horsy," Elsa said.

Ryker swooped her up onto his shoulders. He cheered with

the others and bounced until Elsa giggled and grabbed hold of his ears.

Oh, it was a grand sight, to see the boys in blue marching through the cheering crowd. The women and girls followed Auntie Abigail's example and kissed every soldier within reach. The bugler lost his wind, but the crowd sang without him. They finished *Rally Round the Flag* and then switched to a new song, one that had become the battle cry of the nation. *The Battle Hymn of the Republic*'s words sounded over the parade grounds. *Glory, Glory, Hallelujah, His truth is marching on.*

There was not a dry eye in Fort Abercrombie. How long they had waited, terrified they might never be rescued. What losses and depredations they had endured. And now, reinforcements. Ryker knew that if he lived to be a hundred, he would never forget the wonderful feeling of deliverance experienced that day.

Later, after the men rested and ate, there would be time for the news. He would ask about his brother. Someone might know something.

Captain Vander Horck saluted their commanding officer, still catching his breath from his exuberant dance with Auntie Abigail. He then grasped his hand in welcome. Their officer handed Captain Vander Horck a dispatch pouch. News! Pandemonium broke out again. It was as if the people could not welcome them enough. They touched them, shook their hands, kissed them, and cheered them as conquering heroes. They were their boys. They were Americans who would whip the Sioux for good and let the settlers return to their lives on the prairie.

Ryker lifted Elsa on top of his head so she could see over the crowd. She pulled his hair and kicked her little feet against his neck. The twins climbed a stack of firewood for a better view.

Mathilde Jacobs grabbed a young soldier around his neck and kissed his cheek. Ryker didn't like it. They were just friends, but it seemed untoward for Mathilde to kiss a stranger. To make it even worse, the soldier turned and took her in his arms. He kissed her in return. Only he kissed her full on the mouth.

Ryker's heart thumped in his chest. It couldn't be. He strained for a closer look. He lifted Elsa off his head and handed her to Klara. The soldier wore a beard, but only one person he knew had that mop of yellow hair and lopsided grin.

Martin!

CHAPTER 44

Ryker had to know for sure. "Martin!" He pushed through the crowd "Martin!" His voice was lost in the cheering crowd. Ryker shoved Mrs. Kelly aside and squirmed past Mathilde. He must find out if his brother lived.

He ran after the soldier, who was now kissing Auntie Abigail. Or rather, Auntie Abigail was hugging and kissing him. Ryker grabbed his arm and jerked him around to face him.

"What's going on?" the soldier said. The voice was Papa's, but the face was Martin's.

"Is it really you?"

"Little brother?" Martin said. "Thank God. I've been worried sick ever since I heard about the Indians."

The brothers embraced. It felt like a dream, a good dream that Ryker hoped would never end. Martin alive. Martin here at Fort Abercrombie. It would have been enough to know that he lived, even to have known that he languished in a prison camp, but to have him home again . . . A miracle. Another miracle.

"Your brother?" Auntie Abigail fanned her flushed face with a lacy handkerchief. "Lord have mercy!"

"I knew you weren't dead," Ryker said. "You couldn't be."

"Dead?" Martin said with a dismissive shake of his head. "Taken prisoner, not killed. Damn Rebs. Didn't you get my letters?"

The brothers hugged again. Martin almost crushed Ryker with his bulging muscles. He had grown into a man. He smelled

245

of tobacco and stale sweat. Dirt and dust encrusted his uniform. A jagged scar stretched across his left cheek, mostly hidden by a heavy beard.

The twins, with Elsa in tow, exploded onto Martin. The happiness that Ryker felt equaled the degree of sadness felt with Papa's death, the Tingvolds' massacre, Johnny's torture, and Mama being taken. Ryker turned his thoughts away from the sorrows of recent weeks and focused instead on the pure joy of Martin's return.

"Look how you've grown!" Martin twirled Klara around and gave Sven a playful punch. "You're almost as tall as I am."

"Horsy." Elsa squealed and jumped up and down. She had been newborn when Martin left home. She clung to Ryker's legs when Martin tried to pick her up.

"Don't give me that," Martin said. He kissed Elsa and jiggled her to stop her crying. "I'm your older brother." Elsa howled and stuck her finger into his nostril.

"Ouch!" Martin said. "Give me a break. I've just marched across Minnesota to rescue you."

"Horsy," Elsa said, reaching for Ryker.

"You want a horsy ride? I'll show you horsy!" Martin lifted her onto his shoulders and galloped around the twins. "You're not a baby anymore."

Martin paused to catch his breath. He looked past them. "Where's Papa and Mama?"

The bad news lodged in Ryker's throat, as surely as the rutabaga had choked Brimstone.

He did not know how to begin.

Martin asked again. Ryker stumbled for words. Martin turned wary, his voice a half-step higher when he asked a third time.

Should Ryker tell him about Papa first, or about Mama? What would be the kindest way to tell his brother? The bugler and fiddle player launched into *O Susannah* with such vigor that conversation became impossible, especially a conversation about tragedy and loss.

Auntie Abigail suggested they go into the empty blockhouse. "You need family time," she said. "Everyone else is out here."

Martin looked toward his regiment, where Mrs. Kelly distributed hot food to hungry men. They ate wherever they could find a place to sprawl on the ground, huddling out of the wind behind firewood stacks and earthworks.

"I'll bring your food inside," Auntie Abigail said.

They closed the door behind them.

Ryker slipped into Norwegian, the language of home. He spoke the words that turned their joy into grief. The reality of Papa's death and Mama's kidnapping became real with the telling. The twins cried, Ryker mopped tears off his face, and Elsa howled. Ryker did not know how much Elsa understood, but he could see she was upset.

Martin lifted a shaky hand to his forehead and slouched to the bench. He looked more like his old self and less like a cocky soldier. Rivulets of tears ran down his dirty face, leaving streaks of white amidst the dirt. "My God, I can't believe it."

They sat in silence, except for an occasional sniffle.

Then Martin's eyes took on a hard glint, and Ryker realized that Martin would be a formidable foe to face on the battlefield.

"Tell me what happened," Martin said grimly. "Don't hold anything back. I want to know everything."

CHAPTER 45

"We left Papa in the root cellar," Ryker said after Martin heard the entire story. "Papa told me to get help. After he died, I did what he said."

"You did right," Martin said with a firm nod and set jaw. "Mama depended on you."

"He's in a tomb," Klara said. She started to put her thumb in her mouth but instead sat on her hand. "Like Jesus."

"We dug that root cellar," Martin said. "Happy times, they were."

Sven reminded them how Mama screamed when a snake slithered into her bread pan the first morning of living in the dugout. Klara remembered being afraid to fetch potatoes from the root cellar during the cold of winter because of the spider webs and mice.

"Papa will rest easy amid the memories," Martin said. "We'll seal it up and put a marker at the door." Martin nodded at Ryker and the twins. "You did well. All of you. If I were your commanding officer, I'd give you each a medal."

"But Johnny might be alive if I had listened," Ryker said. "He wanted to escape from the Indian woman sooner."

"It's war," Martin said, and his expression steeled. "People die. You did the best you could. Papa would be proud. I'm proud of you."

A weight lifted off Ryker's chest.

Martin had to return to his unit. "Don't want to be listed

absent without leave on my first day in Fort Abercrombie."

"But what if they send you back to the war?" Klara said. She clutched his hand, refusing to let go, even if he were only going to the barracks.

"I'm back for good," Martin said. "We were released by the Rebs to fight the Sioux," he said, "on condition we wouldn't return south. Thank God. I've had more than enough of that hell hole."

"There's something else." Ryker cleared his throat. "Papa said Mama was having another baby."

"I hope it's a little brother this time," Sven said. "I've had enough of baby sisters."

"Maybe another baby sister like Elsa," Klara said. Elsa clapped at the sound of her name.

Martin rose to leave the blockhouse. "Now we find Mama."

Auntie Abigail hurried inside when Martin left. She prodded for information, itching for tidbits to share with the others. Auntie Abigail wasn't exactly a gossip, but she loved to be the bearer of news. Her kind heart overflowed with sympathy for those with troubles and rejoiced with those who shared successes.

"The whole fort is buzzing about Martin coming back to fight the Indians," she said. "He's one of ours." She said that another soldier in Martin's unit told how Martin returned with the others. "The Rebels agreed to send three hundred prisoners back to fight the Sioux. Martin wasn't picked but snuck into the train when one of the chosen men died." Her laughter cackled through the blockhouse. "Martin was that determined to come home."

"Mama's prayers," Klara said. She stuck her thumb into her mouth.

Ryker expected to sleep like a baby that first night after the siege lifted. Instead, he tossed and turned, dreaming terrible dreams about Mama crying out for help and no one to rescue her. He went outside for a bit of fresh air.

He stepped outside of the blockhouse and looked up at the prairie sky. A billion stars glittered in a cloudless night. A harvest moon rounded fat as a pumpkin over the horizon. A white layer of frost covered the ground and turned every breath into a cloud. Out of habit, he looked toward Slabtown. No lights showed.

Ryker must return to the homestead to dig the potatoes. They might be able to eke out the winter if there were even a few bushels in the ground. They must be harvested before a hard freeze ruined them. Rutabagas and carrots were sweeter after the first dip in temperature. He tried not to think about the burning haystacks. If only the Sioux had left one of the stacks unmolested. The price of hay would be sky high since the Sioux ruined so much of it.

The sentries called out their positions. Ryker noticed Captain Vander Horck walking from sentry to sentry, encouraging the men. The captain's face showed in the small glow of his cigar.

Captain Vander Horck greeted Ryker as he passed the blockhouse. He stopped beside him, rocking back on his heels and looking up at the stars. "Couldn't sleep?" He puffed on the cigar and exhaled a stinky cloud.

"Guess not," Ryker said. "Wondering what happens next."

"Ah, yes," Captain Vander Horck said. "If we only had a crystal ball."

They stood in silence for a long while, until Ryker felt nervous, as if he should be saying something. Captain Vander Horck was an important man, and Ryker was just an immigrant boy, maybe an orphan. Ryker tucked his hands under his armpits to keep warm.

"Your brother came in with the Exterminators," Captain Vander Horck said.

"Ya," Ryker said. "Though I didn't know their name."

"Hmmm, nothing official," Captain said. He puffed a last drag on the cigar and ground the butt under his heel. "Here to eliminate the Sioux once and for all."

A shooting star streamed across the sky. They watched it drift beyond the horizon. The first glimpse of daylight colored the tip of the eastern horizon. An owl hooted by the river.

The Lord's Prayer said to forgive as we are forgiven. Ryker remembered the faces of the Indians who killed Johnny, and the ones who murdered the Tingvolds. It was hard to forgive the Sioux after what they had done to Papa. To Mama.

"Will you look for our mother now?" Ryker said. His voice cracked, so that he began as a man and ended squeaking like a boy. Again the embarrassment of stating the truth that needed telling. "The baby," he said. "I don't know when it will come."

"I see." Captain Vander Horck lit another cigar, striking a lucifer on the sole of his shoe. "We'll look for her," Captain Vander Horck said. "And find her if she lives." He puffed a dark, stinking cloud. "Hundreds dead. The Sioux whipped, but barely."

Another cloud of cigar smoke enveloped them.

"How old is Martin now?" Captain Vander Horck asked as he stomped the butt of his cigar beneath his heel.

Ryker paused and figured on his fingers. "Seventeen, almost eighteen. Why do you ask?"

Captain Vander Horck said that there might be a way for Martin to be released from the army owing to the fact that he was still underage and much needed by his family. "It's nothing for certain," Captain Vander Horck said, "but I'll do my best."

He walked off then, stopping to speak to the next sentry, calling out to the men reporting for guard duty, instructing the bugler to sound reveille. "We're going on patrol with first light," Captain said. "Ready the men."

CHAPTER 46

Hannibal waved back as the men marched out on patrol in the freezing weather. Small bursts of vapor hovered before the soldiers' mouths like white clouds. They marched with enthusiasm, as if glad to leave Fort Abercrombie. It had been over a month since they had been away from its confines.

Ryker spotted Martin on guard duty next to the horse barn. Ryker pretended to have business at the barn and took the opportunity to chat with his brother. He needed to talk to Martin about their future.

"They wouldn't let us go along today," Martin said in disgust. "Said it was our turn to man the fort." He cleared his throat and spit into a pile of horse manure. "We came to fight Injuns. Not to stand guard over women."

Ryker had wanted to go along, too. Of course civilians weren't allowed. The women in the blockhouse chattered like a flock of magpies, planning their return home, packing small items in readiness.

"They're not going home," Martin said. He never ceased scanning the open ground beyond the stables, the area he was responsible for guarding. "It's not safe on the frontier."

"That's what I wanted to talk to you about," Ryker said. He told his brother about the potatoes in the field, the coins around his neck, and his desire to take the younger ones home to the homestead.

"That's crazy," Martin said. "You'd never make it alone.

What about firewood? Milk or eggs?" He spit again. "I've a little back pay coming. Maybe enough to keep you at the fort over winter."

"Doesn't look like there's room for us," Ryker said. "Your unit will need the blockhouse once winter sets in."

"Maybe that nice Mrs. Kelly would take Klara and Elsa," Martin said. "I'd pay for their room and board. You and Sven might bunk with one of the hostlers and work for your keep."

Ryker shook his head. He did not like what he was hearing. "But the farmstead," he said. "Papa said stay together."

"Impossible. You're too young to be responsible."

Martin's commanding officer neared the horse barn. "Go back," Martin said in a hurried whisper. "I'll get in trouble if you're here."

Ryker left, of course. He had no choice. He had wanted to speak to his brother about Captain Vander Horck's suggestion that Martin might be released from the army. Together, he and Martin could surely keep the farm going. He had been responsible for the younger children since his father's death. He had brought them through tall-grass prairie. They had survived. He had proved himself, no matter what Martin might say. They needed to stay together, not send the girls away with Mrs. Kelly. That's what Papa would have wanted.

A niggling thought refused to leave his mind. Papa had put him in charge. It wasn't Martin's decision to make.

That day Auntie Abigail waited for news about her son, Robert, who had been missing since the first attacks. The twins chattered about Mama's soon return. Surely the soldiers would bring her back with them. The Jacobs family packed and made ready to leave as soon as Captain Vander Horck returned.

"I hope your cabin is standing," Ryker said to Mathilde. Really, he looked for any excuse to talk to her, and it seemed a safe thing to say. "It looked all right when I was there."

"Papa says we'll rebuild if it's burnt." She tucked a lock of stray curls back into her braids. "Do you know what you'll do?"

"We're returning to the home place as soon as we can," Ryker said. He didn't mention Martin's plan to send the girls away. "We'll make it somehow." He hoped his words were true. They mostly burned cow patties for fuel. He calculated how they might gather enough wood or cow patties to keep the stove going over the winter.

Mathilde was the one good thing about being at Fort Abercrombie. She smiled at him, and his heart raced. He needed to speak up while he had the chance. It felt dangerous, somehow, as if, if he said the wrong thing, it would all fade away.

"Now that I know where you live," Ryker said before he lost his courage, "maybe I can visit."

Mathilde turned a pretty pink. "I'd like that," she said.

The bugler sounded the men's return. It was almost dark. The settlers hurried to the parade ground, anxious for news. No settlers returned with the men. Ryker swallowed a huge gulp of disappointment.

Captain Vander Horck pulled up the reins and spoke from the saddle. Everyone quieted, straining to hear his every word. "We saw no hostiles," he said. Everyone cheered. He raised a restraining hand as a signal for quiet. "But we saw horrific damage, death, and senseless violence." It grew quiet as a grave.

"Any word about my Robert?" Auntie Abigail called out the question on everyone's minds. "What about our missing loved ones?"

"No sign of anyone, but the dispatch brought news about two hundred eighty-eight whites recovered at a place called Camp Release." Captain Vander Horck paused for breath. Ryker noticed how tired he looked. "Maybe your son is at Camp Release. We haven't heard specifics. It all takes time."

"When can we go home?"

"Burial details go out tomorrow." Captain Vander Horck paused and fingered the bridge of his nose. He slapped the reins, and his horse headed toward the barn. "Don't expect to leave anytime soon."

"You can't keep us forted up this way," Mr. Jacobs said in his thick German brogue. "We might yet something of our crops salvage."

"Impossible," Captain Vander Horck said. "Military tribunals are going on in Mankato, but we can't be sure all the hostiles are apprehended."

A low grumble started in the back and grew to a roiling protest.

"Like it or not," Captain Vander Horck said, "you're stuck in Fort Abercrombie for a while longer."

CHAPTER 47

A group of immigrants returned to St. Cloud guarded by a small detachment of soldiers. The nice woman who had nursed Elsa was among them, going back to her aunt's farm until the trouble on the frontier settled. The others waited to return to their farms in spite of the danger. Auntie Abigail planned to move into one of the tiny houses on the edge of Slabtown as soon as the captain allowed. She would do laundry in exchange for rent. She invited Ryker and his younger siblings to join her.

"We'll be snug as a bug in a rug," she said in a hearty voice. "Captain will give permission soon."

Ryker noticed the droop in her shoulders and heaviness in her steps that betrayed her real feelings in spite of her joviality. There had been no word of her missing son. Ryker had found Auntie Abigail weeping behind the haystack, just that morning. Mama would know how to comfort the good woman with an aching heart.

Ryker hugged Auntie Abigail around the neck and kissed her cheek. "Thank you," he whispered. "He'll be back—you'll see."

More waiting. Martin left for an extended foray after the Sioux. They marched out of the fort with a sharp step but returned a week later, footsore and bedraggled. They told of burned homes, missing settlers, and burial duties. They had not seen a single hostile.

"Did you find Mama?" Klara said while hanging onto Elsa to prevent her from running out in front of the horses.

"No sign of her," Martin said. "Any word from Camp Release?"

"Not yet," Ryker said. "Captain Vander Horck says we should hear any day now."

Martin plodded toward the bunk house with the other men. How tired he looked. Ryker hesitated to bother him, but he needed to talk to him while he had the chance. For all he knew, Martin might be sent out again soon. Ryker ran to catch up to his brother and grabbed his arm. Martin shook him away and turned to him with a look of exasperation on his face. He reeked of sweat and cooking fires.

"We need to go out to the home place and see how things stand," Ryker said. "Maybe the cattle survived. There might be potatoes or carrots. Something."

"You heard the captain," Martin said with a snort. "Not allowed."

Ryker didn't like when Martin got bossy. Papa had left Ryker in charge, and Ryker had a deep-down feeling that unfinished business remained at the homestead. "Even a couple of days would be enough. It only makes sense to gather food."

"You're crazy."

"I'm going to ask," Ryker said.

Martin argued that Captain Vander Horck wouldn't give Ryker the time of day. He reminded Ryker that he was just a kid, and the army gave no credence to civilians.

Ryker disagreed. He had grown up over the last months. Not only were his trousers inches too short, but his voice was changing, too, and he must ask Martin about borrowing his razor. But it was more than all of those things. Ryker had learned to carry responsibility over the journey to Fort Abercrombie. A boy would not speak up, but a young man would dare to approach Captain Vander Horck and present his case.

After supper, Ryker squared his shoulders and walked over to

Captain Vander Horck's billet. Ryker tapped on the door. It wasn't too late to turn back. Maybe Martin was right.

No . . . Ryker strengthened his resolve. He would ask his question in a respectful manner. The worst that could happen would be that Captain Vander Horck would refuse.

"Who is it?" Captain Vander Horck called out.

"Ryker Landstad," Ryker said.

"Come in out of the wind," Captain Vander Horck said. "Excuse me for not getting up. Gout is giving me fits."

The man sat in his shirtsleeves reading dispatches, with his boots off and his feet propped up on a stool. The man's big toe escaped through a hole in his sock. The room stank of cigar smoke and wood smoke.

"There are lots of mouths to feed here at the fort," Ryker said. His voice cracked, and he cleared his throat. "There might be garden produce to salvage on the farmsteads." He cleared his throat again. "We'll need food to survive the winter. You might consider allowing farmers to return home to scrounge what's left."

"It's unsafe," Captain Vander Horck said. "You heard—"

"In the company of an armed soldier or two." It was rude to interrupt, but Ryker felt he had no choice. "Just long enough to dig the potatoes. It would bring peace of mind to the settlers and add food to the larder."

Captain Vander Horck removed his glasses and rubbed the bridge of his nose. He sighed. The smell of horse manure wafted up to Ryker's nose. Ryker shifted his weight and wished he had scraped his shoes before entering the captain's room. Captain Vander Horck said nothing. A clock ticked on the mantle. Martin had been right. It was prideful to think the good man would pay attention to a boy. Ryker turned to leave.

"Wait," Captain Vander Horck said. "It makes good sense. Not everyone at once, mind you, but staggered out over a couple of weeks." He replaced his glasses and picked up the dispatch again. "Clear thinking, son. I should have thought of it myself." Ryker was almost out the door when the captain spoke again. "Keep it under your hat until I can work out the details."

Captain Vander Horck gathered the remaining settlers the next morning and announced his plan. Ryker would be the first to return home in the company of two armed soldiers. "Only the men allowed to go," Captain Vander Horck said. "No women or children."

Ryker watched Martin's face darken. He didn't understand why Martin would be angry about Captain Vander Horck's decision. Could it be that Martin was jealous?

Hannibal and Martin were assigned to accompany Ryker. They would leave before first light.

"Anything to get out of the fort," Hannibal said. "I've got a good case of cabin fever, and it's only October."

Ryker rode an ancient army horse, one long in the tooth and mean of temperament.

"Hang on for your life," Hannibal said with a loud guffaw. "He's a race horse."

"Don't leave us in the dirt," Martin said. "We'll never keep up with such an old nag."

Ryker had never ridden a horse before. Their teasing made it harder for him to ask advice about how to manage the reins. Ryker took a breath. He would figure it out on his own. It couldn't be that hard.

Captain Vander Horck waved and nodded as they rode out of the fort. "Think about what I said," Captain Vander Horck called out to Martin. "It's not too late."

"What did he mean?" Ryker said, turning to look at his brother. "Your discharge?"

Martin glared. "You a mind reader?"

"Don't you know that Ryker and the captain are on speaking

terms these days," Hannibal said in his wheezy voice. "They take tea together in the afternoon like gentlemen."

"Don't think you're a man, just because you talked the captain into letting you go out to the farm," Martin said. "You're still wet behind the ears."

They rode in silence past Slabtown. Martin pulled his horse to a stop and turned to face Ryker. "If you must know, Captain Vander Horck pulled strings to release me from the army." He pulled his collar to protect himself from a sudden rising wind. "I refused."

"But, Martin . . ." Ryker said. He could not believe his ears. Martin was the oldest son, the one to take the responsibility. Martin knew how to manage everything. "The little ones need you. Mama . . ." He gulped. "We all need you."

"I worked it out," Martin said. "The girls will go with Mrs. Kelly, and the hostler will take you and Sven." He shivered in the cold and pulled his collar over the back of his neck. "Besides, Abe Lincoln needs me more than you do. I'll finish what I started at Shiloh, even if it means fighting Sioux instead of Rebs."

"We're staying with Auntie Abigail at the fort over the winter," Ryker said. He sat up straighter and gripped the horse's mane with both hands. A flock of geese flew toward Whiskey Creek, honking a sad and lonely song. "You can keep your money."

"But I told you," Martin said.

"Papa left me in charge," Ryker said. "It's not your decision."

CHAPTER 48

Martin jabbed his boot into his mount's side and cantered ahead. Ryker could see his brother's anger in the way he stuck out his jaw and jerked the reins. Ryker felt as if he had been kicked in the stomach, too.

Gray clouds layered the sky like pond scum, and a cold wind burned their ears and noses. The prairie stood forlorn and forsaken, the grass brittle and dry with the frost, and the wild flowers dried stalks of dull colors. A red fox scurried across their path, and a flock of geese flew overhead, winging southward to avoid the upcoming winter. Their haunting cries fitted Ryker's mood. *Vonlaus.* How could he manage without Martin's help? How would they ever find Mama?

It was like Martin to do what he wanted, even if it meant others had to pick up his tasks. Like running away from home to escape the farm. Like refusing to come home to help with the children. Ryker looked at Martin's silhouette ahead of him and did not like what he saw. Mama always said that Martin took after Papa. Maybe she was right.

They cut across the prairie on the route Hannibal had used the time he ran away from the army. "Your ma talked me out of it," he said. "Said it was safe at the fort." He snorted in his wheezy voice.

They rode all morning and came up to the homestead from the west. A thickness of memories choked Ryker's throat: the feeling of sun beating down as they raked hay; the smell of

Mama's bread baking in the oven; the taste of warm milk from Marigold; and the sound of Papa's weeping in the dark of night after he learned Martin was missing. The haystacks had turned to black circles of ash. A flock of blackbirds pecked in the barley field. Martin shooed them away, and they rose like a black blanket shaken in the wind. Martin fingered the stalks but came up empty handed.

"Nothing left," he said with scorn. "All that work, and nothing to show for it."

Ryker bit back the words pointing out it was not Martin's work that had been lost. Papa, Sven, and Ryker did it all, with Mama and Klara working to keep them fed. The blackbirds settled back on the field to resume their pecking and scratching. Papa had been right. Wild things did not bother the hay. It made sense to concentrate on next year's hay crop. He would plant enough grain for their own use and rig a scarecrow to keep the blackbirds away.

They left their horses in the tool shed, at the end of the hayfield. Hannibal insisted they secure them out of sight. "No need to get stranded afoot. It's a long hike back to Fort Abercrombie."

Wild animals had rooted in the west garden, but Ryker pulled a fat rutabaga. Its pungent smell so enticed him that he shook off the dirt and bit into the tangy vegetable. "Look," he said. He kicked through the dead cucumber and bean vines. "Rutabagas, carrots, and potatoes."

They would come back and dig the vegetables after they looked over the home place. They would stay overnight in the soddy and get an early start in the morning. They plodded toward the root cellar, no one speaking, everyone dragging their feet. They stood next to the willow tree with its yellow fall leaves and gathered at the closed wooden door that led into the root cellar.

Ryker steeled himself to open the door and remove the body for burial. He didn't know if he could muster the courage. Ryker had left Papa with his hands resting on his chest and covered with the burlap sack. Beside him, he heard Martin sniffling.

"It's his grave," Martin said. He wiped his nose on his sleeve and sniffed again. "Not right to disturb him."

"He'd stink," Hannibal said in a matter-of-fact way. "Best to leave him unhindered."

At least Ryker didn't have to make the decision. They piled stones in front of the small trapdoor, and heaped dirt on top of the stones to seal Papa's grave. Tears and strong emotion surprised him. Grief, regret, and a sudden anger sprung up and spilled out of his mouth.

"You broke Mama's heart when you ran away," Ryker said. "Papa's, too." The anger settled thick as a blanket after Martin enlisted. "And when we heard you were missing . . . Mama blamed Papa." How long ago it seemed, although it was only a few months. "I heard Papa weeping in the night when he thought we were asleep."

"Well, what did you expect me to do?" Martin said. "Stay on this farm and make hay all my life? I wasn't about to waste my life out on the prairie. I'm a better soldier than a farmer. It's all I ever wanted to do."

Before Ryker could answer, a low mooing sounded behind the outhouse. Brimstone. No sign of Fire, but Brimstone stood chomping dried weeds. Ryker hugged him around his neck, patting the scars on his side. The ox looked skinny but healthy. "Don't go eating any turnips," Ryker whispered into his ear. Brimstone answered with a low moo.

"We can't lead the ox back to the fort," Martin said. "He'll slow us down, and I have to get back for guard duty tomorrow night."

"We're not leaving Brimstone," Ryker said. "Think of Papa's

263

winter at the logging camp to pay for him." Ryker took a breath and squared his shoulders. "I'll bring him myself if I have to. He won't make it through the winter once the slough freezes up and snow covers the dried grass. I need him for spring planting."

"You can't be serious," Martin said. His lopsided smile turned into a grimace.

"You'll see," Ryker said. "Papa said to hang on to the farm. I aim to do it."

The black hen scurried into the dried prairie. Three brown eggs lay in a hidden nest under the outhouse wall. Broken egg shells were scattered around the small hideaway where invading animals had robbed the broody hen. The frost had taken its weedy camouflage, leaving it open and exposed. Ryker placed the eggs in his pocket with a chuckle. "Patsy's nest right under our noses. Klara searched for it all summer."

He told Martin and Hannibal how he would capture the hen and bring it to Fort Abercrombie to help feed them through the winter.

"An egg is a beautiful thing," Hannibal said. He cleared his throat and looked intently at Ryker's pocket holding the small treasures. "How long has it been since I've tasted one?"

Ryker ignored the hint. He would bring them to Auntie Abigail in appreciation for letting them stay with her over the coming months. She might make a cake or a pudding. *Katt* streaked past and hid under the willow branches.

"*Katt!*" Ryker said. A fierce joy bubbled within his chest. The Sioux had not taken everything. "She's grown wild."

"You're crazy," Martin said. "I'm not Noah, and this ain't no ark. I won't be toting animals back to Fort Abercrombie."

"Don't worry," Ryker said. "I'll do it myself." The bubble of happiness changed to a growing awareness of his brother's shortsightedness. A good cat kept rats out of the grain and flour. A daily egg meant the difference between food and no food. After what Ryker had been through in getting to Fort Abercrombie, he felt fearless. He had faced and triumphed over impossible problems. He could do it again if he must.

"Oh, oh," Hannibal interrupted before Martin could answer. He pulled his sidearm and pointed toward the soddy. "We've got company."

A plume of smoke puffed above the mounded roof, then died away. Someone was trying to start a fire in the stove. They weren't doing a very good job.

"Injuns," Martin said. He pulled out his revolver, too. "Should we go back for reinforcements?"

"We can handle a stray Injun or two," Hannibal said, while pulling his side arm.

Ryker doubted it was an Indian. An Indian knew how to build fires. He recalled the efficient way Good Person managed her camp. "Might be a survivor taking shelter," Ryker said. "A woman or child who needs our help."

"We'll find out. You stay with the horses," Martin said. "If it goes south, go to Fort Abercrombie for help."

Ryker glanced toward the shed, where the horses were safely tethered. Martin wasn't the boss of him. He would look through the side window if he wanted. If he saw Indians, he would return to the horses. He wished for Beller's warning growl.

Hannibal and Martin crept to the front door. Ryker followed from a distance, quiet lest they order him back to the horses. The door sagged on its hinges, sure evidence of wild things, or wild men, inside. A bucket of water sat outside the door beside a pitiful stack of corncobs and cow patties.

"Don't startle him," he heard Hannibal whisper. "Even a rat fights when cornered."

Ryker dodged to the backside of their prairie home. He heard a crying baby. He crept up to the small window. He peeked inside. A woman wearing a blue kerchief hunched over the stove with a newborn baby in one arm, while stirring the coals with a poker.

"Mama?" Ryker said. He looked again. He felt like the time he had fallen from the tree and was seeing double. He blinked hard and squinted through the filmy glass. Then he leapt to his feet and called out to his brother. "Don't shoot," he said. "It's Mama."

He ran to the door, laughing with glee. Martin and Hannibal urged caution, but Ryker shook off their clutching hands. "It's Mama," he said. "It's really her."

He pushed through the sagging door and stumbled over the threshold, as clumsy as Johnny Schmitz. Mama turned toward the commotion, holding the poker like a weapon. No recognition flashed in her eyes, only fear in the pathetic way she positioned to defend her baby, like a muskrat caught in a trap.

Mama had lost flesh, her cheeks hollow. Gray lines shadowed her mouth. Another gap showed when she opened her mouth. Her ragged dress barely covered her body. The newborn baby was shriveled red as a dried plum.

"Mama!" he said. "It's Ryker."

Mama dropped the poker. She gripped the edge of the stove. Her knees started to buckle. "I prayed you'd come."

Ryker caught Mama in his arms before she fell to the floor. Her weight felt wispy as a cloud. The baby howled.

"Take your brother before I drop him," she whispered. Ryker took the baby, wrapped only in an animal skin. Mama gripped Ryker's arm with fingers as skinny as old bones. "Tell me," she said, and the light in her eyes sent a shiver through Ryker. She looked near death and reeked of cooking fires, dried blood, and unwashed body. "Tell me at once. Do the children live?" Mama said. "Did you find Elsa?"

"Ya, Mama." Ryker couldn't tell her about Papa yet. "We're all fine."

"Don't lie," Mama said. She gripped his arm and hissed into his face. "I want the truth."

Ryker assured her the children were safe at the fort. He and Martin half dragged, half carried her to the bed, and Hannibal took over the fire building. She slumped onto the mattress, looking dazed and exhausted. Mama's teeth chattered. No bedding remained in sight. Ryker took off his jacket and wrapped it around her shoulders. Martin draped his army coat over her legs and feet and interrupted Hannibal to fetch bedding from the horses.

"She told me," Mama said between clacking teeth. "I didn't know . . . couldn't believe her. Had no choice."

She rambled like a crazy person, like someone who had lost her mind. She stared at Martin without recognition. Then she pointed an accusing finger.

"You did it," she shrilled. "You took my baby."

"It's me, Martin," Martin said. "Home from the war."

"Martin?" Her wails sounded as loud as when she learned he had gone missing. She reached out and fingered his beard. Martin folded her into a bear hug. "Is it really you?" Her voice muffled in Martin's chest.

"I'm home. We're all safe."

Mama sobbed huge gulping sobs, clutching frail arms around his chest.

"I had to do it," she said. The wild look in her eyes brought a lump to Ryker's throat. Maybe she never would be herself again. "The bad men wanted Elsa. I had no choice." She wrung her hands and reached for the new baby. "Give him back! You can't have him." She settled the baby to her breast and rocked back and forth. "Johann will never forgive me."

"Rest now," Martin said. He stood up and put the kettle on

the stove. "Hannibal, fetch tea leaves from my saddlebag." Ryker asked Martin to cook the eggs for their mother as Hannibal jogged toward the horses.

Ryker held Mama then, cradling her and the new baby in his arms and rocking her back and forth. Lice crawled through her tangled hair showing beneath her kerchief. Poor Mama, always so meticulous about her grooming.

"Killed them. Women and children. Burned the Schmitzes'," Mama said. Her eyes locked with Ryker's, and her voice shuddered. "They were taking Elsa away, the woman said so. Said Elsa would be lost forever."

"Rest, Mama," Martin said. Ryker noticed his shoulders heaving, though he turned his face.

"What woman?" Ryker said. Mama was making no sense.

"Why the one with the kind eyes," Mama said in a far-away voice. She picked the front of Ryker's shirt with filthy nails, as long as bird claws. "She said, 'Don't be scared to let Elsa loose on the prairie like Moses's mother put her baby in the bulrushes.' I didn't know if I could trust her." Mama pinched Ryker's skin through his shirt, reminding him of the nipping geese when they had harvested feathers. Mama rambled about the bad men and the woman. "She said, 'Hurry up, before they come.' "

"Oh, Mama," Ryker whispered. He kissed her forehead. She must have been so scared. He swallowed hard, but the lump in his throat refused to leave.

"Angels stirred the clouds," Mama said. "She had the kindest eyes." She dissolved into wild weeping. "They couldn't find her." She clutched Ryker's arm and cackled like a crazy woman. "I wouldn't tell. Couldn't make me tell." Her laughter was worse than her crying.

"You did the right thing. Elsa is safe at the fort." Someday Ryker would tell her that he saw angels, too, and about his climb up the cottonwood when Beller came to him. "And the twins."

"We all made it," Martin said. He put the eggs on to boil. He wiped his sleeve across his eyes and turned away, stirring the fire until the metal pipe glowed red hot. Hannibal returned with the bedding, and they covered Mama and the baby as best they could. Mama lay back on the bed. Ryker folded his jacket for a pillow.

"Thank God." Mama grew very quiet. Her sobs ended. She looked around with a furtive glance as if they were in danger. Then she motioned Martin nearer.

"What about your father?" Mama whispered. "Where's Johann?"

"We'll talk about it later," Martin said. "Now you must rest."

"*Nei,*" Mama said. "Tell me. I can't rest until I know."

Martin avoided eye contact. Then he turned away and slouched by the door with Hannibal.

Martin, always so brave, left Ryker to tell Mama what had happened. There was no way around the impossible task. Ryker must be the one to break his mother's heart.

Ryker took a deep breath and told her what happened, watching Mama flinch with grief and pain.

"Did he suffer?" Mama whispered. "Don't spare me. I want to know."

"He lasted one night, with time to say good-bye and give each of us his blessing." As Ryker spoke the words, he remembered again the instructions Papa had given him about keeping the farm at all costs.

"We should have stayed in Norway," Mama said in a flat voice. "We'd be together in Norway."

The baby shrieked like an attacking Sioux. The baby's cries changed to contented sucking noises as he found Mama's breast.

"Your new brother," Mama whispered, her voice barely

audible, and her eyes almost closed. "What do you think of Baby Johann?"

The knot loosened in Ryker's throat, and he kissed the top of the baby's fuzzy head. "Named for Papa."

"Ya," Mama said. Then she began mumbling again, about Norway and angels, Beller, and needing to hide Elsa. "I had to let her go," Mama pleaded. "I had no choice."

"Hush," Ryker said. He smoothed Mama's forehead. Mama's frantic murmurs turned to silence. She lay back on the bed, gripping the baby to her chest. Her eyes closed, and her breathing slowed.

"Mama," Ryker said. There was another story to tell. "How did you get away from them and find your way back home?"

"Why, Good Person and Finds the Knife," Mama said as if surprised that Ryker didn't already know. "She brought proof you were alive." She pulled the tattered copy of *Uncle Tom's Cabin* from underneath the edge of the cornhusk mattress. Ryker recognized the torn cover.

"A true friend." Mama's voice was so weak that Ryker bent his ear to catch her words. "I owe her my life."

A million questions swirled through his mind, but they had to wait. Mama slept.

CHAPTER 49

"Look at her!" Martin said. "Damn the *skraeling*s." He stomped around the little dwelling, cursing the Sioux and vowing to get even. He acted just like Papa.

Ryker bit back his words about Good Person rescuing Mama, that all Sioux were not murderous, and that the whites had broken the treaty in the first place. But Johnny Schmitz's death loomed too fresh in his mind for him to defend the Indians.

Ryker stayed with Mama as Martin and Hannibal left to dig vegetables from the garden. Martin seemed relieved to get away and slammed the broken door on his way out.

Ryker pulled the door closed and retied the leather hinges. He pulled the scratchy wool blankets tighter around Mama's shoulders and made sure the covers tucked around the baby. Little Johann slept in the crook of Mama's arm, making sucking noises in his sleep. Like Ryker, the baby had Papa's chin. Dark hairs were plastered on his scalp. Maybe Baby Johann would be a black Norwegian, too.

"I wouldn't have trusted Good Person," Mama said. Ryker had thought she was asleep. "Feared trickery, but then the book."

"How could you understand her?" Ryker said. "She doesn't speak your language."

"A missionary woman translated." Mama lay back on the mattress. "Or a preacher's wife."

Ryker pressed again, anxious to understand.

She paused and took a long breath before continuing. Ryker helped her sip hot tea. "They took me with the Jensen girls, they . . ." Mama paused again, and her voice drifted off. "They were unkind."

Mama shifted the baby to her other arm, looking away and almost forgetting to speak. "Finds the Knife traded me for a fresh bear hide," Mama said. "The bad men wanted me, but he talked them into selling me." She slipped into silence again. "Told a wild story of my children living in trees by Whiskey Creek." Mama took a breath and pulled the blanket around the baby's head. "Said my dog fought the bear with the quill beard, gave his life for my return."

Ryker poked another handful of corncobs into the firebox. They sparked and flamed like the Tingvold farm on the day of the massacre, like the flames racing toward the river during the windstorm.

"He convinced them that I had strong medicine because of the bear," Mama said, and her hysterical laughter startled the baby. Her laughter quieted. "Good Person brought me home after the baby came."

Mama asked Ryker to start at the beginning and tell the whole story. Ryker agreed, if she would eat an egg and finish her tea. She nibbled as he told about gunshots during school and finding Papa wounded. He told of their wild escape across the prairie, finding Elsa alone, seeing Beller in the clouds, and how Good Person rescued the girls from warriors. He left out the part about Johnny's death and the Tingvold massacre. He spoke instead of safety at the fort, the kindness of Captain Vander Horck, and Auntie Abigail's invitation to stay with her over the winter. He ended with their glorious reunion with Martin, who came with the Exterminators.

"When you're well enough to travel," Ryker said, "we'll go back to the fort. The twins and Elsa will be overjoyed." He looked toward his mother, but she was asleep.

He opened *Uncle Tom's Cabin* but could not concentrate on Topsy's plight. The Norwegian Bible stood on the shelf.

Happiness surged through Ryker. Something survived. Something important. He turned to the family record on the inside cover of the holy book. One page listed wedding dates. Ryker traced the record of Johann and Marie Landstad's holy matrimony on December 26, 1842. He turned to the pages listing family births and deaths going back five generations.

Each name showed birthdate, baptismal and confirmation dates, and cause of death. He saw his father's neat record of Sissel's and Bertina's deaths by smallpox. He thanked God they had not lived to be mistreated by the Sioux. He looked over at Mama and prayed the Indians had not outraged her, or the Jensen girls. The thought made bile rise in his throat. And Papa—he had no words for how he felt about Papa's death.

Mama cried out in her sleep. Ryker set the Bible aside and sat beside her, holding her hand and assuring her that everything was all right. When they returned to the fort, he would haul water so that she could have a full bath. Auntie Abigail would see to the nits in her hair.

Mama woke and clutched Ryker's hand. He reminded her that everyone was safe, and Martin was in the garden digging potatoes.

"Do you know something?" Mama said. "I didn't think of Norway while I was in the hands of the Sioux. I was homesick for this, our prairie home, and my dear family." She kissed his hand, and her tears wet Ryker's skin. "And now, just when it feels like home, I will lose it."

"Why?" Ryker said. "We have shelter. The title is free and clear."

"But how can we manage?"

"Papa made me promise not to give up the homestead."

Ryker calculated the coins in his pouch; the money promised by Martin; what he and Sven might earn at the fort over the winter. "I'll plant your lilacs. Everything will be all right. You'll see."

"I'm so sleepy," Mama murmured. "I'll rest if I hear your voice."

And so Ryker told her about Mathilde Jacobs, and how Hannibal helped them on their journey to Fort Abercrombie. He told about Auntie Abigail, and the way Good Person and Mrs. Kelly shared milk with Elsa. "Your good deeds were returned a hundred times."

He told her that he might start a small school for the children at the fort over the coming winter. Ryker had not thought of this before, but speaking to Mama always brought clarity to his mind. Though Ryker had much to learn, he would share what he knew with the others. Captain Vander Horck owned a whole shelf of books. Perhaps he would loan them to the children.

When he was sure Mama slept, Ryker rummaged for the ink pot and quill hidden behind the stove. He opened the Norwegian Bible and recorded the date of Papa's death. It was more difficult to put into words the cause of death. Unlike smallpox or fever, typhoid or childbirth, the tangled mess about the Sioux war had no single description. Human greed, the War of Rebellion, broken treaties, and Norwegian stubbornness all played a part. If only they had stayed in Norway, if they had heeded the call to come into the fort for protection, if only . . .

Ryker dipped the quill and carefully penned the reason Papa's life ended on September 6, 1862: Sioux arrow.

Ryker must ask Mama about Baby Johann's birthdate before he added his brother's name to the family record. He blew over the page to dry the ink. He would make sure Johann was baptized as soon as they could find a pastor. Then he closed the Bible.

It seemed Martin had made up his mind not to return to the

farm, even after the war ended. Like Papa, Martin did not see the angels.

Ryker sighed. Nothing had turned out as expected. Papa must have felt the same way. At least they were not left as orphans. Mama would be there to steer the family in the right direction. He and Sven would raise this new brother. Klara would help them.

Ryker would tell Little Johann about their father and how happy he had been before life grew so overwhelming. Ryker would teach him how to make hay: cutting the prairie grass before daylight with a scythe honed razor sharp, raking the fragrant stems into windrows to dry in the hot sun, and how to gather haycocks into gigantic stacks compacted to shed wind and weather.

Ryker would teach Mama the American words, and in the cold winter days when outside work was impossible, Ryker would write their story. He would begin with the northern lights of Norway and their journey to frontier Minnesota. He would end with the brilliant colors of prairie sunrises and sunsets. In between he would paint the glory of tall grass and angels hidden in shifting clouds, intertwined with their escape to safety at Fort Abercrombie.

The baby squirmed and fussed. Ryker carefully lifted his baby brother and snuggled him against his chest. "Look," Ryker said. He held Little Johann nearer the window and pointed to a swirling cloud. "Angels hide in the clouds," Ryker said. "I'll teach you to see them."

The little one jammed a fist into his mouth and sucked the side of his hand. When he found no milk, he let out a howl as loud as any Sioux warrior.

Ryker kissed his forehead and looked into his eyes. "Don't cry, Little Brother," Ryker whispered. He kissed him again. "I'm here."

ABOUT THE AUTHOR

Candace Simar nurtures a passion for history and the way things might have been. She is the author of the Spur Award–winning *Abercrombie Trail* series: *Abercrombie Trail; Pomme de Terre; Birdie* and *Blooming Prairie.* Her latest historical novel, *Shelterbelts,* was a finalist for both the 2016 Midwest Book Award and 2016 Willa Literary Awards in Historical Fiction. Candace lives in Pequot Lakes, Minnesota. For more information see www.candacesimar.com.

The employees of Five Star Publishing hope you have enjoyed this book.

Our Five Star novels explore little-known chapters from America's history, stories told from unique perspectives that will entertain a broad range of readers.

Other Five Star books are available at your local library, bookstore, all major book distributors, and directly from Five Star/Gale.

Connect with Five Star Publishing

Visit us on Facebook:
    https://www.facebook.com/FiveStarCengage

Email:
    FiveStar@cengage.com

For information about titles and placing orders:
    (800) 223-1244
    gale.orders@cengage.com

To share your comments, write to us:
    Five Star Publishing
    Attn: Publisher
    10 Water St., Suite 310
    Waterville, ME 04901